Merciless Past

AN ASHA KADE PRIVATE DETECTIVE MYSTERY THRILLER

TIKIRI HERATH

REBEL DIVA ACADEMY

Merciless Past

Asha Kade Private Detective Mystery Thriller Series

www.TikiriHerath.com

Copyright ©2022 Tikiri Herath

Edition: 2022

Library & Archives Canada Cataloging in Publication

E-book ISBN: 978-1-990234-01-9

Paperback ISBN: 978-1-990234-13-2

Hardback ISBN: 978-1-990234-14-9

Audiobook ISBN: 978-1-990234-04-0

Large Print book ISBN: 978-1-989232-42-2

Author: Tikiri Herath

Publisher Imprint: Rebel Diva Academy Press

Copy Editor: Stephanie Parent

Back Cover Headshot: Aura McKay

Tikiri

A Gift For You

Thank you for picking up my latest novel. There's a gift for you for picking up this book!

HER DEADLY END is a 250-page twisty serial killer thriller about an unusual murder-suicide case that Tanya (Tetyana), Asha, and Katy accidentally stumble upon while vacationing in Paradise Cove.

It's a pulse-pounding, nerve-shredding mystery of a devious serial predator stalking a small seaside town in Washington State.

You'll learn about the characters in the Merciless murder mystery series which features private detectives, Asha Kade & Katy McCafferty, and those in the new Tanya Stone FBI K9 series which features Special Agent Tanya (Tetyana) & Max, her K9 German Shepherd.

Join the VIP Red Heeled Rebels Club and receive your exclusive gift. Click the link below to join.

HER DEADLY END: A gripping thriller with a twisty end
https://books.tikiriherath.com/ts-b0-mmm-herdeadlyend

There is no explicit sex, heavy cursing, or graphic violence in these books. There is, however, a closed circle of suspects, many twists and turns, fast-paced action, and nail-biting suspense.

NO DOG IS HARMED IN THESE BOOKS. EVER. But the villains always are.

The Red Heeled Rebels Universe

The Red Heeled Rebels universe of mystery thrillers, featuring your favorite kick-ass female characters:

Tanya Stone FBI K9 Mystery Thrillers
www.TikiriHerath.com/Thrillers
NEW FBI thriller series starring Tetyana from the Red Heeled Rebels as Special Agent Tanya Stone, and Max, as her loyal German Shepherd. These are serial killer thrillers set in Black Rock, a small upscale resort town on the coast of Washington state.
Her Deadly End
Her Cold Blood
Her Last Lie
Her Secret Crime
Her Dead Girl
Her Perfect Murder
Her Grisly Grave

Coming soon!

—⊷⊶—

Asha Kade Private Detective Murder Mysteries

www.TikiriHerath.com/Mysteries

Each book is a standalone murder mystery thriller, featuring the Red Heeled Rebels, Asha Kade and Katy McCafferty. Asha and Katy receive one million dollars for their favorite children's charity from a secret benefactor's estate every time they solve a cold case.

Merciless Legacy
Merciless Games
Merciless Crimes
Merciless Lies
Merciless Past
Merciless Deaths
One more to come.

—⊷⊶—

Red Heeled Rebels International Mystery & Crime - The Origin Story

www.TikiriHerath.com/RedHeeledRebels

The award-winning origin story of the Red Heeled Rebels characters. Learn how a rag-tag group of trafficked orphans from different places united to fight for their freedom and their lives, and became a found family.

The Girl Who Crossed the Line
The Girl Who Ran Away
The Girl Who Made Them Pay
The Girl Who Fought to Kill
The Girl Who Broke Free
The Girl Who Knew Their Names

The Girl Who Never Forgot
This series is now complete.

The Accidental Traveler

www.TikiriHerath.com

An anthology of personal short stories based on the author's sojourns around the world.

The Rebel Diva Nonfiction Series

www.TikiriHerath.com/Nonfiction

Your Rebel Dreams: 6 simple steps to take back control of your life in uncertain times.

Your Rebel Plans: 4 simple steps to getting unstuck and making progress today.

Your Rebel Life: Easy habit hacks to enhance happiness in the 10 key areas of your life.

Bust Your Fears: 3 simple tools to crush your anxieties and squash your stress.

Collaborations

The Boss Chick's Bodacious Destiny Nonfiction Bundle
Dark Shadows 2: Voodoo and Black Magic of New Orleans

Tikiri's novels are available around the world, on all Amazon stores everywhere. The nonfiction books are available on Apple, Kobo, Barnes & Noble, Indigo Chapters, and all good bookstores around the world.

All these books are also available in libraries everywhere. Just ask your friendly local librarian or your local bookstore to order a copy via Ingram Spark.

MERCILESS PAST

A MERCILESS MURDER MYSTERY THRILLER

The First Kill

Today is the day I die.

This was the only thought racing through her mind as she stumbled through the woods.

Her shirt was ripped, and her shoulders were bloodied. Scrapes crisscrossed her bare thighs and bruises covered her face. The ropes had left red marks around her wrists. Still raw.

The wintry morning air was cool and crisp, pinching her skin where it was exposed. Even Mother Nature was being unkind.

But she didn't feel the pain.

She couldn't feel anything other than one simple urge.

I want to live.

The ominous footsteps crashed through the trees behind her. They were getting close. A flash of terror blazed through her spine like a lightning strike, threatening to implode inside her head.

But she didn't dare look back.

Not now.

Her focus was in front as she dodged between the snow-laden fir trees, trying not to fall into hidden snowbanks.

Oh no.

She grabbed a tree branch and stopped just in time.

The ravine.

She'd forgotten the river that cut through the mountain.

She teetered at the edge of the cliff and stared into the abyss. Everything was white around her, blindingly white, except for the riverbed fifty feet below.

This water never froze. It burst through the narrow galley, crashing over the raggedy black rocks like a furious river god, mad at the world.

Her chest heaved.

She could barely breathe.

What do I do now?

She turned her head.

It was a fleeting sound, but she heard the crack of a twig. A dark shadow loomed from behind the tree.

Then came the hand, reaching to her back.

She opened her mouth to scream, but no sound came out.

One quick thrust was all that was needed.

Her feet gave way.

She hurtled into the gully, clawing at nothing, her mouth wide open in a terrified but silent shriek.

She plunged headfirst through the frigid water. The river gods swirled around her, pushing her forward, pulling her under.

She flailed her arms. Dying to breathe. She came up for a second and tried to yell for help, but fistfuls of icy water pounded down her throat.

She gagged.

Her head bashed against a boulder. Water filled her lungs.

It only took a minute. The current's pull was too strong.

The world soon turned black.

Fifty feet above the gully, at the exact spot where she fell, stood a tall dark shadow, watching her body disappear down the raging river.

This is a beautiful place to die.

A slow smile cracked on their face.

One down. Two more to go....

Chapter One

"How come Victoria's wedding isn't at Cedar Cottage?"

Katy turned to me, a frown on her face. My best friend was sitting in the front passenger seat, fiddling with her phone, trying to get it to work.

I kept my eyes dead straight ahead.

Navigating a winding road on a mountainous terrain in New Hampshire with snow coming down was tougher than I expected.

We had rented an all-wheel drive at the airport. It was one of those oversized SUVs hockey moms love to drive around the city, but unlike them, I was using this vehicle for what it was built for. Still, this machine was having a hard time chugging up the steep and slippery slope.

"Was wondering the same thing," I said. "She lives in a manor. Huge grounds. Lots of space for everyone to stay the weekend. Cedar Cottage is the perfect venue for a Christmas wedding. It could be on the cover of a bridal magazine."

"I'd have thought Chandler Rupert would host their wedding at his mega ski resort in Falcon Hills," said Katy. "A lodge doesn't sound romantic, especially in the middle of a snowstorm."

"Maybe because it's a small affair?"

"I think she deserves better."

I had to agree.

Victoria had had a tough life—a past we'd all rather forget.

Her parents hadn't just abandoned her, they had shipped her off to a psychiatric hospital with the help of a local physician with more love for cash than scruples. She had only been nine. A perfectly healthy but unwanted child ruthlessly discarded by her own flesh and blood.

That had to leave deep scars.

She had barely survived her incarceration at the mental institution when she learned she was the only living heiress to her parents' estate in the White Mountains. That one-hundred-and-eighty degree turn had been a shock to the system, too.

Could someone truly recover from a horrific childhood trauma, despite the wealth they had inherited? I worried about her.

"I just hope Victoria made the right decision," I muttered to myself.

Katy let out an annoyed hiss in reply. "What's wrong with this place?"

I knew what had put my friend in a bad mood.

She was feeling guilty for not being at her daughter's school nativity play, especially since we were only a week away from Christmas. Then again, neither Katy nor I could say no to a good friend's once-in-a-lifetime wedding either.

When Victoria had called me three months ago in New York to tell me she'd found her true and forever love, I'd been so happy for her.

Her voice had been bubbly. I could hear her beautiful and beaming smile over the phone. Though a part of me wondered if getting engaged to a man she'd known for only six months was a smart move, I'd pushed those thoughts to the back of my mind as she gushed over the fairytale gown she was getting made.

She was marrying local royalty, the richest family in Falcon Hills, after all.

"Still not working?" I said.

Katy let out another frustrated sigh.

I didn't want to tell her that no amount of clicking or turning the phone on and off would help. We were on high elevation, surrounded by a winter forest, driving next to a deep and narrow canyon, with storm clouds hanging low above us.

These were not the ideal conditions for a perfect cellular connection.

"Thank goodness, Peace found time off work," said Katy. "Chantelle will have one of us in the audience, at least."

"She'll understand. She's a smart kid."

"We're taking her snowboarding after this. Maybe that will make up for me missing the play."

"They should have Wi-Fi at the lodge," I said. "You can call her from there."

"They had better," grumbled Katy.

I turned my attention back to the road.

It was nice to be on a road trip with my friend, especially after the week we'd had.

I hadn't slept for days, my mind rumbling with worries. My deepest fear of our past catching up to us swirled constantly in my head, and I couldn't shake off the feeling someone was watching us.

The prank call that had come to my bakery several months ago had annoyed me. The poison pen letter that had followed it weeks later had bothered me, and the anonymous email after that had unsettled me. But it was the graffiti I'd discovered on my bakery's wall three days ago that had shaken me.

I hate you all. Burn. Kill. You'll pay.

It was a vicious message. Even the local beat cops agreed.

Who had sprayed those sick words on my bakery's side wall? Was it targeted at us? Or was it just another hopeless kid from the streets unleashing their fury at the world, using my small business premises as their anarchic billboard?

The police seemed to think so. I disagreed. But they had nothing to go on and had bigger criminals to catch.

My fiancé, David, and my friend, Tetyana, hadn't wasted one minute after the two constables left. Within forty-eight hours, they had worked their contacts, made the right calls, and secured our brownstone building with enough electronic surveillance equipment to make a small spy agency jealous.

I was glad my friends and family were taking these anonymous threats seriously, but it still didn't help me sleep at night. Fear crawled up and down my spine, and I couldn't help looking over my shoulder.

A cool burst of air swirled around my neck.

"Hey, what are you doing?" I said, turning to Katy.

Katy was holding her window button down.

I shivered. "Put the window up."

"I'm trying to get a signal."

"That won't help."

"You don't—"

A loud splash outside silenced her.

Then came a muffled yell from somewhere in the gully. It was so faint I was sure I'd imagined it.

I took my foot off the gas, spun my head around, and glanced through Katy's window.

"Did you hear that?" she said in a whisper.

"Sounded like something fell into the river."

"Did someone cry for help, or am I going crazy?"

I turned the wheel, stopped the car on the side of the road, and peered through the windshield.

Looming high above us was the craggy mountain peak. The snowfall had never let up. The ski lodge was several miles ahead. Everything around us was so white it was hard to see where the forest ended and the ravine began.

No one should be wandering outside in this weather.

We waited in silence. For what, I didn't know.

Did something fall in the river? Or was it someone?

"Over there!" gasped Katy, clutching my arm.

I followed her finger.

A shadow.

Is it a man? A woman?

The shadow had flitted through the woods quickly. One second, something moved, the next, it vanished, like a phantom.

My stomach tightened. I could feel it in the pit of my gut.

Something was wrong.

Someone was in trouble.

After surviving a childhood of trafficking, one that still gave me nightmares, and after fighting gangsters to keep my family, friends, and myself safe, I trusted my instincts more than ever.

I zipped up my jacket and turned around to pluck the Glock from my purse in the backseat.

"What are you doing?" said Katy, staring at my sidearm in alarm.

"Finding out what the heck is going on here," I said, opening the door and stepping out.

Chapter Two

"Are you sure this is a good idea?"

Katy was at my heels, sticking close to me.

I was petite and almost a foot shorter than her, so she couldn't hide behind me, though it never stopped her from trying whenever she thought we were in a sticky situation.

During winter, when I wasn't at a client meeting, I wore jeans, a jacket, and my favorite red boots. Putting my long black hair in a casual ponytail got me regularly carded as a teen at bars and restaurants. But I was a grown woman in my thirties, engaged to my childhood sweetheart, and running two businesses.

Katy was the opposite of me. With her freckled face, arresting green eyes, and fiery red hair, strangers mistook her to be a plus-sized model from New York and wondered if she was someone famous.

My best friend had had a rough life. Only I knew of her dark secret of fighting bulimia as a teen. Like me, she'd been orphaned at a young age. She'd battled side by side with me, against the gangs who'd tried to take us captive when we were young and vulnerable.

But her fighting Irish genes had cooled after she married Peace, my business attorney, and had become a mother. Right now, I knew she'd rather be in the warm car than traipsing along this desolate road.

"We're late as it is," said Katy. "Shouldn't we get back in the car?"

"Stay back," I whispered. "And watch out for the cliff."

We crept in between the trees to where we'd spotted the shadow, but there was no one. I was just about to head back to the car when I saw them.

"Footprints," I said, pointing at the marks on the fresh snow. "Someone was here."

"So, we didn't imagine it, then?" said Katy.

"It's a kid," I said, placing my foot next to a print. "It's almost my size. Six."

"Could be a small woman too," said Katy. "You're not the only pixie girl in town."

Ignoring her comment, I followed the prints on the ground, my ears and eyes on full alert now. A few feet in, I halted and put an arm out to stop Katy.

"Don't take another step."

"Oh, my goodness," she said, putting a hand over her mouth.

I hadn't realized how close we'd been to the edge of the gorge.

I peered down at the muddy river seething below us. It crashed against the boulders, its thundering sound echoing through the narrow valley that seemed to wind its way through the mountain.

"Did someone fall in?" whispered Katy, as we peered over the edge, holding on to each other.

Her guess would have been as good as mine.

There didn't seem to be another human being in the vicinity. If anyone had fallen, the current would have swept them up or dragged them under by now. I shuddered at the gruesome thought.

"This place is haunting," whispered Katy, gazing down. "Beautiful but haunting."

My spine suddenly tingled.

I whirled around, expecting to find someone watching us, but there was no one.

I scanned the woods.

The immense coniferous trees were heavy with snow, looking like rows of proud Christmas trees waiting to be lit. Against the breathtaking backdrop of the White Mountains, it was like we had walked into a magical winter wonderland. Maybe Victoria had good reasons for hosting her wedding here.

But Katy was right.

Something was odd about this place. Instead of feeling like we had stepped into a blissful Christmas card, I felt goose bumps rise all over me.

"What's over there?" whispered Katy.

I turned around to see a wooden structure, partly obscured by the trees, about twenty yards from us. It looked like a small, dilapidated building, forgotten in time.

"Maybe that's where the shadow went," I said, gripping my gun.

"Maybe we should get in the car," said Katy, not letting go of my arm.

"Good idea. Get back, lock the doors and stay inside till I return."

"What are you up to?"

"I won't sleep tonight if I don't find out what's going on here."

"Nothing's going on here."

"We heard something, and we saw something."

"You're not sleuthing on your own again."

"You're welcome to stay."

I turned in the direction of the cabin.

"I swear you're going to get us killed one of these days," grumbled Katy, her boots crunching on the snow behind me. "Everything's an investigation for you. You need to learn to relax."

She was right. I loved my job.

While Katy managed my bakery in Harlem, I spent my time working in my private investigation firm. She disapproved of some projects I took on, but my detective business paid better than my cakes and crumpets. I'd make even more if I advertised my work, but I catered to the bakery's wealthy clients who sought discretion over all else.

Ignoring Katy's rumblings, I crept in between the trees, my eyes scanning the area. It took us five minutes to get close enough for a good look at the wooden structure.

Part of me felt silly.

That shadow could have been a cross-country skier who'd got lost and had been trying to find their way. Someone could have been out on a morning walk, on a break from the festive overeating and partying, and had returned to the lodge. It could have even been a deer or a bear, not a human shadow.

We probably looked like idiots, walking stealthily like this.

But I couldn't ignore the warning flags coming from my gut. The closer we got to the shed, the harder my heart beat.

There was something in there.

Katy was holding on to my shoulder now. That was not a good idea if I had to take swift action, but I didn't have the heart to tell her to let go. She was scared. I should have left her in the car.

We were thirty feet from the shed now.

"Get behind that," I whispered, pointing with my chin toward a large fir tree. "Keep your eyes and ears open."

Katy scooted toward the tree without hesitation.

I stepped up to the structure.

The shed had a derelict wraparound porch with five steps that led up to the door. One wall had moss growth, now partially covered by the snowdrifts. Sharp icicles hung from the roof, like translucent daggers in a row. The place looked sad and secluded, like it hadn't had visitors for months.

I peeked around the porch. The cabin's lone window was shuttered and curtained. *Who puts curtains in an abandoned cabin in the woods?*

I walked up and tried the door. It didn't budge. That was when I noticed the lock. Someone had put an expensive, modern electronic lock on this ramshackle of a shed.

Strange.

I turned to head back to Katy when I saw them again.

More footprints.

They were the same boot marks on the snow, only a few feet from the structure.

I stepped down from the porch and kneeled on the ground next to the markings. The small shoe prints were mixed with the markings of a larger boot print. The snow had been disturbed heavily, like someone had fallen or some people had tussled on the ground.

A dry brown leaf, a leftover from the fall, was stuck under the snow, its pointy ends sticking out. But it was the dark red spot next to it that caught my breath.

Blood?

I whipped out my phone and took a picture. The splotch of red was so small, it was hard to say, and I didn't dare touch it. I slipped my cell back into my pocket and glanced around me.

The woods were silent. The tall trees stared back at me, as if they were mocking me for being so paranoid.

I could imagine Katy cursing me from behind her hiding spot. A lecture was waiting for me when we got back in the car, I was sure. She always thought I was too quick to suspect the worst and conjure up crimes when there were none.

I got to my feet and walked back to the tree, catching a frightened eye peeking from behind.

"Shed's locked," I said, as I joined my friend. "Didn't see anyone, but I saw more footprints."

"Could be a hunting cabin," said Katy.

"Hunting season's over."

She blew a raspberry.

"Can we go back to the car, please? Victoria's waiting for us and I'm freezing."

I nodded and turned back to the main road. Katy fell in step with me, her teeth chattering, but still grumbling.

"I tell you, every time—" she was saying when she lurched forward. I grabbed her by the shoulder just in time.

"You okay?"

"Stupid root," she said, kicking at something on the ground.

I stared at what she had tripped on. We were almost at the road and the wood thinned here.

"That's not a root," I said, moving the snow aside with my boot.

Concealed underneath was a thick burlap sack that seemed to encase something.

"What is it?" she said, peering over my shoulder.

I bent down and pulled the cloth away.

"My goodness," gasped Katy.

"It's a hatch," I whispered.

We stared at our find.

It was a small wooden door, large enough for an adult to crawl out of. Or in. The steel ring on top was what Katy had tripped on.

"Why would anyone put a door out in the woods?" said Katy, her brow furrowed.

It was clearly an entrance, but an entrance to what?

"An underground cellar?" I said and turned back to the shed that was shrouded behind the trees now. "Another entrance to that cabin?"

I bent back down and tried the steel ring.

"Asha?"

I looked up. Katy was hugging herself and hopping from foot to foot.

"I don't care what this is," she said, "but I don't want to hang around here anymore."

"Don't you want to see what's inside?"

"You're not on a job. We came for a wedding, remember? And we're already late."

"Aren't you curious?"

"No!"

Flashing me an annoyed look, Katy spun around.

"This is exactly the place a serial killer would bring their victims," she said as she stomped toward our car. "These woods give me the creeps."

Chapter Three

"Good thing Tetyana was too busy at work to come," said Katy as she slammed her door shut.

"That's a bit mean, isn't it?" I said, slipping back into the driver's seat.

"With the two of you together, you'd make me hang out in the woods, hunting wild shadows all day."

"Now she's got an FBI badge, she won't be interested in my little investigations," I said with a rueful smile. "I sure miss her. She would have broken into that shed in a heart-beat."

"See, that's your problem. We're going to a wedding and all you see is trouble. Can you try to have some fun for a change?"

"My job is fun," I said as I slipped my Glock back into my purse.

I pushed the key into the ignition and turned it on, relieved to hear the car purr to life. I blasted the heat and rubbed my hands to warm myself.

I had made one good decision that day.

Katy had wanted to rent the cute yellow convertible in the corner of the rental lot. The bored service rep didn't seem to care either way and had mumbled something about it having winter tires. But I'd held firm.

I turned the wheels and moved us back onto the road. Though I was still curious about what the woods held, it was good to be enveloped in the warm and safe cocoon of our vehicle again.

"Ten minutes to the lodge," I said, glancing at the GPS on the dash. "Keep an eye out for anything suspicious out of your window, just in case."

"I think we imagined that shadow," said Katy. "Could have been a moose."

"We didn't imagine that creepy shed or the weird hatch."

She fell silent.

The incline was getting steeper and more slippery. As I pushed into a higher gear, the engine whined in protest.

"Going downhill is going to be worse," I said, peering through the windshield.

"Hey!" shouted Katy suddenly. "You missed the road!"

I turned around, startled.

She was pointing at something behind us, on her side. I slowed down, peeked out through her window, and gave her a quizzical look.

"What road?"

"Didn't you see the sign for the ski lodge?" she said.

"GPS says it's straight up."

"I saw the sign. It clearly said we were supposed to take that road."

I brought the car to a complete stop, and double-checked my GPS.

"But there are no other roads around here," I said, frowning.

"I saw it," said Katy, jutting her chin out stubbornly. "It went that way."

"Through the woods?"

"All I'm saying is the sign to the ski lodge was that way and you missed it."

I put the car in reverse and backed down the mountain, foot by foot.

"Hope no one's coming up or we'd be in real trouble," I said, my eyes on the rearview mirror.

Katy had her face pressed against her window, watching the road, and signaling with her hand for me to keep backing up.

"Just a bit more and you'll see it," she said.

I reversed a few more yards.

"There!" she said, pointing. "See?"

I stared at the sign.

Cloud Cabin Ski Lodge.

"I told you," said Katy. "You need to believe me more often."

Cloud Cabin Ski Lodge was where Victoria was waiting for us, where the wedding was to take place in a few hours.

I frowned at the screen on my dash. The software came pre-installed with the car. Shouldn't it be more reliable than a sign on the road? Or did the computer have an outdated map?

"Doesn't look like a road," I said, peering over Katy's shoulder.

"Tire marks," she said, sitting up straight and tapping her finger on the window. "Someone's already gone that way. Maybe the other guests who came before us. Let's follow it."

"How come I don't see it on my screen?"

"The Google car hasn't come this way yet."

"GPS is satellite. This isn't Google maps."

"This is a shortcut up the mountain. We're already late for the wedding. Are we going to try it or not?"

I turned the wheels.

Driving in the lowest gear, I followed the smaller road that cut through the narrow opening in the woods. It seemed more like a dirt road than a paved one, but since ice and snow coated the entire mountain, it was hard to say.

I scanned the surroundings, wondering why anyone would carve this side road when the main road worked perfectly well.

I glanced at my GPS. According to it, we were moving away from the ski lodge.

My gut was signaling to me again. Something didn't feel right.

We had driven fifty yards through the isolated route when I crawled at a snail's pace.

"Why are we slowing?" said Katy, turning to me.

"I don't like this, Katy. We need to get back on the main road."

"But the sign says—"

"A sign is easy to move. A road isn't. I don't think this is going anywhere."

I put the car in reverse before she could protest, and pressed on the gas pedal. My wheels ground in the snow.

"Shoot," I said, easing off the accelerator. "I think we're stuck."

I reversed a bit and tried again. That was when the wheels caught on a snowbank and fishtailed on the icy surface.

"Watch it!" shouted Katy, grabbing on to the dashboard.

I scrambled to straighten the car, turning the steering wheel to its limit, but the tires were sliding. We were slipping down the slope, backward.

I braked hard.

Too hard.

The car swung around on the ice, making a complete U-turn.

Katy screamed.

We were facing the wrong direction, heading straight toward the canyon.

"Stop the car!" shrieked Katy.

I put all my weight on the brakes.

My heart was hammering. Perspiration streamed down my face. I clutched the steering wheel with my sweaty hands, but they were threatening to slip any moment.

The tires finally caught traction.

A root.

I'd hit a tree root.

The car screeched to a halt.

We stopped ten feet from the edge of the bluff.

Katy and I stared at the abyss, not breathing.

If I'd been driving at normal speed or if that root hadn't been jutting out of the snow, we'd have hurtled into the gully below and smashed into smithereens by now.

I looked around me. There were no warning signs, nothing indicating this was a danger zone. To my right was the lonely shed, but there was no sign of anyone.

I swallowed hard and wiped my hands on my jacket.

"That was close," I said.

Shortcuts never work. I knew that. That's the last time I listen to directions from Katy.

"We're getting out of here," I said, putting the vehicle in reverse. It took several tries to turn around inch by inch, without getting dragged toward the edge, but we finally got back on the main road.

We drove in silence after that.

One thought was buzzing through my mind.

Who put that sign there? Did someone move it deliberately?

Chapter Four

"Gosh, it's beautiful," gasped Katy.

"This isn't a lodge," I said as I pulled into the driveway. "This is a luxury Swiss chalet."

Katy turned to me with a bright smile, our recent ordeal all but forgotten. "This isn't so bad. Good for Victoria."

I turned into the parking lot and eased into an empty spot between a Mercedes sedan and a vehicle protected by a cover embossed in a luxury logo.

"Fancy," said Katy, with an appreciative glance at the Porsche emblem. "These people must be loaded."

"Not the best car for these parts," I said, and turned around to point at the super-sized Humvee we'd passed by the entrance to the driveway. "Now, that's the one I'd take if I needed to get down in a hurry."

The Humvee's winter tires were strapped in chains and were as tall as the Porsche beside us.

"That horrible gas-guzzling monster truck?" Katy said, making a face. "Can you make an uglier thing?"

I put our car in park and unbuckled my seat belt with a grin. My friend had strong opinions about vehicles, none of which had anything to do with their utility.

That was when the ping came from my phone.

Victoria?

I turned around to pluck my cell from the backseat and read the text message out aloud.

"Welcome to Cloud Cabin Ski Lodge. This will be a wedding to remember."

"Who is it?" said Katy, leaning over.

I showed my screen to her. She gave me a puzzled look back.

"Unknown number," I said. "I have Victoria's cell programed in, so it isn't her."

"Maybe it's one of her new in-laws."

"I haven't even met them yet. They can't have my private number."

"What about Jim and Nancy? They're here. Didn't she say Nancy's her maid of honor? Jim's in the wedding party too, I think."

Jim and Nancy were Cedar Cottage's young caretakers. Victoria's inherited manor was grand but wasn't a place for a single girl. I was glad the couple, whom I trusted, had stayed with her, so she wouldn't be alone in that big house in the mountains.

"Doesn't sound like anything they'd send," I said.

"The good news," said Katy, unbuckling her seat belt, "is this means there's better cellular reception up here."

I nodded absentmindedly, as I typed a polite but noncommittal message into the box.

Thank you. Can't wait for the ceremony.

"It's been a while since I saw Victoria," I said, slipping the phone into my pocket. "Maybe she changed phones, or she's using Chandler's."

Katy pulled her handbag from the backseat and took out her makeup mirror and lipstick.

I sat silently, my mind elsewhere.

We'd had a strange trip and my brain was swirling with questions. We'd been very lucky to not end up at the bottom of that gully.

I surveyed the chalet in front of us, one finger tapping on the steering wheel.

It was a sprawling, one-story building with vaulted ceilings and large bay windows that overlooked the woods. A beautiful stone chimney rose high from the side of the structure.

An electric generator and a stack of wood kindling sat next to the lodge. By the generator were a row of red gas cannisters and an ax stuck on a stump of wood.

Scattered across the grounds were a dozen smaller log cabins. The closest one to the main lodge had its lights on, but the others looked dark and empty.

Several yards behind the main lodge lay the wintry forest that grew along the mountain slope. The trees crouched close together here, casting dark shadows on the grounds and the building.

From what I'd read, Chandler's family had made their fortune on ski resorts and had built this lodge as their private haven—a getaway from the common crowds that flocked to the hills in winter.

We had passed the ski resort owned by the Rupert family on our way here. Located at the base of the mountain, it was surrounded by chain hotels, fast-food joints, children's play parks, and everything families on winter holidays look for. It had been buzzing with people.

This place was different.

This was a rich man's getaway.

It gave off a quietly opulent vibe, but it was eerie. If I hadn't seen the cars or the lights, I'd have thought no one lived here.

"You look awful, Asha."

I turned to my friend.

"Thanks," I said, with a grimace. "Didn't sleep much last night."

I rarely did, even though I popped sleeping pills after dinner every evening. My childhood nightmares that visited me every night made sure I didn't rest.

"You've got to freshen up then, girlfriend. Come on. Do it for Victoria."

I groaned.

I loved to play dress up, maybe not as much as Katy, but there were times I just wanted to get cozy in my comfy pants and woolen top. After the day we'd had, this was one of them.

Our dresses were hanging on the door hooks at the back of the car, uncreased and secure inside their garment bags. It was a good thing we'd brought our winter coats too because no one could survive this weather in cute little black dresses.

"Ooh, check out those lovebirds."

I peered through the back window, expecting to see Victoria.

A tall, blond man in a black tuxedo was standing by the rhododendron hedge by the parking lot. He was grinning at someone behind the bushes. A piece of bright pink chiffon fluttered out from the bottom of the hedge. Whoever it was, was wearing a long pink gown, but we couldn't see their face.

As Katy and I watched, the man leaned forward, yanked at the woman's arms, and pulled her up for a kiss.

Katy turned around with a raised eyebrow.

"Best men fooling around with the bridesmaids. Happens all the time. Love blossoms at weddings."

She jabbed me with her elbow.

"Hey, isn't it time you and David planned your big day? Seven years is a long time to be engaged, hun."

She took her hairspray out and sprayed the top of her head.

I sneezed and reached for my purse, where I had my lipstick and face powder, the most I wore, if I could help it. I put on my lipstick, knowing better than to encourage her.

All my friends chided David and me about our extra-long engagement. I was the holdout. With a successful bakery to run and a private investigation firm that was getting busier each month, I didn't have time to plan a weekend getaway, let alone the wedding everyone was expecting me to have.

I opened my door.

"Let's go," I said. "We're going to a wedding, not to a modeling gig in New York."

Getting our dresses, we slipped in between the cars and walked toward the main lodge.

We were halfway up the pathway when I noticed the middle-aged woman in a black fur coat watching us from the front steps. By her feet was a large tan dog whom she was holding by the collar.

"Gosh, is that a wolf?" whispered Katy. "It looks mean. Her too."

She was right. The frown on the woman's face was clear.

Despite that anonymous text message, Katy and I weren't welcome here.

Chapter Five

We strolled toward the main entrance in silence, smiles frozen on our faces.

The woman didn't move, but the closer we approached, the deeper her frown got.

Her light Scandinavian blonde hair had been done up in an elegant updo. She wore a magnificent three-strand pearl necklace that peeked out from the beautiful fur coat draped around her shoulders.

She looked dressed to welcome the queen. I felt inadequate just to be in her proximity.

I knew this woman. I'd seen her face on local online news channels as she presented big blown-up checks to local charities. This was the matriarch of the family.

Victoria's new mother-in-law.

We were ten feet from her when she let go of the dog.

Katy scooted behind me. I braced myself for angry barking.

Instead, the German Shepherd jumped down and ran toward us, tongue lolling, tail wagging, like he hadn't seen visitors his entire life. I bent down and petted his massive head as he sniffed around us, feeling thankful there was at least one friendly face at this lodge.

Maybe Victoria's mother-in-law wasn't that mean after all, I thought as I tried to not get entangled in between the dog's legs. Anyone who owned a friendly pup would have to be good folk.

"Good morning," I called out, waving to the woman on the steps. "We're Victoria's friends."

She didn't smile back.

"She mentioned you," she said in a crisp, cool voice. "I didn't realize she actually invited you to a private family function."

I raised an eyebrow.

Private family function?

Katy shot me a worried look.

"We came all the way from New York," I said, keeping my smile intact. "Flew in early this morning. Couldn't miss her wedding for the world."

The woman's face remained stoic.

"You'll be leaving after the ceremony, then?"

That wasn't a question. It was a command.

Katy and I exchanged a glance.

"We were hoping to stay the weekend. Victoria asked us...." I stopped. It was time to try another tactic.

I walked toward her.

"Hi. I'm Asha Kade and this is Katy McCafferty. It's a pleasure to meet you."

Still no smile. She must have been the unhappiest rich woman I'd ever met.

"You must be Chandler's...?" I trailed off, hoping she'd finish the sentence.

"I'm the mother of the groom," she said, a side of her mouth curled up. "Barbara Rupert."

I walked up the steps and offered my hand. It was the polite thing to do. To my surprise, she held out hers with some reluctance, but that nose in the air told me she clearly disapproved of our presence.

I was just about to shake her hand when a shrill scream came from somewhere on the grounds.

We whirled around, startled.

A rake-thin young woman in a pink bridesmaid's gown was scampering our way, waving her arms. She tripped over something in the snow, caught herself, and kept running toward the lodge.

What was she doing out in the cold dressed like that?

The dog jumped around her, barking excitedly. Barbara turned to it with an annoyed frown.

"Down, Max," she said in a stern voice.

"I... s... saw in the... the r... river!" stammered the woman as she got closer.

A chill went through me.

Maybe there was something to the splash we heard, after all.

The young woman's face was flushed, and she was stuttering, barely able to get a complete sentence out.

"I... I d... I... s... saw—" She tried in vain.

"What are you playing at now, Mia?" scolded Barbara. "I don't have time for your silly games."

Mia turned away, as if frustrated at not being able to find her words. I wondered if this was a speech impediment or a result of her nervousness.

"What did you see, hun?" I said.

"A b... b...." stuttered Mia hopelessly, pointing toward the woods.

Her eyes were wide, and her face was flushed. Whatever she had seen had troubled her. She wasn't lying.

"What was it?"

"Some... s... s... I s... swear... it was a b... b..."

"Stop this," said Barbara, her voice sharp. "You know better than to act like this in front of guests."

"Not at all," I said, jerking my head her way. "We heard a splash on our way up. We were wondering what it was."

"Local kids playing pranks," said Barbara, turning her cool blue eyes on me.

Kids? That would explain the small footprints.

"These hooligans throw rocks down the cliff, ride their mountain bikes all summer and snowmobiles during the winter, raising hell on the mountain," said Barbara, giving me a disapproving look like I was one of the hooligans. "They heard you coming and knew you were from out of town. You were pranked."

"B... but... but.. I'm t... telling you, I —" Mia didn't get to finish.

"Ah, the fibber is in full form today."

It was a male voice.

Katy and I turned around.

It was a sandy-haired tuxedoed man, looking a lot like the man we'd seen kissing a girl behind the rhododendron bushes. He strutted up to us, hands in his pockets, a cocky look on his handsome face. He looked like he'd just walked off a photo shoot for an upscale men's magazine.

"So, you're the ladies Victoria's been babbling about," he said, holding out his hand amiably.

I shook it, but not before giving the young woman beside him a discreet glance. She looked distraught. Why were they ignoring her?

The man saw me look. He put a hand to his head, twirled a finger, and mouthed *cuckoo*.

Mia's face turned bright red. She hadn't missed the man's gesture or his words. Tears welled in her eyes. I realized that despite the heavy makeup and the fancy dress, she wasn't more than eighteen years old. I felt for her.

Was it her behind the rhododendron bushes by the parking lot?

Before I could say anything, she turned away, staggered up the stairs and disappeared inside the lodge, her hands covering a sob.

"Don't mind Mia. She's just looking for attention," said the man with a grin. "Every family has a crazy and my sister is it in mine, I'm afraid."

"You must be from the groom's party?" I said, ignoring his nasty jab at the poor girl.

Barbara turned to me, a proud look on her face.

"Chandler is my one and only son. He just got back from New York. He's been busy, doing very well for himself and us, I might add."

She gave a small, fake laugh.

Did I hear her right? Did she say Chandler?

Barbara beamed at her son.

"He's a hedge fund manager for one of the biggest firms in the country. Can't make a mother more proud."

Chandler's grin widened as he soaked up the praise.

This was the groom. The man about to marry Victoria. I must have stopped breathing because I felt my chest tighten.

I'd seen Victoria's wedding gown. She'd shared a dozen photos of it, bubbling with excitement. I distinctly remembered it wasn't pink. That meant whoever Chandler had been flirting with behind those bushes hadn't been his bride.

"How did you and Victoria meet?" asked Katy, turning steely eyes on Chandler.

"I was in town and met her at some charity shindig. We locked eyes across the room, and as they say, the rest is history."

His grin remained intact, but his eyes weren't smiling.

The man was lying.

"Are you and Victoria planning to go to New York after the wedding?" asked Katy, her voice hardening.

I knew she was struggling to stop herself from lashing out and demanding what we both wanted to know.

"Of course not," said Barbara, with a dismissive wave of her hand. "Do you think I'd allow that?"

"Your wish is my command, Barbara," said Chandler with a small bow.

Barbara?

Most people called their mothers *Mom*. Or, *Mother*.

Odd.

"He's staying right here," said Barbara, reaching over to squeeze Chandler's arm and giving him a fond smile. "He'll take over the family business and my husband can retire. I want grandbabies, Sunday family dinners, and picnics in the summer."

Her eyes were glued on him, her entire focus on her son. It was like we weren't even here.

"For the first time in a long time, I will have everyone around the dinner table. I've been dreaming of this for years."

My mind whirred.

We'd only seen the man near the bushes from behind.

Had I mistaken him for someone else? Maybe he had been one of the groom's men?

Something about his story didn't feel right.

Chapter Six

Chandler gave me the side-eye.

He'd noticed me scrutinizing him.

"The ceremony is about to start," he said, stepping away, his grin disappearing. "A snowstorm's on its way and we don't have time for chitchat."

"But we're still waiting for—" Barbara didn't get to finish.

Chandler shook his head. "The show must go on."

He leaped up the steps, accidentally stepping on the dog's tail as he did. Max let out a whelp.

Instead of stopping to see the damage he'd done, he gave the dog an impatient kick before striding inside. Max scurried behind Barbara, his ears and tail down.

I glared at Chandler's disappearing back.

What a jerk.

Without a word at us or a look our way, Barbara whirled around and followed her son inside.

Katy and I exchanged a shocked glance.

What a welcome.

I stepped up to the dog and stroked his head.

Max wagged his tail gently and licked my hand, but kept his head down, like he was afraid I'd strike him too. I wondered if he'd been kicked before. And I wondered what kind of family Victoria was marrying into.

"Hey, you two!"

I spun around.

It was someone we hadn't seen in a long time.

"Nancy!" shrieked Katy as she ran up to her, her arms wide and ready for a hug. I dashed down to join them.

Nancy was in a pink gown, in the same style and color as Mia's—the same type of cloth we'd seen flutter from behind the rhododendron bushes only moments ago.

When we saw Nancy last, she had been in overalls and rubber boots, cleaning the stables at Cedar Cottage. She looked gorgeous with her dark hair elegantly done up and a pink rose pinned to the lapel of her dress that flowed to her heels.

It was nice to see a familiar face, one I trusted for a change.

This place was getting to me.

The woods were dark and foreboding, even without a creepy shed and a mysterious underground hatch. This lonely ski lodge set high on the mountain and away from civilization didn't make me feel any safer. But it was the churlish son and the haughty mother who bothered me the most.

"How's Victoria?" I asked Nancy once we'd hugged and said our hellos.

"She's sick," she replied, turning worried eyes on me.

"What? How?"

"Food poisoning from the reception dinner last night. It's not just her. Jim and I are fine, but some others got it bad."

"Poor girl," said Katy, her face falling, "on her wedding day too."

"She'll be okay. Just needs a break after all this is over." Nancy smiled. "She'll be so happy to see you. She's been dying for you to meet Chandler."

"Oh, we just met him," I said, without smiling back.

Nancy raised her brows. She turned from me to Katy and back.

"So, you felt it too?" she said.

"What's he like with Victoria?" said Katy.

Nancy looked away. "She's head over heels over him and all, but he's not very..."

We waited.

She sighed. "He doesn't think much of Jim and me. Barely talks to us. I'm scared he'll convince Victoria to let us go after they get married."

"Fire you, you mean?" gasped Katy. "She'd never allow something like that. Who'd take care of Cedar Cottage then?"

Nancy gave us a wonky smile and waved dismissively.

"Forget what I said. We're here for a wedding. The happiest day of Victoria's life."

I pulled my phone out of my pocket.

"Hey, Nancy, did you send me this text, by any chance?" I asked.

Nancy peered at the screen and shook her head.

"Was it Jim?"

"He's more the *hey, can't wait to see you* kind of guy." She shrugged. "Wrong number maybe?"

About the wedding?

"It's weird," I said, slipping my phone back into my pocket with a frown. "Where's Victoria right now?"

"She's waiting for you," said Nancy, turning around and gesturing for us to follow her to the cabin nearest the main lodge. Katy and I trailed behind her, carrying our gowns.

The log cabins scattered across the grounds had a foot of snow piled on their slanted roofs. They looked like cozy, modern-day versions of a mountain hobbit's home. If I hadn't had an unpleasant taste in my mouth, I'd have thought this to be a perfect winter vacation destination.

"Victoria's cabin is the closest to the lodge. Ours is the fourth down," said Nancy as she led the way.

She opened the door to Victoria's cabin and Katy walked in after her. I followed them inside, taking in the compact interior. The whiff of expensive perfume and makeup permeated the air.

A queen bed took most of the space. Across from it was a chest of drawers with a large mirror, and next to that was a closet filled with a jumble of men's and women's clothes.

Paintings of skiers and mountain sunsets decorated the walls. The small door next to the entrance was closed, which I gathered to be the ensuite bathroom. On the wall by it was a red fire extinguisher.

These cabins looked like rustic ski huts on the outside, but they had all the amenities of a well-equipped five-star hotel room on the inside.

"Is she in the bathroom?" I said, pointing to the closed door.

Nancy leaned her ear against the door and tapped gently.

"Hey, sweetie, Asha and Katy are here."

Silence.

"Victoria, are you feeling all right, honey?"

No answer.

Nancy's brow furrowed. She knocked again.

"Flush the toilet, or open a tap hun, if you don't feel like talking."

Nothing.

I stepped up, reached over, and pushed on the door handle. I peeked inside and dropped my garment bag in shock.

Victoria was bent over the toilet, her face down. I didn't have to get close to spot the blood on her veil.

I rushed inside.

"Victoria!" Katy cried as she dashed in after me.

She was dressed in her beautiful white bridal gown. She even had on her sparkling shoes and silk veil held in place by a silver tiara. But her makeup had been rubbed all over her face, like she had hastily wiped her mouth and cheeks.

The three of us surrounded her when she put a hand out, as if to ask for space.

Katy and I shuffled to the side.

"Oh, my gosh, you scared me," said Nancy. "What are you doing in here, sweetie? Are you still feeling sick?"

Victoria raised her head, but her eyes remained closed.

"Are you okay, honey?" said Katy.

Victoria opened her eyes. They widened as she saw us. She placed her arm out, reaching toward us. I grabbed her hand and helped her to sit up on the side of the bath.

"You need to lie down," I said.

"What you need is water," said Katy, turning toward the sink.

Victoria gave us a dazed look.

"Honey," I said, leaning forward. "What happened?"

She shook her head, like she was too exhausted to reply.

"Maybe you need to postpone the wedding," I said. "You need to get better first. That's your priority."

Those words had a strange effect on her. She sat up straighter and pushed me away.

"No," she said in a hoarse voice.

"Drink," said Katy, leaning over with a glass of water. While Katy cajoled Victoria to take a few sips, Nancy got a wet towel to wipe the blood off her veil.

I waited for Victoria to drink and settle herself.

"Where's the blood coming from, hun?" I said, easing the veil away from her face to see if she had any bruises or wounds.

Victoria turned and glanced at her veil like she was seeing it for the first time.

"She was throwing up all morning," said Nancy, looking up from rubbing the stain. "We thought she was done and got her dressed up, but I guess she had to go again."

"She vomited blood?" I said, frowning. "That's serious. Is there a doctor at the lodge?"

Nancy gave a quick shake of her head.

"Not that I—"

A bang on the door made us all jump.

"Hurry, girls!" came a male voice from the outside.

It was Chandler.

"Coming soon!" shouted Nancy.

He banged on the door again. I was losing respect for the groom fast.

With an exasperated sigh, Nancy turned around and walked out of the bathroom, the wet towel in her hands.

"No!" cried Victoria, a panicked look on her face. "Don't let him in!"

I bent down to her level, took her hand, and looked her in the eye. "Why, sweetie? Is he giving you trouble?"

"A groom shouldn't see the bride in her dress," she whispered hoarsely. "It's bad luck."

Chandler banged on the door again.

Katy and I exchanged an incensed look over Victoria. If I'd thought the man was a boor before, he was confirming my theory.

I heard the outside door open. Katy gently closed the bathroom door halfway so Victoria wouldn't get more flustered. He couldn't see us, but we could hear him.

"We need a little more time, Chandler," Nancy was saying. "Can you keep everyone entertained for another half an hour at least?"

"What the hell is taking so long?"

I grimaced, wishing more than ever to punch him in the face.

"She's not feeling well. You know this. Give her time."

"Well, hurry up, for heaven's sake."

"What the heck is his problem?" I hissed, wishing I'd met him earlier, so I could have investigated him and warned Victoria off him.

We heard Nancy close the door and lock it. She stepped into the bathroom, a pained expression on her face.

"Is he always like that?" I said.

"What kind of man goes around banging on his bride's door when she's sick?" said Katy.

Nancy gave us a sad look.

But Victoria remained silent.

Chapter Seven

"It happened so quickly," said Nancy in a whisper.

"The engagement?" asked Katy.

"All of it."

I popped my head out of the bathroom to check on Victoria. She was in bed, lying on her back, worn out after another bout of vomiting.

Her eyes were closed. Her chest moved up and down as she wheezed. She needed the rest.

Nancy, Katy, and I had huddled inside the bathroom after we cleaned her up and took her to bed. I was dying to know more about the Rupert family, especially Chandler.

"In all of six months," said Nancy in a low voice, "she met the man, got engaged, and planned the wedding. Just like that."

"I don't like the guy," said Katy, making a face like she'd just bit into something rotten.

Nancy sighed.

"You should have seen her the past few weeks. Glowing. Over the moon about the wedding and Chandler. Said she met her soul mate and all that."

"Sounds like she really loves him," I said.

"Jim and I have been watching him for a while," said Nancy, dropping her voice even lower. "He acted like Prince Charming at the beginning. Wooing her with flowers, gifts, trips. Took her to Venice, even. Did you know this is just the first wedding?"

"First wedding?" said Katy and me at the same time.

"Chandler's flying the whole family to Paris tomorrow, where they'll have a grand wedding party at a five-star hotel."

Was that what Barbara meant when she called this a *family function*?

"Are you going too?" I asked.

Nancy made a face.

"They will never invite us. They're not too happy with her choice for maid of honor, I can tell you. As far as Barbara is concerned, Jim and me are just help."

"But you're family!" said Katy, putting an arm around Nancy's shoulders.

"I didn't expect this," I said, shaking my head. "I thought Victoria would know better...." I stopped and swallowed, feeling bad about speaking about her behind her back.

Nancy leaned in closer.

"We told her to take more time before saying yes. I know he's a super successful hotshot and all. Made millions trading stocks or something. I can't make head or tail of what he does, but because he comes from a well-known, wealthy family, they're the perfect couple—if you listen to town gossip, that is."

"How did they meet?" I said.

"He came to Cedar Cottage in his fancy Porsche one day. Said he knew her grandmother, Madame Bouchard. Supposedly he had met her in New York and wanted to say hello to the family."

"He said they met at a charity shindig," I said.

"He was lying," said Katy. "I saw it in his eyes."

Nancy shrugged. "Don't believe a word he says, if you ask me. All talk but hollow as a whistle."

"What does Victoria see in him?" asked Katy.

"He visited her with the biggest flower bouquet and invited her for lunch. That turned into a dinner date, more gifts, expensive jewelry and all that, and that snowballed into the engagement. Poor Victoria. You know how she grew up. This is her fantasy come true. She's star struck."

"In six months?" said Katy.

"She just had her thirtieth birthday," said Nancy, giving a quick side glance out of the bathroom door. "She said she wanted to settle down, have kids, and live a normal life for once."

Katy sighed. "Who can blame her after all that happened?"

"That's what I said to Jim."

I frowned.

"Why didn't they have the wedding at Cedar Cottage? You've got plenty of rooms. And it's a beautiful location."

"That's exactly what Jim said to her," said Nancy, poking my arm with her finger. "But Robert, Chandler's father, said we have to come to the ski lodge. He promised a cozy, fairytale winter wedding. He's paying for everything, and Victoria never says no to Chandler, so here we are."

Katy opened her mouth to speak when we heard a low groan from the room.

I stepped out of the bathroom and walked over to the bed. Victoria turned her head and gave me a weak smile.

I wanted so badly to open up to her, but I was getting the distinct feeling she wouldn't welcome us questioning her in-laws or her fiancé, least of all on her wedding day.

"How are you feeling, hun?" I said, sitting on the edge of her bed. "Better?"

Nancy came over and helped her sit up. Victoria leaned her head on Nancy's shoulder and gave us a wistful smile.

"I'm so sorry, guys."

"Hush," said Katy, leaning over to squeeze her arm. "You have nothing to apologize for. We just want you to feel better."

Victoria looked up at her, then at me.

"I'm so happy you came."

"We'll always be here when you need us," I said.

She turned to Nancy.

"Hey, sweetie, can you redo my makeup for me?" she asked. "You spent hours on it and I messed it all up already. Sorry."

"That's what I'm here for," said Nancy, getting up and reaching for the makeup kit that lay open on the chest of drawers. "You just make yourself comfortable, and we'll take care of everything."

I stood back and watched as Nancy and Katy got busy, cleaning Victoria's face and reapplying her makeup.

I was torn.

Victoria had been an unwanted child, abandoned by her own parents who didn't want her around, reminding them of their biggest mistake. She had only been nine when she had been shipped off to the asylum.

I'd been there to rescue Victoria from her troubled past. Nancy and Jim had been there too. Together, we'd formed a bond and become almost like a family. I hated to see someone I cared about making the wrong decision.

Neither Katy nor I had told her what we'd seen in the parking lot yet. All I'd got was a quick glimpse. I wish I had snapped a photo, so I'd have evidence.

Now as I watched Victoria sit impatiently, eager to start the wedding, as Nancy and Katy fixed her makeup, I questioned my own eyes.

We saw that man lean in. But we didn't catch his face. Who was the woman, anyway? It couldn't have been Mia, his own sister. Then who was it?

If that had been Chandler, I was obligated to tell her what we saw. It was what I'd expect from my friends.

Victoria's eyes turned to me, and a small smile broke out on her lips.

"Stop moving, hun," said Nancy. "We're almost done."

"Hey," I said, looking Victoria in the eye. "How long have you known Chandler?"

Her eyes flittered. Then she let out a heavy sigh.

"I know what you're all thinking," she said in a soft voice. "It happened fast. But Chandler treats me like a queen. No man's talked to me like he does. I love him and he loves me."

"Do you have a prenup?"

Victoria jerked her head up. The eyeliner in Nancy's hand made a black swoop across her forehead. Nancy shot me an annoyed look.

"Asha!" said Victoria, her face a picture of dismay. "Do you think I can't take care of myself?"

"That's not what I meant," I said, half kicking myself, wishing I'd been more diplomatic.

"I've been dreaming of this day since I was nine. Even if I throw up a hundred times today, I'm going through with this. Besides, I'm not planning to eat anything. That should settle my stomach back to normal soon."

No one spoke.

"I just want you all to stop worrying," continued Victoria, flashing her beautiful smile at us. "Take lots of amazing pictures and relax, and I'll soon forget I was sick. This is my day."

I tried to rustle up a smile for her and keep my voice casual.

"So, who's in the wedding party?"

"Other than Nancy and Jim, you mean?" she said.

I nodded.

"Chandler's three sisters are the bridesmaids."

"Sisters?" I said, arching an eyebrow. "All of them?"

She nodded.

"Does he have brothers?"

"He's the only son." Victoria shot me another smile from under Katy's arm. "I wanted to ask you and Katy to be my bridesmaids, but I know how busy you are."

"Don't think twice about it," said Katy, busy with the compact powder and brush.

I swallowed hard and took a deep breath in to steel myself. It was time to speak up.

"Victoria, do you trust Chandler?"

Victoria's smile disappeared.

There was no other way to say it than directly.

"This isn't easy to say, but I think I saw him flirt with one of the bridesmaids," I said.

Her laugh caught me off guard.

"Is that what you're so worried about?"

Katy and I exchanged a quizzical glance.

"He's their only brother and they're all affectionate," Victoria chattered, her smile returning. "Besides, they haven't seen each other in ages. They're playful, that's all."

I raised a brow.

Playful was not the word I would have used to describe Chandler or any of the family members I'd met so far.

Victoria reached under Nancy's arm and squeezed my hand.

"You're my only family. Chandler's side will be filled with his people. Jim will be on my side, but he'll be lonely. Can you just come and enjoy the ceremony?"

"That's why we're here, honey," said Katy, picking up a lip gloss. "We came because we love you and want to be with you for your special day."

At those words, Victoria's shoulders relaxed.

"Stay still," scolded Nancy, as she wiped the black liner mark from her forehead.

I watched them get Victoria ready, with a sinking feeling in my stomach.

This is why divorce was invented, I thought grimly.

If things went south, she always had a way out. In the meantime, I was going to watch Chandler like a hawk.

I hadn't realized then that something more sinister and much darker than a simple divorce would soon rip us all apart.

Chapter Eight

It was the smallest wedding I'd ever attended.

Despite the snow and cold, the Rupert family were hosting the ceremony outdoors.

A handful of people tucked in smart winter coats, hats, gloves, and designer scarfs milled on the grounds of the main lodge. Someone had draped multicolored Christmas lights around a large fir tree. Though we were in full daylight, the twinkling lights among the snowy branches brightened up the grounds.

The air smelled cool and fresh. The sound of light classical music came from stereo speakers installed on the patio ceiling. A white garden arbor was draped in gossamer cloth and decorated with rows of pink roses. A dozen white chairs were arranged in front of the arch.

Behind the trellis lay the wintry forest, its trees coated by what looked like layers of frosty icing sugar. The mountain peak towered over us, draped in fresh snow.

I could hear the rush of the river below. The ravine wasn't too far from the wedding ceremony, hidden behind those snow-laden trees.

Despite my gloomy feelings, I had to admit it was a gorgeous setting.

The sound of water running through the woods should have been soothing, but my mind wandered to the splash we heard in the car, the disappearing shadow in the woods, and Mia's incomprehensible cries of seeing something in the river. What troubled me most was the way Chandler and Barbara completely dismissed the girl.

I shook my head to clear the cobwebs.

If anyone had fallen into the river and had gone missing, they would have noticed by now. Just because I didn't like this family didn't mean I had to be paranoid.

Victoria had recovered from her bout of vomiting. She'd got her color back and was bright-eyed and bushy tailed, keen for the ceremony to start. My cautious words hadn't deterred her one bit.

After cleaning her up, we'd bundled her into her faux fur-lined white shawl and escorted her to the main lodge. Jim had been waiting for us as we'd walked in, looking dapper in a new three-piece suit. Since Victoria had no parents, he was playing the father of the bride that day.

Victoria was alone with Nancy now, seated inside the dining room behind the patio doors, waiting for her walk down the aisle. When we left them to join the rest of the wedding party, they were warming their white-gloved hands over the fireplace.

I stepped out of the lodge with Katy and Jim and surveyed the grounds.

The event was so bare bones, there wasn't even a photographer. Strange for the nuptials of the only son of the wealthiest family in the region.

Then again, most people didn't hold two weddings, one for their family at a private ski chalet and another lavish affair at a luxury hotel in Paris.

"Are we the only guests?" asked Katy, looking around.

"Yes, sirree," said Jim. "They made it clear that this is a family affair."

"Barbara wasn't happy to see us," I said.

Jim let out a heavy sigh. "They're not too keen about me walking her down the aisle either, if that makes you feel better."

"You're Victoria's only family," I said. "How could they say no to you?"

He gave us a wonky smile.

"Victoria's marrying into a big family, though I hear business isn't so great for them these days." He shrugged. "Anyway, as far as they're concerned, I'm just help."

"Help?" cried Katy. "How can they even—"

Jim motioned her to keep her voice down.

"They don't like outsiders very much." He paused. "I heard them argue about you too."

I raised a brow. "Really?"

"Chandler and Barbara were in her cabin. It was four nights ago, my first night here. Nancy and I were walking over with hot chocolate when we heard them arguing through the window."

"What were they arguing about?"

Jim let out another sigh and rubbed his forehead.

"We weren't eavesdropping, so you know. Chandler was so loud anyone walking by would have heard him."

"What was he saying?" I said.

"I hate to gossip like this."

"Tell us, Jim," said Katy, shaking him by the arm.

Jim looked down at his shoes.

"Apparently Chandler didn't know Victoria had invited you two, and he was mad. Really, really mad. He was telling Victoria to uninvite you."

"*Uninvite* us?" said Katy with a huff. "Did they want her to get married alone?"

"Victoria was crying. She was refusing, saying you're her only friends, other than us. Chandler wasn't too happy. That's all we heard."

"Chandler sounds like the typical narcissist," I said, trying not to seethe. "Isolate her from everyone so she is dependent on him, then keep her tight in his clutches."

"You don't want to know what I think of that—" Jim halted abruptly.

I looked up to see what stopped him in mid-sentence.

"There you are," said a deep baritone voice.

A well-dressed, silver-haired man was walking toward us. He exuded the epitome of a retired wealthy businessman.

This was the father of the groom.

With a squeeze of my shoulder, Jim stepped away before Robert Rupert approached us. I watched Jim walk back to the lodge, his head down, wondering what kind of life Victoria had signed up for.

"We weren't expecting you, but welcome," said the older man, his smile deepening as he got close. "Did you have a pleasant drive over?"

Unlike his wife, Barbara, this man emanated warmth and congeniality. Or so it seemed.

"I was looking forward to meeting you lovely young ladies from New York." He offered his hand.

Katy and I smiled back politely.

"It was good of you to come and it's nice for Victoria to have her friends at the ceremony." He paused and flashed another smile. "I just didn't expect to be in the presence of such beautiful guests."

Chandler had inherited from both his parents. The haughtiness of his mother and the charms of his father, the same charms he'd turned on to woo Victoria.

But like his son, who didn't hesitate to kick a dog in his way, I couldn't but help wonder if Robert was putting on his own façade.

"It's a small event, but everyone who needs to be here is here," said Robert as if he was reading our minds. "Even the wedding officiant, our local Justice of the Peace."

I glanced over his shoulder to spot who he was waving at.

It was a man in his sixties, wearing an old-fashioned top hat and long-tailed black coat, talking to Barbara. He looked like a character out of a Dickens' novel.

Chandler didn't have any groomsmen.

My heart skipped a beat.

Did this mean it was definitely Chandler who we saw kissing the woman behind the bushes?

I turned to look at the bridesmaids.

Young Mia was standing away from the group, looking distinctly unhappy. She was plucking petals from the roses in her bouquet, a strange thing for a bridesmaid to do. I watched the petals rain on Max, who was sitting quietly by her feet. That bouquet would be a skeleton of stems if the function didn't start soon.

Next to her, looking bored and annoyed, was a taller bridesmaid, twirling her clearly dyed platinum blonde hair. She didn't look that much older than Mia but was heavily made up with pointy thin eyebrows and blood-red lips.

She looked like the stereotypical mean girl from high school, one who'd been roped into a family event and couldn't wait to return to her room. I wouldn't have been surprised to see her popping gum.

Something about these two young women bothered me.

Who had Chandler flirted with? The mean girl looked most likely.

But wait.

Didn't Victoria say there were *three* bridesmaids?

With a start, I realized what was bothering me. Robert, Barbara and Chandler were all tall and big boned. They had the imposing size and features that said they must have Nordic blood.

But the two young women were short and petite.

"Are those your daughters?" I said, turning to Robert.

The man's eyes flittered for just a second, then turned to stare at the two young women.

"Tiffany and Mia," he said with a shrug.

Odd.

"You have three daughters, I hear?" I said.

"Rebeca's in her room, sick and stubborn as a dog. Doesn't want to come out, even for her only brother's wedding ceremony."

Was it the sick girl with Chandler behind the bushes?

"Poor girl," said Katy. "Food poisoning too?"

Robert let out a sigh.

"I hired one of my chefs from the resort to cook for us this weekend. He had a family emergency and couldn't make it, so I ordered the food to be delivered, and now everyone's dropping like flies."

"It could have been sitting in the van for hours," I said.

He nodded.

"They don't know it, but the chef and his team will be losing their jobs tomorrow morning, once this is over."

"Hope everyone recovers soon," said Katy.

"I feel fine, don't I?" said Robert, slapping his chest. "Kids these days don't have the solid constitution we used to."

"The ceremony will start," came a voice from near the arch.

We all turned to look at the wedding officiant, gesturing for everyone to sit.

"Come, ladies, let me take you to your seats," said Robert, ushering us toward the chairs.

Katy and I followed him toward the seating arrangement, when the officiant walked up to us.

"Michael," said Robert, putting a hand on his shoulder. "Have you met Katy and Asha yet?"

"Well, well, well," replied the older man, his eyes on Katy.

He stepped closer to her and leered. She smiled back awkwardly. It's never fun when men ogle, especially those old enough to be your father.

With no warning, he slipped his hand around Katy's waist and squeezed her. She pushed him away and stepped toward me with a grimace.

"Excuse me?" I said, glaring, but I didn't get to finish.

A bone-chilling shriek came from the woods.

The hair on my neck sprang up.

Chapter Nine

K aty grabbed my arm.

"What was that?" she said in a terrified voice.

I scanned the grounds, regretting my decision to leave the Glock in the car trunk.

To my surprise, Chandler gave a nervous guffaw. Barbara, who had clutched her pearls at first, let out an embarrassed laugh.

Everyone who'd initially jumped in fright settled down quickly. Chandler strolled over to the arch while Barbara took a seat in the front row. Mia went back to plucking her petals while Tiffany, the second bridesmaid, returned to twirling her hair and looking bored.

"Almost gave me a heart attack," said Michael, turning to Robert with an embarrassed grin.

"Made me jump, too," said Robert with a shake of his head.

"That sounded like a woman screaming," I said, frowning.

Without waiting for them to answer, I turned around to march toward the woods.

"Fisher cat," called out the officiant. "Screams like a banshee. You should hear them at night."

I turned back to look at him.

"Fisher cats?"

He wiggled his bushy eyebrows. "Damn things are as small as weasels, but they'll tear into your pets and kids if you don't watch out."

"Don't listen to Michael," said Robert. "He's heard one too many old wives' tales. It was probably a fox. Everyone blames the fisher cats for everything around here. But I tell you, foxes are the worst."

He pulled two empty chairs on the left side of the wedding aisle.

"Why don't you ladies take your seats? We will start soon. This will be a wedding to remember."

With a small bow, he turned around and walked toward the arch, his hands behind his back, shoulder to shoulder with the officiant.

This will be a wedding to remember.

I'd heard those words before. I took my seat, pulled out my phone, and opened the text app to read the last message.

Welcome to Cloud Cabin Ski Lodge. This will be a wedding to remember.

I scanned the crowd. Everyone was busy getting ready for the function.

Did Victoria give my number to her new father-in-law? Why would she? If she did, why would he send me a message like this?

I was racking my brain when my phone vibrated. I stared at my screen. Katy leaned over and gasped. She took my phone and read the message out in a low voice.

Someone's missing from the party. Wanna guess who it is?

Katy and I exchanged a glance. This was getting stranger and stranger.

Robert's words flashed to mind. *It's a small event, but everyone who needs to be here is here.*

"Is this a prank?" I said. "But who'd do something like this?"

"I know who's missing," whispered Katy. "We haven't seen the third bridesmaid yet, have we?"

"What I want to know is who's sending me these texts," I said, frowning at my mobile. "And how did they get my number?"

Before she could respond, the officiant called out.

"All rise for the bride."

Katy and I got up and turned around.

Victoria was standing by the lodge's patio doors, one arm on Jim's, her dress and veil set perfectly around her. Jim wore an awkward smile, but the happiness on Victoria's face was unmistakable, despite her stomach troubles. In that stunning gown and shawl that flowed to her toes, she looked every bit the fairytale princess.

She sailed by us with her dazzling smile, her eyes on Chandler. Only Katy and I could see the dark spot on her veil, the stain Nancy had tried hard to get out with soap and water.

My gut churned, like it was sending another warning flag.

When Victoria got to the front, Chandler held out his hands and pulled her in close. The officiant opened a thick book and raised his right hand, signaling for silence. We sat back down.

That was when I noticed Mia.

She was standing to the left of Tiffany, only a few feet in front of us. She had kept half of her bouquet intact, but she was wavering on her feet, swaying. Her face was pale and haggard, despite the makeup.

"Gosh, Mia looks really sick," whispered Katy.

The officiant began his speech, but I couldn't take my eyes off the youngest bridesmaid. As I watched, her eyes rolled up. She staggered back and let the bouquet fall.

Max jumped in surprise as it hit his head.

Someone yelled from the groom's side.

I leaped toward the trellis and caught her just before she hit the ground.

A murmur rippled through the crowd.

Katy came running over and held her up on the other side. Suddenly, Mia's head lolled back.

"Fainted," I said. "We need to get her inside."

I looked up to see the entire wedding party staring at us. Victoria had her hand over her mouth, horror etched on her face.

"What happened? Is Mia okay?" she said.

"Don't worry," I said to her. "We'll take care of her."

Relief crossed Barbara's face. Robert gave me a thankful nod. Chandler just watched on, his face cold and his eyes dark, like he was accusing Mia of ruining his moment.

I turned my attention back to the girl.

Her chest was heaving. She was still alive. I patted her cheek a few times. When her eyes flittered opened, Katy and I pulled her to her feet.

"We got you," I said.

"D… d… don't… p… please don't…" she stammered.

Her words were low and slurred.

"We're going to get you to your room, sweetie," said Katy. "All you need is water and a warm blanket, and you'll feel better already."

Mia's knees buckled, but we caught her before she collapsed again.

She swallowed hard, then closed her eyes, and clutched my arm, her nails digging into my skin.

Chandler and the officiant were scowling at us now.

"Can we start?" said Chandler gruffly.

"Let's get her out of here," I said, turning to Katy, trying not to grit my teeth. Victoria and Nancy were the only people showing a modicum of sympathy for the young bridesmaid.

Holding Mia on both sides, Katy and I steered her away from the wedding trellis and toward the lodge.

"You'll be fine," Katy said to the girl. "Just keep walking, hun."

Mia remained silent, but her breathing was getting faster and shallower. Not good.

A hostile silence had fallen behind us, and I could feel everyone's eyes boring into our backs.

A cold shudder went through me.

Something was wrong with this place.

Something was wrong with this family.

Chapter Ten

When we got to the patio doors, Mia tried to break from our grasp.

"N... N... No..." she stammered.

She didn't want to leave the ceremony.

"You need to be in bed," said Katy in a firm voice, as we tried to calm her down. "You can't even stand, sweetie."

Mia gave her a distressed look. Her eyes were so glassy, I wondered if it was food poisoning or something else.

"This way," I said, pointing my chin toward the front entrance.

Katy and I ushered her out of the lodge and down the small path that led to the cabins. Dumping her in the dining room didn't feel right. We walked slowly as Mia put one foot in front of the other, clinging to us.

"Which is your cabin, hun?" I said.

Mia took her hand off my arm and pointed a shaking finger.

"Oh, good," breathed Katy. "Not that far."

We escorted her toward the cabin three doors down from Victoria's.

That was when I noticed that each of the cabins had wooden nameplates on the doors. Victoria's cabin had Chandler's name. Next to hers was Tiffany, then Rebeca, and finally Mia.

"Here we are," said Katy, reaching over to open Mia's door. We half carried her inside and helped her lie down on her bed.

While Katy went to fetch a glass of water and a towel from the bathroom, I glanced around the room. The cabin was smaller than Victoria's and the furnishings were cheap in comparison, like they'd been bought from an assemble-your-own furniture store.

I wondered why either parent hadn't expressed more concern or followed us here to find out how their youngest daughter was faring. I also wondered how the wedding ceremony was panning out.

"Drink," Katy said, as she offered the girl a glass of water.

Mia turned her face away but pulled at Katy's arm like she wanted to tell her something. I walked over to the bed. Katy put the glass down on the bedside table and wiped the girl's forehead with a towel.

"What is it, Mia?" I said.

It took a while for her to get her words out.

"No b... nobody... nobo... b... b... believes... m... me..."

"Believes what?" I said.

Mia's frightened eyes flitted from me to Katy, then back again, as if she was gauging whether to trust us.

She must have been seventeen, eighteen at most. It must be frustrating to not be able to articulate her thoughts.

"You can talk to us, hun," said Katy in a quiet voice. "We're trying to help you."

Mia stared at her like she wasn't sure if she could believe her.

"Hey, Mia," I said, softening my voice. "You were by the cliff an hour ago and saw something in the river, didn't you?"

Her lips quivered, but she nodded.

"Was it a rock?"

She shook her head.

"Was it a log, an old tree trunk?"

She shook her head again.

"Was it an animal? A fox? One of those fisher cats?"

She took a raspy breath in and shook her head again, fidgeting with her dress.

"Was it a body?" I asked.

Mia didn't answer right away, but stared at her hands. I didn't have much to go on, but my gut was turning, sending me warning flags.

I should have checked that shed and the hatch. I should have taken that shadow more seriously.

I felt my chest tighten.

"What did you see, Mia?"

She shrugged, either to say she didn't know or she was done answering my questions.

"You know who it was, don't you?" I asked.

She shook her head vehemently this time.

I tried again. "Was it a man or a woman?"

"D... don't... c... couldn't... s... see."

"Are you sure it was a body?" I said.

Mia gave me a doleful look and shook her head.

Katy narrowed her eyes. I knew what she was thinking. It was hard to rely on Mia's words. Her manner didn't inspire confidence.

But I couldn't imagine why she would lie about something like this. She wasn't the attention vying type, no matter what Chandler had said.

"If you saw someone in trouble," I said, speaking slowly, "we have to call the police. We have to tell them what happened. Can you do that?"

Mia let out a loud sob.

Keeping her head down and whimpering like a wounded animal, she pulled away from us.

"We'll stay with you, hun," said Katy, reaching out to her. "You don't have to be scared."

Mia wiped her cheeks, smudging the mascara across her face.

"Hey," I said. "Can I ask you another question?"

No answer.

"Were you flirting with Chandler today?"

She pulled back sharply, like I'd slapped her.

"N... n... no!" she cried, waving her arms. "No!"

"Asha," said Katy, shooting me an annoyed look.

"Sorry," I said, putting my hands up and stepping back. "Didn't mean to upset you."

"It's okay, sweetie," said Katy, reaching for her arm. "No one's accusing you of anything. No need to be scared, hun."

But Mia's lips turned down and her eyes welled with tears. Large droplets fell down her cheek, making her black mascara run.

I watched her, feeling bad for her, but my concern for Victoria was eating me inside out. Our friend was making a big mistake. I felt it in my bones and until I found out what and why, I couldn't let it go.

Mia pushed Katy's hand away and pulled on her coverlet. As we watched, she rolled over and buried herself under her covers, until all we could see were a few hair strands on her pillow.

I took my phone out, debating whether to call for help.

Mia was an unreliable witness, one her own mother and brother didn't respect. Robert Rupert also gave the distinct impression he cared more for his successful son than for his three daughters. He and Barbara would start hopping like mad if we called the authorities.

"What do we do?" said Katy, turning to me.

"Officer Jensen should still be in Falcon Hills," I said, trying to think. "But he might not come all the way here on Mia's words alone, especially when her own family thinks she's loony."

With a resigned sigh, I wrote a message to Tetyana and my fiancé, David.

At ski lodge. Got here OK. Strange place. Weird family. Worried for Victoria.

"David's going to get nervous now," said Katy as she read my text. "He'll be calling Tetyana to helicopter over and to bring an FBI SWAT team while she's at it."

I typed some more.

Nothing urgent. Just goings-on. Stand by.

"He's still going to worry," said Katy, biting her lower lip. "He'll call Peace and the two of them will drive each other stir crazy."

"They're good men," I said, not looking up. I had another task to do. "That's why we picked them."

"These messages bother me," I said, as I forwarded the two anonymous texts to Win, my computer security expert, back in New York. "Maybe she can find out who it is."

"It's not a crime to send anonymous texts, is it?" said Katy.

"No, but I feel like we're in the middle of something going very wrong."

I slipped my cell into my pocket.

"Let's get back to the ceremony."

"What about her?" whispered Katy, glancing at Mia, who had completely buried herself under the layers of covers and cushions.

I leaned over and tapped her pillow.

Nothing.

I pulled the coverlet a few inches and peeked underneath.

Mia had fallen asleep.

With her messed-up makeup, she looked like a college kid, sleeping off a hangover after a wild party. I reached over to check the pulse on her neck. She didn't even stir, but she was breathing, and her heart was beating.

"Barbara and Robert need to know how their daughter's doing," Katy was saying. "Someone needs to look at her. Like a doctor or a nurse."

"I don't like leaving her like this," I said, scanning the room.

Two keys dangled from a keyring on the door. I took one out and slipped it in my pocket. With a last glance at the sleeping girl, we stepped outside, and using the spare key, I locked Mia's door behind us.

Katy and I stepped on the path that led to the main lodge and started walking back.

"Rebeca's room," said Katy, as we passed her cabin.

The third bridesmaid.

Her window was dark, and the curtains were drawn. Was she asleep inside?

An image of a woman in a bridesmaid's dress falling into the river flashed across my mind. I shook my head to clear it. This place was driving me nuts.

"Wait," I said, stepping up to the door.

"What are you doing?" whispered Katy.
I reached over and tried the doorknob.

Chapter Eleven

The door didn't budge.

"Locked," I said.

I stepped away from the cabin and we returned to the lodge in silence, a sense of foreboding gnawing inside of me.

When we got back to the wedding, the ceremony was over. Nancy and Jim were standing to the side, their awkward but polite smiles still on. I couldn't help but admire their grace, given how the in-laws were treating them.

Victoria was bent over a small table next to the wedding arch, signing a paper.

The marriage license.

Chandler watched over her shoulder, a serious expression on his face. When she finished, she flashed a bright smile at her new husband, who scooped her in his arms for a kiss.

While I looked on, the officiant snatched the license from the table, folded it, and stuffed it inside a large brown envelope. He turned to Robert, who was watching the couple, and gave him a thumbs up. Robert winked back. Chandler glanced over Victoria's head at the two older men, a wide grin on his face.

"I told you," said a voice by my ear.

I turned to see Nancy next to me.

"I told you this was too rushed," she said, watching Chandler twirl Victoria around.

"Lunch prep, please," said a sharp voice.

We spun around.

Barbara pointed to Nancy and Jim. The couple stood to attention, like a drill sergeant had just called their names. My distaste for Barbara grew even deeper.

"We'll be taking pictures outside," she said. "Make sure lunch is ready in half an hour."

"Barbara," I said, stepping toward her. "Mia's sick. She needs medical attention."

"What that girl needs is sleep," she replied with a scowl. "Cavorting around all night."

I stared at her in surprise.

Didn't she see how Mia had fainted?

"I'm not sure you understand how bad—"

"I understand perfectly well," snapped Barbara. "She's my daughter. Leave her be."

She turned to Nancy and Jim.

"What are you waiting for? Snap to it then."

"Gotta go," whispered Nancy, picking up her skirt and walking back to the lodge. With a small shrug, Jim followed his wife inside.

Not giving me another glance, Barbara twirled around and walked over to join her husband.

Michael and Robert were standing by the wedding arch, their hands clasped behind their backs, their heads touching, deep in discussion while Chandler, Victoria, and Tiffany scattered across the grounds to take pictures.

I knew Victoria wanted us to join in the photo taking, but I followed Jim and Nancy inside, leaving Katy to keep an eye on the bride.

"Hey," I said, walking into the kitchen. "You guys okay?"

Nancy was taking sandwiches out of a box and arranging them in a tiered silver tray.

"We're only here because of Victoria," she said in a dull voice.

"Thank goodness we don't have to make anything," said Jim, opening the oven and pushing in a tray of ready-made pastries. "I don't think I could stomach cooking for this family."

I stood back and watched them prepare the sandwiches, scones, and jams. A double-layered butter cake sat at the edge of the table, waiting to be sliced. For a family that could afford a truckload of gourmet dinners, this was an odd way to cater a wedding.

"Is this food from the same place as last night's dinner?" I said.

"Came in the same delivery truck yesterday, but from a different kitchen," said Jim, busying himself with the jam jars.

"Aren't you worried they'd be spoiled too?"

"I'm making myself a sandwich," said Jim, pointing a butter knife my way. "I suggest you do the same."

"A cup of Ceylon tea would be great."

"I found a tin can of English Breakfast tea behind the coffee cannister," said Jim, turning the kettle on. "Is that good enough for you?"

"Perfect, thanks," I said, leaning against the counter. "Guys, Mia's in terrible shape. She needs a doctor, but no one seems to take her seriously."

"Barbara decides how and what everyone feels in this house, and what Barbara wants, Barbara gets," said Nancy, making a face. "I'm not one to argue with that woman."

She squeezed my arm as she bustled by me.

"I know they're not the nicest folk, but you need to let it in one ear and out the other, like we're doing. We're going home tomorrow and that's all I care about."

And Victoria will be alone with this family.

"I'm happy to get kitchen duty," said Jim. "Can you imagine being forced to hang out with that bunch all weekend?"

"Victoria's excited and all, but she deserves so much better," said Nancy, shaking her head. "This doesn't feel like a wedding to me."

"More like a wake," said Jim.

It took a while for everyone to gather in the dining-hall for lunch.

A large Christmas tree stood in the corner, decked in gold tinsel, and red and white ornaments, and a gold star on top that just about touched the ceiling. The massive wood fireplace in the corner was burning brightly, radiating a glow around the room.

Despite the ambiance and the fire, I was cold.

This family barely tolerated our presence. I couldn't help but feel they were only doing so because Victoria had stood her ground.

I glanced around the hall.

Someone had decorated the walls with strings of white lights and set enormous fall-themed flower vases across the room. They smelled pleasantly of roasted nuts, cinnamon, and vanilla. Other than that, it wasn't the spectacular wedding venue I expected Victoria to enjoy.

Maybe that was reserved for Paris?

We took our seats around the dining table, facing the silver food trays. Nancy and Jim had done a great job. They were mouthwatering to look at, but I knew better than to touch anything.

Five minutes after the table had been set, Victoria and Chandler came inside, giggling and holding hands. Max tumbled in next, wagging his tail, followed by Tiffany twirling her hair, her permanent pout intact.

Victoria didn't seem to mind the bridesmaid's dour attitude. Either that or she was ignoring her, just like she was overlooking a whole slew of red flags in this family.

Chandler pulled chairs for both women, then strode to the front of the room and stood by the fireplace. He cleared his throat.

The room fell silent.

Even Max sat down, his ears perked up.

Chandler stood quietly for a few seconds, his chest out, hands on his lapels, a proud smile on his face. Then, he turned to Robert Rupert, seated at the head of the table.

"Father," he started. "You've been my mentor, my guide, my teacher, and my partner in crime."

I glanced around the table while he talked. No one seemed hungry. The food remained untouched on most plates, but the wineglasses were being refilled at a fast rate.

Chandler droned on, like he was giving a talk to Congress. Victoria was smiling at everyone, and especially Chandler, but her sickly pallor gave away her discomfort.

She looked my way briefly. I pointed at the food and shook a discrete finger. She nodded and blew a kiss my way.

I sat back with a heavy sigh.

"I learned everything in life from you. My success is all due to your teachings," Chandler was saying, addressing his father. "Thank you for everything."

Barbara clapped. The officiant joined her. The rest politely followed suit. I cringed.

Chandler hadn't said a word about his new bride, his mother, or anyone else in the family. To hear him ignore the women who should have been the focus of this day made me burn with anger.

Nancy and Jim were right. There was a strange undercurrent to this shindig.

Chandler sat down and Robert Rupert got up to give the father-of-the-groom talk. I was listening to Robert drawl about Chandler's star qualities, and not a word about Victoria, when my phone vibrated.

I pulled it out of my pocket and clicked on the text app, hoping Win had cracked the code and found the name of the person sending me those strange notes.

I read the text.

How'd you like the speech? Good, eh?

I raised a brow.

That wasn't Win. It was from an unknown number, just like the ones before.

Whoever sent that note had to be in this room.

I glanced up and looked at each of the wedding guests around the table. All heads were turned to the front, like they were listening intently to Robert. With everyone's hands in their laps, it was hard to see if any of them held a phone under the table.

My heart beat a tick faster.

Who is the texter? What do they want?

I nudged Katy and showed her the message. Her eyes widened.

I hadn't told anyone here I was a private investigator, but I wondered if someone in this lodge knew of my occupation.

"Excuse me," I whispered to the diners closest to me, "bathroom's just outside, right?"

Nancy nodded.

Jim cocked an eyebrow.

Barbara shot me an irritated look.

Ignoring her, I eased out of my chair and headed toward the open door.

Chapter Twelve

I slipped out of the hall, feeling Barbara's annoyed eyes on my back.

I was in the corridor with the large windows that looked out to the cabins and parking lot.

A few feet in front of me was the main entrance. The kitchen was on my left and to my right were the toilets. Past the bathrooms were a series of rooms. Robert and Barbara's private wing, I gathered.

I turned right.

It was time to do some sleuthing.

I'd just passed the women's washroom when I heard footsteps behind me. I swiveled around, my heart missing a beat.

"Katy," I said in relief.

She scurried over, a napkin crumpled in her hands.

"I was waiting for all that rambling to be over," she said, rolling her eyes.

She pulled at the corner of the napkin to show an uneaten sandwich.

"Good job," I said. "Don't want to end up sick like Mia or Victoria."

She pushed the women's bathroom door open and stepped inside, and soon I heard her flush her lunch down the toilet.

I took out my phone to see the cellular reception bar was flickering between green and red. I stepped up to the windows Then I shook the device.

That didn't help. I had to do with what I had. It was time to find out who was messaging me.

I hit the call button.

While I kept one ear glued to the phone, I strained to listen to what was going on in the dining room. But whoever it was had turned their ringer off.

All I could hear was an inaudible murmur of voices.

I hung up and clicked on the number again. Sometimes people pick up on the second call.

I leaned against the window and waited, one ear cocked toward the dining room, but this time, the call dropped after two rings. I frowned as the reception bar on my mobile flickered and turned red.

I peered out the window.

Low, heavy clouds hovered near the peak, blocking the sun and making me feel claustrophobic. The snowfall was light, but it was going to get worse.

The bathroom door opened and Katy stepped out.

"Do you have a signal?" I asked, showing her my phone.

She plucked her cell from her pocket.

"A little." She brandished it up, as if that would help.

"Call Win," I said.

I leaned close to Katy, as she dialed our friend and put the phone to her ear.

"Hello?"

Relief washed through me as I heard Win's voice.

"Hey Win!" squealed Katy.

"Hello?" said Win again.

I took the phone.

"Win, it's Asha, can you hear us?"

"Hello? Who is it?"

"It's Asha. At the lodge. I need you to check on—"

The line went dead. I pulled the phone from my ear and stared at the screen. The bars had turned red on this one too.

"Did my phone just die?" said Katy, glancing over my shoulder.

"It's the snowstorm coming in," I said, handing it back to her, and gestured for her to follow me.

I stepped gingerly along the corridor, but I didn't have to go far before I found what I was looking for. I stopped in front of the second door, turned the handle, and peeked inside.

It was a large room that smelled of firewood, cigars, and whiskey.

An imposing U-shaped mahogany desk took up most of the space. Behind it was a leather executive chair, and on the wall by the desk were photos of Robert shaking hands with men and women in business suits.

This had to be Robert Rupert's den.

I pushed the door open and stepped inside, with Katy at my heels.

Baseball paraphernalia adorned the other walls. At the far end of the room above the fireplace was a mantle lined with framed photographs. The only light came from a green banker's lamp and a fireplace which was burning low, the logs almost extinguished now.

"Fisher Cats," said Katy, examining a branded baseball bat hung on hooks on the wall like a precious Samurai sword.

"Must be the local baseball team," I said, walking up to the desk where an old-fashioned phone sat among a pile of papers.

Exactly what I was looking for. Old tech.

I picked up the handset and held it to my ear.

Nothing.

I turned the headset off and on, and held it back to my ear.

There was no dial tone.

How did that happen?

Putting the headset down, I followed the wires from the base to see if it had disconnected somewhere, but the wires weren't broken, and the phone was plugged in.

I peeked under the desk, behind it, and scanned the top shelves, but there was no sign of a wireless or Internet router anywhere. I scanned the desk, but other than loose papers, manila files, and a cigarette lighter, I didn't find any electronic devices. Not a laptop or a tablet to be seen.

I frowned. The Rupert family wasn't Amish or Mormon, from what I knew. Their ski resort down the mountain was a glowing display of modern technology.

I pulled open the first drawer on the right-hand side.

A letter opener lay among a mishmash of paper clips and an assortment of pens.

I opened the second drawer.

A handful of car keyrings greeted my eyes. One had a Porsche logo and another a Mercedes one. Robert may be a Luddite, but he liked his cars.

I pulled the third drawer open and took a sharp breath in.

A revolver with a carved wooden handle, one I'd expect to see in an antique show, glinted under the dim light of the banker's lamp. Robert had polished it recently. I was about to take it out to examine it when Katy called my name.

"Check this out," came her voice from the other end of the room.

I turned around to see her standing by the mantle. She picked up a photo and turned it toward me, a strange expression on her face.

"Mia, Tiffany, and the one we haven't met yet," she said, as I walked over. She thrust the photo in front of my face. "I thought something was weird, but I see it better now."

I stared at the three young women in long summer dresses, standing shoulder to shoulder with awkward smiles—the kind you'd give when you're forced to smile in public and you didn't feel like it.

"They don't look too happy," I said.

"Look closer," said Katy. "They're supposed to be sisters."

That was when I saw it.

"Gosh, you're right. They look nothing like each other. Very different features."

"None of them look like Chandler either," said Katy. "They have no resemblance to the rest of the family."

"Adopted?"

"Maybe," said Katy, putting the photo back on the mantle.

"That could explain the way Barbara and Robert treat them," I said.

Katy picked up another photo. "But I found this."

I took the second picture and stared at it.

"Robert and Mia?" I said, feeling my stomach turn.

"Weird, isn't it?"

"Maybe this family is the kissing-in-the-mouth kind. Don't they do that in Europe?"

"Of course not, silly," said Katy, her face scrunching in disgust. "No one does this."

Katy pushed a third photo my way.

This one showed the daughter we hadn't met yet with Robert. Kissing again on the mouth. He had his hands on her shoulders and was grabbing her tightly, while her own arms lay limp by her sides, like she had no choice but to acquiesce.

I shook my head.

"I'd normally say to each his or her own, but this is creepy."

"Maybe he's abusing them," whispered Katy.

"Why take pictures, frame them, and stick them in a place anyone can see?"

"We're not supposed to be here," Katy said, giving me a warning look.

I swiveled my head around, but we were alone. I listened in, but the corridor was silent.

"Strange Barbara would let this go on under her nose," I said, turning back to my friend. "Makes little sense."

"It's sickening," said Katy with a grimace. "Even if they're not his real daughters."

I turned around to see if I could spot anything else that would tell us more about this strange family.

That was when I noticed it.

The wire that went from the phone plug near the floor toward an exit by the window was broken. It had been holding in place so well, I hadn't noticed it before. I walked over to the window to scrutinize it. I touched the wire. The breakage was clean.

Someone had cut the wire.

I caught a movement from the corner of my eyes and snapped my head up.

Someone was walking down the path toward the cabins.

Chapter Thirteen

"Someone's left the luncheon," I said, scooting behind the curtains on one side.

Katy scurried over to the other end. "Who is it?" she said, peeking out from her end of the window.

We peered at the silhouette of the man outside, strolling along the pathway.

"It's that old creep. The wedding officiant," said Katy. "What's he doing out there?"

We watched silently as Michael Brown slinked by Victoria's cabin. He stopped for a second and swiveled his head around, like he knew we were watching.

Katy and I drew back hurriedly, but he wasn't looking our way. His eyes were on the main entrance. After another furtive glance around him, he stepped up to Mia's cabin.

My heart went to my mouth as I watched Michael try the doorknob. He hadn't bothered to knock.

I slipped my hand inside my pocket and felt around for the key. It was still there, thank goodness.

"What does he want with her?" said Katy, pursing her lips. "Checking if she's feeling better?"

Failing to open the door, Michael stepped around and tried the side window.

"The creep factor just ratcheted up." I frowned.

I was glad I'd closed her curtains and checked the latches. I wondered if Mia was awake and had heard the man trying to get in, but was staying quiet, terrified.

"What a sicko," hissed Katy from behind the curtains. "She's what? Eighteen? There's no reason for him to be there."

After trying the door again, Michael turned around and walked back up the path toward the main lodge.

"He's coming this way," said Katy, her face darkening.

"Let's go," I said. "I have some questions for him."

Before we left Robert's office, I reached over and snagged the metal letter opener from his desk and a paper clip. These could come in handy.

I closed the door and walked swiftly toward the entrance, following Katy, who looked like she was ready to punch the man.

Just as she got to the door, Katy jumped back, almost hitting me.

Michael stepped back in alarm, seconds before he slammed heads with her.

He moved swiftly for his age.

"Hello, Michael," I said. "Nice to see you."

"Aren't you supposed to be at lunch?" he said in an annoyed voice.

"And you?" I asked. "Missing out on lunch too, I see. Where were you?"

He looked away quickly. He was going to lie.

"I always make it a habit of going for a walk after eating."

His eyes darted back-and-forth.

"We saw you go to the cabins in the back," I said, trying to keep my voice casual.

"Oh?" He frowned and peered at me. Then, as if he was done with us, he pushed us aside and stepped inside.

"What did you want with Mia?" I said.

He stopped in his tracks but didn't turn.

"Did you want to see her about something?"

Michael jerked his head back and glowered at me.

"What are you two doing, snooping around in the corridor?" he growled.

"We were in the women's," said Katy, pointing at the bathroom door. "Came for a quick bathroom break before dessert is served."

"And you?" I said, keeping my gaze steady.

Michael furrowed his brows and glared first at me, then at Katy.

"I, er, forgot my book. Mia borrowed it last week, so I went to get it back."

"What book was that?" asked Katy.

Without replying, he spun around and stomped into the dining-hall. I could almost see steam coming out of his ears. He was angry at being caught.

"Thank goodness we locked her cabin," said Katy, shaking her head. "I can't wait to get away from this place now."

I couldn't wait either.

But while Katy and I could leave at any moment, these three girls lived here. This was their family. And now, Victoria had become part of this strange clan.

"I think it's time to talk to the third girl," I said, as I stepped out through the main doorway.

Katy took the stairs with me. "Brrr.... shouldn't we get our coats?"

"That would tell them we're heading out. Barbara doesn't want us interfering with Mia, even when she's sick. Let's keep this visit quiet."

"We're not going to just barge in, are we?" she said, as we marched along the path toward Rebeca's cabin, trying not to slip on the snow in our kitten heels.

We passed Victoria's cabin, then Tiffany's, and came to the cabin next to Mia's.

"Rebeca," said Katy, reading the carved nameplate on the door.

I stepped up and knocked lightly.

No answer.

I knocked harder.

Nothing.

"She's been sick since last night," whispered Katy. "Maybe's she's sleeping it off?"

I pulled Mia's key from my pocket and tried it on Rebeca's door. No luck.

But I had one more trick.

I hadn't escaped gangs and gangsters in my youth without learning a few guerrilla tactics.

I pulled out the paper clip and slipped it into the keyhole. While Katy kept watch, I bent down and rattled the lock, thankful these cabins didn't have the more high-tech systems of a hotel. In two minutes, I was done, and we were in.

"Empty," said Katy, twirling around. "It's like no one was even here."

The interior of the cabin was designed exactly like Mia's. The only difference was the bookshelf, which stood against the far wall.

But Katy was right.

The coverlet hadn't been touched, the closet was shut, and her makeup kits were arranged in a neat row on the chest of drawers.

"She's super neat," said Katy, as she stepped across the room.

"Either that," I said, "or she hasn't been here for a long while."

Katy opened the top drawer of the bedside table.

"A Bible, a small flashlight, and a tissue box."

I scanned the bookshelf, wondering if it would tell us anything about Rebeca, but all I could make out was she enjoyed cozy mysteries. There were no phones, tablets, laptops, or any electronic devices here, either.

Strange, I thought, maybe the entire family is technophobic after all.

Katy had opened the wardrobe and was going through her clothes.

"Summer dresses," she murmured as she went through the items. "She's bigger than Mia but smaller than Tiffany, but I knew that from the photos."

I whirled around, trying to take everything in and catch anything important, but nothing in this room was giving me any clues to her whereabouts.

Where would a sick girl go?

If she had been knocked out by the same food poisoning as Mia and Victoria, she would hardly have been able to walk. It had taken all of Victoria's energy and determination to go through with the ceremony, but neither Mia nor Rebeca had the same motivations she had.

So where was she?

I stepped up to the chest and opened the top drawer, expecting to find lipsticks, brushes, and eyeliners. Instead, it was something else that greeted my eyes.

I pounced on my discovery.

Chapter Fourteen

"**T**his one's medium, but this one's a plus size," I heard Katy murmur to herself as she rooted through the closet.

"Probably working on her weight," she muttered. "A regular gal like the rest of us."

I slid my hands into the drawer and pulled out the spiral notebook.

The word *Rebeca* was written in sprawling loopy letters on the cover. There was a small golden lock on the side, the kind that served only an aesthetic purpose.

Finally, we would learn something about this missing girl and this mysterious family.

Those anonymous texts were trying to tell me something. Was Rebeca secretly messaging me from somewhere? Was she trying to warn us about Victoria's marriage?

Seeing Chandler lean in to kiss the woman in the pink dress had me worried sick, and the creepy photos on Robert Rupert's office mantle hadn't helped.

Victoria and Chandler's marriage license was only a few hours old. Maybe there was a way to annul it. I didn't know if that would be possible without a divorce, but I wasn't about to leave this lodge without making sure Victoria was safe.

"Oh!"

I turned around to see Katy staring at something inside the closet, a shirt in her hand.

"Look at this stash," she said, pushing several dresses to the side.

I walked over and peeked in.

A small medicine cabinet was affixed to the closet wall in the back. Behind its glass doors was a plethora of pill and syrup bottles.

"She's a hypochondriac," said Katy, reaching in, snapping the cabinet door open and plucking a bottle out.

"Thorazine," she read the yellow label out loud. She placed it back and turned the next bottle around. "Haldol, Trilafon, more Thorazine...."

She turned to me with a quizzical look.

I shrugged. "Your guess is as good as mine."

I took my phone out and snapped a picture of the labels. "We'll get Win to check them out as soon as we get a signal."

I waved Rebeca's journal at Katy. Her eyes widened.

"A diary? Now you're snooping."

"We broke into her room and have been sniffing around for the past fifteen minutes. It's a bit too late to worry about that. Besides, I have a funny feeling this will solve our puzzle."

Katy hung the shirt back in the closet and put her hands on her hips.

"Look at us," she said, giving me an exasperated look.

"What?"

"What happened to us? Sneaking into people's rooms. Checking out their medicine cabinets. These people aren't criminals. We're being paranoid."

"When it comes to Victoria's safety, I'd rather be paranoid."

"Don't you think we're overreacting just a tad? I know this family is creepy and all, but Chandler's a typical hotshot who got rich fast and thinks he owns the world. He has an ego, but doesn't every man?"

"Not Peace," I said. "A successful attorney in Manhattan and not a nasty bone in his body."

"That's why I married him."

"David doesn't either," I said.

"Victoria will straighten Chandler out," said Katy. "Give her a month and he'll be a lamb eating from her hand."

I'd heard that before, but I knew people didn't change overnight, if they changed at all. If anything, they held on to their habits with even more fervor when pushed. And sometimes they got aggressive. Even violent.

I perched at the edge of the bed and flipped the book open.

Scraggly lines greeted my eyes, like Rebeca's pen had run out of ink and she had tried to make it work. I turned the page to the first journal entry. It was written on the first of January and referred to a walk in the woods.

I flipped to the next page.

She hadn't journaled regularly. A few entries talked about Max getting attacked by a raccoon and recovering. A few more were about her discovering a rare wildflower by the riverbed.

It was when I flipped to the last few entries I felt goose bumps on my arms.

"This isn't good," I said, as I read the entry she'd made five days ago.

"What is it?" said Katy, coming over and sitting next to me.

I jabbed at the paragraph.

Katy read it out aloud.

Wish I'd never been born. I can't bear this. What did I do to deserve this? I want to end it now.

Katy's eyes widened. "My goodness."

I flipped the page and read the next day's journal entry.

If I end it all, what will happen to Mia? She's scared too. She'd be all alone if I go.

We stared at the page for a few seconds, digesting the words.

"*End it all?*" said Katy. "Does that mean what I think it does?"

I turned the page.

Robert has a gun in his office but sleeping pills will be easier. That's the fastest thing to do. Go away painlessly. And go away forever.

"She's suicidal," I said, feeling sick to my stomach.

"She needs help," said Katy. "But where is she?"

I read the next entry.

Poor Victoria. She has no idea.

Katy gasped.

I read the line again, my heart beating a tick faster.

"What does she mean by that?" said Katy, grabbing the book and flipping through the rest of the journal, but the remaining pages were blank.

The last diary entry had been made the day before the wedding, the day before our arrival. That meant Rebeca had been in her room yesterday, but something had happened between then and now.

"Victoria's in trouble," I said, suppressing the panic and horror snaking up my spine.

Katy flipped through the journal furiously, looking for more clues. I got up, thinking it was high time I retrieved my Glock from the car, when something soft landed by my feet.

Katy swooped down and picked it up.

"Fell from inside the book," she said, holding the white envelope to the light. "It's sealed."

Katy and I stared at each other for a few seconds. We both knew it was illegal, not to say immoral, to read other people's correspondence, but I was having a hard time suppressing the urge to let it go.

Before I could say anything, Katy ripped the envelope open and pulled out a thin white paper, almost translucent.

"A letter?" I said, looking over her shoulder. "To whom?"

It had the same loopy handwriting as the entries in the diary. It had to be by Rebeca.

We read it silently.

Please don't hate me. Please don't blame me for what I'm about to do.

I can't live like this anymore. I'm so sick of this. I don't know how you stay sane, because I'm going crazy. Real crazy. None of my pills are going to help me through this.

And now, they're making it worse. They have that new girl. They'll do the same thing to her like they did to us. I can't bear to watch this.

I wanted to say goodbye. I will miss you. Please don't hate me.

Love always.

Chapter Fifteen

There was no greeting or signature on the letter.

Katy flipped the paper over, but the other side was blank.

"Who's it for?" I said, picking up the envelope and scrutinizing it. There was no address or name on it either. "She wrote it, but never sent it."

"What did she mean by *new girl*?" said Katy, her face pale. "She means Victoria, doesn't she?"

"I can't think of anyone else," I said. "What if Rebeca's done something to herself, but the others are covering it up for the wedding to go on?"

"You'd have to have a cold dead heart to do something like that, though I wouldn't put it past this lot."

"Or they don't know yet," I said. "Everyone's sure she's sleeping off the food poisoning in her room."

"Except Mia."

"Maybe she knew what Rebeca had been planning, and seeing whatever she saw at the bottom of the gully terrified her."

"We didn't spot anything when we looked," said Katy.

"The river runs fast. It could have carried her away before we spotted her."

"What did Mia see then?"

I rubbed the sides of my head, feeling a migraine coming on.

"I wish she would talk to us."

"She's just a kid, and she's scared about something," said Katy. "Plus, she stutters. Good luck getting her to open up."

"What about those text messages?" I said. "What are they trying to tell us?"

"*This is a wedding to remember*," said Katy. "I don't like the sound of that anymore."

I didn't either. The red flags in my gut had turned into ringing alarm bells now.

"Whoever sent those messages is warning us about something. But why be so cryptic? Why not just come out and tell us?"

"It's like someone's playing a game with us," said Katy, shivering. "I don't like it here."

A loud bark startled us.

I turned my head.

"Max?"

More barking.

I jumped to my feet and peered out the window.

"What's he doing by the woods?" said Katy, joining me.

I opened the window and leaned out.

"Hey, Max," I called out. "What's up, buddy?"

Hearing my voice, he came bounding through the snow.

It took a while for him to wade through the drifts piled up in the back. He stopped when he got close to the cabin, panting hard. He barked twice, then turned around.

We watched him trundle through the snow for about twenty feet when he stopped and cocked his head our way. He whined and turned to head back in the direction he came from.

Toward the woods.

"He wants us to follow him," said Katy.

I placed the journal back in the drawer and shut it.

"First, we need to see Victoria," I said. "Talk some sense into her so she knows what she's getting herself into."

We stepped out of Rebeca's cabin and scurried toward the main lodge. It was cold and still snowing outside and we were in our party dresses and shoes. I badly wanted to change into pants and a warm top, but Victoria was our priority.

We'd just turned a corner on the path when we bumped into her.

"Victoria!" cried Katy.

Chandler was twirling her around in front of their cabin, both giggling like teenagers. Victoria's eyes were lit up and on Chandler, and his were on her. They didn't even notice us.

"Hey, Victoria," I said, stepping close to the couple.

She lifted her head from Chandler's chest and flashed me a smile.

"Did you like the ceremony?" she said, her voice bubbly. "Wasn't it so sweet?"

She was drunk. Her eyes were glazed and her words were slurred. She hadn't even remembered Katy, and I weren't present, helping Mia to her cabin.

"Hey, congratulations," I said with a smile, extending my arms and stepping toward my friend, ignoring Chandler's glare.

"Can we get a hug from the bride?" said Katy, catching on and stepping closer. "This is so exciting."

"Do you mind?" snapped Chandler, turning around to face Katy and me. "It's our wedding dance."

Yes, I do mind.

I curled my hand into a fist and took a deep breath.

"Honey, don't talk to them like that. They're my friends," said Victoria, slapping his chest gently and fluttering her lashes. "They just want to spend time with me."

"Well, I want to spend time with my new wife," said Chandler, swinging her away and twirling her round and round, making Victoria burst into laughter.

My mind buzzed trying to think of how to get her away from him when he pulled her to the cabin door, kicked it open, and pushed her inside.

"Hey, Victoria?" I called out. "Where's our hug? It will only take a minute."

Another giggle came from inside.

"Let them come in, babe," said Victoria, laughing.

"Come on, Chandler. Be a sport," I said.

Chandler's face popped out the door. He wasn't smiling anymore.

"It's our wedding night. Leave us alone," he snarled before slamming the door on our faces.

The ominous sound of the door bolting came next.

A shiver went through me.

It sounded more like a jailer locking their prisoner inside.

Chapter Sixteen

I stepped up to the door and knocked.

"Hey, Victoria," I called out.

Silence.

"Victoria," I called again, thumping on the door. "Can we talk for a minute?"

A door banged inside. Did someone go into the bathroom? Or did Chandler push her in and close the door?

My mind buzzed with wild thoughts. I thrust them to the side. I couldn't let my fear overtake me. Not now.

"We're only going to rile him more," said Katy. "There has to be another way."

The bathroom door banged again.

What's going on inside?

"We need to get her alone," I said, staring at the closed door, the knot in my stomach tightening. I turned to Katy. "It's time for Plan B."

"What's Plan B?"

"I'll figure it out," I said, turning around. "But first I want to chat with Nancy and Jim. We need reinforcement."

We walked toward the lodge, holding on to each other. I cursed my kitten heels as I tried not to slip on the ice gathered on the pathway. I was glad it was only past noon. We still had daylight and a few hours left before darkness settled on the mountain.

There was only one thing I wanted to do now. That was to bundle Victoria, Nancy, Jim, and Katy in our car and head down before anything happened to any of us.

Just as we stepped inside the lodge, Robert marched out of the dining room, and turned right on the corridor. We watched him stomp toward his office, a deep frown on his face. He had been so absorbed in his thoughts he hadn't even noticed us. The door slammed shut behind him.

Katy and I exchanged a glance.

"Something's brewing," whispered Katy.

I felt it too.

The lights were still on in the dining-hall and the music was playing at low volume. We made a beeline toward the room.

Barbara was at the dinner table talking to Michael. Tiffany was more engrossed in her nails than the conversation.

Nancy and Jim, I was sure, were hiding in the kitchen. I couldn't blame them.

As we walked up to the table, the officiant pushed his chair back and strode out, giving a nasty glance at us. He was still upset at our earlier encounter.

"Hey, Barbara?" I said, approaching the older woman.

She turned and gave me a sour look.

"You left right in the middle of the speeches," she said in an accusing tone.

"We saw Max running around Rebeca's cabin," I said, ignoring her comment. "Maybe someone needs to check up on her?"

To my surprise, Barbara leaned over and snatched my arm.

I pulled back instantly, but she hung on, her painted nails digging into my skin. I tried not to grimace. I could overcome this middle-aged woman in combat any time, but now was not the time to get into a brawl.

"Stop interfering with my family," she hissed, her eyes boring into mine.

I stared back.

"Rebeca's gone for a walk in the woods," she said. "She takes one every morning with Max."

"I thought she had food poisoning."

Barbara let go of my arm and sat back with a heavy sigh. She shook her head, as if she'd given up trying to convince me.

"She's not sick. That girl can eat anything and will be fine." She paused. "That's not the reason she's not at the wedding today."

She turned her blue eyes on us, looking more sad than angry.

"Rebeca has severe bipolar."

"Oh?" said Katy.

"She has a tendency to stay by herself," said Barbara, her arrogance gone and in its place a melancholy expression. She looked down at the tablecloth, her shoulders hunched. "She goes off on walks all the time."

"Isn't that dangerous?" said Katy. "It's daytime, but she could get lost in the woods, stumble or fall... You never know what could happen."

"She knows her way around."

"Did she take her phone?" I asked.

"She's not a phone person," said Barbara, looking away.

Who in this world doesn't have a phone these days?

"I could never live without mine," said Katy.

Barbara shook her head. "I don't have a phone here. None of us do. We keep the tech stuff away from the lodge. We come here to disconnect from all that."

"You have no communication channels?" I said, cocking an eyebrow. I wondered if she was going to lie about the phone I saw in her husband's office.

"We use a landline for deliveries."

So who has been messaging me then?

"Rebeca grew up at this lodge," Barbara was saying. "She knows the woods like the back of her hand. All three girls do. They love this place. They ski in the winter and hike in the woods in the summer. Can't get them to come home for dinner on time."

Tiffany looked up, a strange expression on her face. She had been playing with her hair while we were talking, not saying a word. She saw me look and turned away with a scowl.

Barbara turned her face toward Katy, then toward me. She looked angry again. Her eyes were dark and her face was flushed.

"If you want to know the real reason Rebeca isn't here, it's because of you two," she spat out.

"Us?" said Katy in a shocked voice.

"She doesn't like crowds, and she hates meeting new people. Gets rattled. When Victoria told us you were coming, she packed a picnic lunch, geared up, and left on a hike."

"I'm so sorry," I said, suddenly wondering if I'd been overthinking everything. Maybe this was why Chandler and Victoria had been arguing. "I didn't realize we scared away your daughter—"

"Rebeca's not her real daughter."

I spun around to Tiffany, but she had gone back to examining her nails, seemingly oblivious to the impact of that bombshell.

Barbara glared at Tiffany.

"What...?" said Katy. "What do you mean by that?"

Barbara let out a heavy sigh.

"We adopted Rebeca when she was seven years old."

"From the Falcon Hills Psychiatric Institution," said Tiffany in a low voice, not looking up.

Barbara glowered, but the truth was out.

Katy let out a gasp.

I leaned away in surprise.

I'd heard that name before.

It was the same mental institution Victoria's parents had banished her to when she was only nine years old.

Chapter Seventeen

"I'll go see if Nancy and Jim need help in the kitchen," I said, squeezing Katy's shoulder.

She caught my eye.

Good.

She knew what to do.

Katy pulled a chair for herself and sat down next to Tiffany.

"What a day," I heard her say as I stepped out of the room.

Katy could watch them while I checked the men out. After a quick scan of the corridor, I turned right.

Low murmurs were coming from the office.

I tiptoed along the wall, stopping every few feet to make sure they hadn't heard me. The door was ajar, but only a few inches, which told me Robert and Michael were expecting us to stay in the dining room, chatting, eating, and drinking.

I leaned my ear against the doorframe.

They were speaking too low for me to make out their words, but the urgency in their voices was unmistakable.

I peeked in.

All I could see through the thin wedge was the office desk. It was empty. I stayed as still as I could, listening to the snippets of their dialogue.

"... airport..."

"... tomorrow evening..."

"... no trouble... I'll take care of it..."

"... Cedar Cottage..."

"Don't worry... they'll never know..."

Curiosity gnawed inside of me and clawed at my throat.

I leaned over and pushed the door with the tip of my index finger. I braced myself, expecting a creak or a groan from the door scraping against the wooden floor.

But it opened, silently.

Feeling bold, I pushed it another inch.

Then another.

Keeping my body shielded behind the wall, I peeked through the small opening with one eye.

Finally, I could see.

The two men were standing by the fireplace, next to the mantle where those pictures were. They were facing each other, standing close, their heads bowed deep in discussion, like they had by the wedding arch after the ceremony.

As I looked on, the officiant plucked a brown envelope from his jacket and handed it to Robert.

The wedding license!

It had to be it.

Robert turned toward the desk and reached for something. I drew back quickly. One look at the door and he would catch me red-handed.

I let a few seconds go before leaning toward the opening again.

Robert was going through a sheath of papers, flipping through them, showing them to Michael. In between the inaudible murmuring, I caught the word insurance, repeated several times.

Insurance?

Would that be health insurance? Home insurance? Life insurance?

Robert sorted through the papers, slipped them inside the envelope, and clasped it to his chest. He beamed like he'd won the jackpot.

The men shook hands and thumped on each other's backs like they were congratulating themselves.

My spider senses tingled.

I wondered if I had been focusing on the wrong man. Chandler may be a cheating jackass, but Robert Rupert was the one who pulled the strings. He was the alpha dog in this pack.

What was he up to?

Michael mumbled something, gave a wave, and turned around.

He was heading toward the door.

I pulled back quickly.

I spun around and scooted on my tiptoes along the hallway, resisting the urge to look back.

I slipped into the women's bathroom just as Michael stepped out. I stood frozen on the other side of the bathroom door, listening to his footsteps coming down the corridor, my heart hammering.

Part of me felt silly to be snooping around like a schoolgirl.

I'd blown up Saudi trafficking rings, chased criminals across borders, shot at evil men who had deserved their fate, and here I was at my friend's wedding, running around like a Nancy Drew wannabe.

More footsteps.

Robert had joined his friend, and they were returning to the dining-hall, their voices still low but more casual and relaxed.

I waited for their steps to recede before pushing the door open and peeking out.

The corridor was empty.

I slipped out and scurried over to the office. There had to be clues I missed the first time around, clues that would tell me what they were up to. But more than anything, I wanted to see those documents Robert had slipped inside the brown envelope.

I turned the doorknob.

Robert had locked the door.

I looked up and down the hallway. Loud voices were coming from inside the dining-hall now. I hoped Katy would keep them occupied.

I reached into my pocket and reached for the paper clip.

"Can I help you?"

I jumped three feet high. I whirled around to see Robert Rupert standing by the dining-hall door.

"Someone's been in here for a while," I said. "They've locked the door."

Robert stared at me, a puzzled look on his face.

I tapped on the door and cocked my head.

"Anyone there?" I said. "Can you hurry, please? I really have to go."

Robert pointed at the women's only a few feet from him.

"The toilets are here," he said, unsmiling.

I stepped back and stared at the office door, as if I'd just realized my mistake.

I slapped my palm on my head.

"Gosh, what a dork," I said, and turned to him with a wonky smile. "That's what happens when you drink wine too early in the day."

He didn't smile back.

Ignoring his unfriendly face, I stumbled toward the washroom. With an apologetic shrug, I scooted inside and closed the door.

I opened the tap and threw cold water on my face, trying to calm down.

That had been close.

I took a towel and wiped my face, but my heart refused to cool. Suddenly I realized why. I couldn't help feeling Robert Rupert's presence outside the door.

He was waiting for me.

Chapter Eighteen

I leaned toward the door.

Robert's heavy breathing came from the other side. He was standing very close.

I glanced around me.

Space was tight inside the bathroom. There were two toilet stalls, a sink, and an old-fashioned hand dryer. The stalls had flimsy latches, and the main door had no lock. There was no window or any other exits and there was no way to hide in here.

If he barreled in, I'd have to fight him with my back toward the sharp-edged ceramic sink.

Not good.

Why did I leave my Glock in the car?

Though I'd just wiped my hands, they had begun to sweat. My heart was thumping so loudly, I was sure Robert could hear it.

Other than my weekly martial arts training with David, it had been a long time since I'd engaged in hand-to-hand combat with anyone out in the world.

Robert was tall and big-boned, almost three times my size. But he had the typical middle-aged flab that signaled the good life. He may look imposing, but I could fight him any day.

I took a deep breath to settle my racing heart, stepped quietly to the door, and put my hands and one foot on the wood panel to hold it in place.

Come in and I'll rip your eyes out.

"Robert!"

I jerked my head up.

Barbara.

"Aren't you going to join us for the nightcap?"

She was calling from further down the corridor. I imagined her head popping out of the dining-hall entrance.

"Coming," came Robert's voice, annoyed.

I was right. He'd been inches from the door.

What did he want?

It was a relief to hear his footsteps recede. I dropped my arms and wiped my face with my sleeve. This had to be the strangest wedding I'd been to.

Was Robert just a common creep? He was the one kissing his own daughters, adopted or otherwise, on the mouth.

Or had he wanted to confront me, angry because he caught me snooping near his office? That would mean he was hiding something he didn't want me to see.

Either way, while Robert Rupert blustered around like the suave businessman of town, there was a lot more to him than he was showing.

After a quick check on my phone and seeing no reception, I opened the bathroom door. The corridor was empty again.

Before anyone else could come out, I dashed down the hallway toward the main entrance. I jumped down the front steps, trying not to slip and fall.

A beautiful blanket of pure white enveloped the entire grounds. Large fluffy snowflakes fell on my shoulders as I hurried along the pathway, slithering on the snow.

Visibility would soon be nonexistent. Driving down the mountain road would become deadly. No one in their right mind would be out in this weather, even Rebeca.

I doubted everything this family was telling us.

It took a minute to identify our car buried under the snow. With a shiver, I unlocked it, slipped inside, and closed the door. I plucked my sidearm out of the glove compartment and opened my bag to get my outdoor gear.

It was a relief to change into my waterproof ski pants, thermal shirt, and ski jacket. Katy and I had planned on a fun ski day at the resort after the wedding, but that was a remote possibility now.

I kicked off the kitten heels and put on my thick winter socks and heavy-duty hiking boots, feeling infinitely better.

I looked down at my phone, but the bars were still an ominous red. I opened the message app and typed.

"Leaving tonight. Call for help if you don't hear from us in 24hrs."

I hit send and queued the message with the others I'd sent to David, Tetyana, and Win. Keeping my fingers crossed for a signal to come through soon, and sticking the Glock in my jacket pocket, I slipped out of the car.

I stopped by Victoria's cabin, but the curtains were drawn, and the lights were off. It looked like no one was inside. It was hard to say if anyone had stepped out, as the snowfall would have covered any tracks.

I stayed by her cabin door, debating whether to knock or call out. All I had were feelings, suppositions, and Rebeca's diary. I had to get more solid evidence before I could convince Victoria something was wrong with this family.

I hung around the door for another few seconds until I realized I was no better than Robert Rupert listening by the women's bathroom. I snapped around and marched back to the lodge.

To my relief, the corridor was empty. Classical music wafted from the dining-hall with intermittent voices speaking in low volumes.

Who's still inside?

Robert's office door was closed, so it was hard to say if he'd gone back in.

I patted my pocket, feeling the reassuring bulk of my Glock, and ducked across the dining-hall entrance toward the kitchen.

The door was closed.

I reached over and tried the handle, but it held.

Did Nancy and Jim lock up and retire to their cabin?

I tried the handle again and rattled it. This time, the door wobbled. It wasn't locked, but something was holding it in place.

I stepped back, took a swing, and kicked at the door.

It flung open.

"No!" shrieked Nancy.

The kitchen light glinted off the carving knife in her hand.

Chapter Nineteen

"What the heck's going on, Nancy?" I said.

She lowered the knife, relief washing across her face.

"It's *you*," she said. "Scared the blazes out of me."

"The door was stuck," I said.

She put the knife on the table.

"It wasn't stuck. There's no lock, so I put a rag under it."

I raised an eyebrow.

"That way, no one can barge in without me knowing," she said. "You still got me though."

I looked back at the entrance. A crumpled dish towel lay on the ground.

I glanced around the kitchen.

"Where's Jim?"

"Barbara called me to the dining room to serve wine. Jim didn't like me being with them, so he went instead."

"That's good," I said. "Don't like Katy being alone with that crowd, either. I was about to check up on her."

"Jim and me agreed on a secret knock, so I'll know when he comes back."

I stepped toward the door, closed it, and replaced the rag under it, before turning around to join Nancy by the kitchen table.

I examined the butcher knife. Next to it was a half-eaten sandwich on a plate. Nancy was so frazzled, she hadn't even mentioned my change in clothes.

"What's going on here, Nancy?" I asked.

She plopped down in her chair and rubbed her face.

"I've been getting the heebie jeebies ever since we got here. The way Chandler treats Victoria. That creepy Michael fellow hanging around our cabins. The girls getting sick. No sign of one girl at all, like she's a ghost, and Barbara being nasty and telling me we're not part of the family."

I raised an eyebrow. *Did Michael make it a habit to snoop around other people's rooms?*

I put a hand on Nancy's arm.

"Did Barbara really say that to you?"

She looked up, her eyes lined with exhaustion.

"Robert tried to brush up against me one morning. Jim thought I was imagining things at first, but he can't wait to leave too now."

"You look like you haven't slept for days, hun," I said.

"The fisher cats scream every night. It's like someone's torturing them. Can't sleep after you hear that." She gave a shudder, then shot me a worried look. "Did you get Jim's message?"

"What message?"

"He texted you as soon as he saw it."

"Saw what?"

"The rat poison," said Nancy, as if I should have already known.

"Rat poison?"

"Don't tell me you ate from the table." She waved her arms. "I wasn't watching you all the time and I couldn't tell you in front of everyone. If you ever—"

"Don't worry. Wasn't hungry anyway," I said.

I leaned toward her.

"Tell me about this rat poison."

With an exasperated sigh, she pushed her chair back, walked over to the kitchen sink, and opened the small cabinet underneath it.

"See?" she said, gesturing. "It's gone."

I stared at the space underneath the sink.

"When we got here three days ago, there was a can of rat poison sitting right there. I swear I saw it. Barbara said it was to keep the fisher cats away from the lodge."

"And now it's disappeared? When did that happen?"

"Don't know, but Jim noticed it when he came here looking for an extra bottle of wine just after the speeches. He was getting a dishcloth out when he saw it…. or didn't see it."

She shut the cabinet and lumbered back to the table. "He sent you a text soon after."

I glanced at my phone's message app for what felt like the thousandth time that day.

The last note I'd received was the anonymous one I got during the speeches. My phone had gone silent after that with my own messages to David, Tetyana, and Win still in the queue.

"It's catching a signal on and off, but it seems out of range now," I said, slipping the mobile back into my pocket. I glanced out of the kitchen window. "We're at a high elevation with those woods surrounding us and that isn't helping."

But Nancy's mind seemed elsewhere.

"What about Katy? Did she eat anything?"

"Slipped it all into her napkin and flushed it down the toilet."

"Thank goodness."

"Did everyone get sick after dinner last evening?" I said. "Or was it just Victoria and Mia?"

"Victoria threw up a few times. You saw her. I heard Mia was sick as a dog last night too," she said. "Come to think of it, it was just the girls, except for Barbara and me."

"What about Tiffany?"

"Tiffany seems fine. She never talks. Not to anyone. Just gives airs, and keeps to herself, like she's better than everyone."

"Robert said Rebeca is sick and staying in her room," I said. "But Barbara told us she didn't like crowds and went for a walk. Have you seen her?"

Nancy shook her head. "Never seen her or even heard her, and we've been here a few days. I'm beginning to think she doesn't exist."

"There's a cabin in her name," I said.

She shrugged. "This whole place gives me the creeps."

I debated whether to tell her about our discovery in Rebeca's room, that she had vanished without a trace, but I didn't want to frighten Nancy any more than she was.

The diary didn't tell us anything specific. None of the clues we'd found so far did. But when I put everything side by side, I got a strong signal that something sinister was going on here.

"Is there any reason anyone in this family would try to poison Victoria and Mia?"

"All I know is they got sick, and then we find the rat poison gone." Nancy gave me a dark look. "Jim thinks I'm kooky to say this, but I think there's a psycho at the lodge."

"Or a very calculated person," I said. "Maybe whoever did this didn't want to kill them. They wanted to send a message."

"A message?"

"It could be the same person who sent those texts to me," I said.

"What texts?"

I pulled out my phone and handed it to her so she could see for herself. She scrolled through the messages, her eyes widening with each one.

"Do you have any idea who would send these?" I asked.

"I'm beginning to think this place is haunted," she mumbled.

"If it's haunted, it's by the human kind," I said. "Last time I checked, ghosts don't text."

"I'm seriously scared about what Victoria's getting into."

"What do you know about this family?" I asked.

"They've been in Falcon Hills for as far as I can remember," she said, staring at the table, her hands folded in front of her. "This is old money. The kind that comes with a lot of power."

She paused.

"Robert Rupert is pals with the city council members and was the president of the Chamber of Commerce at one point. It's a small town so everyone wants to be his friend and he has pull with everyone."

"But Jim said their business has gone down lately," I said. "How did that happen?"

"A national ski franchise opened a resort about an hour's drive away. Got lots more stuff for kids and families, and he lost quite a bit of business from that."

"When was this?"

"Two years ago, I think. Rumor has it they took out a hefty loan from the bank just to keep things running." She gave a small shrug. "It's all small-town gossip. Just smoke."

The pieces were slowly coming in to focus.

"That's not true," I said, sitting up. "Where there's smoke, there's always a fire."

Chapter Twenty

"Tell me about Chandler," I said.

"Other than he's the biggest A-hole I ever met?" said Nancy. "He went to high school with us, but he took off to the big city the day he graduated."

I raised a brow.

"You knew him? Why didn't you tell me?"

"Not really. He was one of the cool kids and Jim and me were just...." She trailed off. "Heard bits and bobs after he left though."

"What did you hear?"

"He was doing day trading."

I nodded.

"He gambled big and got lucky, then got hired by one of those Wall Street companies who paid him millions to make them even more millions."

She paused.

"That's the story he's been telling everyone in town, anyway. Barbara and Robert are super proud of him. Treat him better than the girls, that's for sure."

"Did the girls go to your school too?"

"Funny thing. Never seen them around before."

"Homeschooled?"

"That's what everyone thought. We all heard Chandler had sisters, but they never came down to town. Seems like they spent all their time at the lodge."

"Barbara told us Mia was adopted," I said. "Maybe they all are?"

She frowned.

"I thought it was weird that Mia and Tiffany look nothing like Chandler or their parents. Thought they were relatives from out of town at first."

She paused and gave me a dark look.

"Did you know Chandler had a rep at school?"

"What kind of rep?"

"Disgusting stuff. Used to touch little girls. When he became a senior, everyone was going around saying he was a player."

"A player?"

"Slept with all the girls just to add a notch on his belt." She shook her head. "Some people said it was jealous talk. He was the rich kid, and no one liked him, except his little posse and a few star-struck gals."

"Where's his posse now?"

"They all wanted the big city life. No one worth their salt stays in Falcon Hills after high school if they can help it."

"Except for you and Jim," I said. "You're worth every ounce of your salt and more, if that makes any sense."

She gave me a concerned look.

"I'm worried for Victoria. The missing rat poison freaks me out. I keep thinking someone tried to kill her."

I glanced at the door.

It was still closed, but I could hear the music coming from the dining-hall. We had kept our voices low, but this place seemed to have ears and eyes everywhere, watching, listening.

I lowered my voice.

"I asked Win to do a background check on the family, especially on Chandler. I also asked David and Tetyana to be on standby. Just in case."

I leaned in closer.

"Katy and I saw Chandler with a woman in a pink dress behind the hedge near the parking lot. We didn't see her face, but they weren't just talking, if you get my gist."

Nancy's shoulders dropped, and she shook her head, like she was disappointed.

"Any idea who that could be?" I asked.

"There's been some funny goings-on in this lodge."

I raised an eyebrow.

"On Wednesday, our first night here," said Nancy, "I caught Robert sneaking out of Mia's cabin in the dead of the night."

"Robert? Are you sure?"

"Those darned fisher cats woke me up and I couldn't go back to sleep," she said. "Was tossing all night and didn't want to wake Jim up. So I got up and stared out the window for a bit, trying to feel sleepy again. That's when I saw him."

"What time was this?"

"Three in the morning. I checked my phone because it was weird. He didn't go in there for afternoon tea, I can tell you that."

"Unless he went to do something else while she was sleeping."

"Like what?"

"Poison her water glass, toothpaste, or something to make her sick today."

"That was three nights ago. She only got sick last night."

"What do you know about the Falcon Hills Psychiatric Institution?" I said.

Nancy jerked her head back. "That's the hospital Victoria got sent to."

"Exactly. Barbara told us they adopted Rebeca from the same hospital when she was a kid."

Nancy's jaw dropped.

"I wouldn't be surprised if all three girls came from there," I said. "This family has a connection with that place."

"Oh no," said Nancy, putting a hand on her heart. "What in heaven has Victoria got herself into?"

"I'm wondering the same thing."

"They're supposed to fly off to Paris tomorrow," said Nancy, shaking her head. "I don't like her being alone with these people one bit."

"The snowstorm will help," I said. "They'll be forced to stay here."

Nancy shook her head.

"I grew up in these parts. It will be over in a few hours. Plus, Robert called for a crew with snow removal machines from the resort to clear the roads tomorrow—"

Someone rattled the doorknob, making us both jump.

"Is that Jim's secret knock?" I said.

"N... no."

The door rattled again.

I pulled out my Glock and stepped up to the entrance.

They were banging on the door now.

Nancy sprang from her chair and grabbed her knife.

Keeping my gun steady, I kicked the rag away and pulled on the handle.

Chapter Twenty-one

"Katy!" cried Nancy and I, at the same time.

"The door was—"

She stopped in mid-sentence and stared.

"Why did you change?"

I thrust my gun into my pocket and pulled her inside.

"What's with the knife?" said Katy.

"Frazzled, that's all," said Nancy, sheepishly putting her weapon down.

Katy walked over, pulled out a chair, and flopped down with a weary sigh. I shut the door, put the rag back in place, and joined my friends.

"Can we go home now?" said Katy, giving me a tired look. "I'm so done here."

"We can't leave Victoria just like that," I said.

Katy blew a raspberry. "Barbara just asked me when we were heading home. I mean, talk about rude."

She shook her head.

"I asked about that third girl, Rebeca, but she blew me off again. If Chantelle was off hiking in the woods in this snow dump, I'd be calling a rescue operation."

"It's time we find her," I said, recalling the diary entries. "Mia can't talk and Tiffany won't. I feel like all the answers lie with Rebeca."

I stepped toward the door. "Coming, Katy?"

She gave me a surprised look.

"We'll stop by the car and get you changed," I said.

Nancy turned to me, her brow furrowed. "What are you planning?"

"No better time for a hike in the woods."

"You don't know the mountain. There's a steep drop not too far from here. You could slip and fall right into the river."

"Whatever has happened to Rebeca has something to do with Victoria's marriage. We can't let her fly out of the country with this family tomorrow."

"Fine, I'm coming with you," said Nancy, picking up the butcher knife.

I shook my head.

"You stay right here with Jim."

"But—"

"Monitor your cell and call Officer Jensen as soon as you get a signal."

Nancy's eyes widened. "Officer Jensen?"

"Remember that young cop who helped us save Victoria? He should still be in town. Too young to retire. He knows who you and Jim are."

"What do I tell him?"

"Tell him a girl has gone missing from the lodge for forty-eight hours. That should bring him up in a hurry."

Katy and I stepped out and waited for Nancy to shut the door behind us before leaving.

Our first stop was at our car so Katy could change. We grabbed our gloves and woolen hats. It was still daylight, but I plucked a flashlight from the emergency kit in my trunk, just in case.

"Let's try Mia before we go. She may be ready to talk," I said, as we walked up the pathway. "She knows something about Rebeca."

Katy and I trundled silently toward her cabin. I wondered how a wedding invitation had turned so quickly into an investigation I never wanted.

Mia didn't answer our knocks, so I pulled the spare key from my pocket and unlocked the door.

We knew something was wrong the second we walked in.

"She's gone!" cried Katy.

We stared at the mess.

Her cabin had been organized almost to a fault, but now it looked like a tornado had ripped through it. A slightly metallic smell permeated the air, one I couldn't identify.

"What happened?" said Katy, picking up a ripped pillow from the floor and throwing it onto the bed. "Just two hours ago, she was too sick to walk."

A cold draft swirled around my neck, making me turn around.

The back window was open.

I walked up to it when Katy gasped out loud. She was on her knees, reaching for something or someone under the bed.

"Mia?" I said, hope rising in me.

"A box full of letters," she mumbled. "Got overturned during whatever happened here."

I turned my attention back to the window. The latch was intact, and the glass wasn't broken. Whoever came in, if anyone had, had their own key.

"Asha?"

"What?"

"You have to see this."

I turned to see Katy waving a piece of paper in the air.

"What is it?"

"You won't believe it."

She came over and thrust the paper in front of my face.

My eyes widened.

"A marriage certificate?" I said.

"Between Robert Rupert and Mia."

My stomach turned.

I grabbed the paper, read it, and re-read it.

"Robert Rupert is a bigamist," I said, finally.

"How can you marry more than once?" said Katy. "Is she even of legal age?"

I scrutinized the signatures at the bottom of the document.

The first one extended outside the signature box. Robert Rupert. Next to it, in tiny, neat letters, was Mia's name, and underneath both was Michael Brown's signature as witness to the marriage and wedding officiant.

"He did it with Michael's help. It says she's eighteen here."

"Doesn't Barbara know?" said Katy, furrowing her brows. "The way she goes on about her family, it's like peaches and cream and apple pie."

"Either she doesn't know, or she's accepted her position. It could explain why she didn't blink when Mia fainted and never even asked about her."

"Do you think Victoria knows?"

I folded the marriage certificate, tucked it inside my pocket, and reached over to shut the window. "Maybe this will open her eyes—"

I stopped and yanked my hand back.

"Jeez!"

"What?" said Katy, looking over my shoulder.

"Blood," I said, pointing at the ledge. "Fresh. That's why I smelled something funny."

Katy leaned over and put a hand over her mouth.

"Whose blood is it?"

"Mia's or someone else's."

Katy clutched my arm. "It's all over the pane. She must have been bleeding heavily. Do you think someone attacked her?"

"I just hope she fought back against whoever it was," I said in a grim voice.

"Where is she, though?"

It was time to call for reinforcement. I pulled my phone out and dialed nine-one-one.

Nothing.

The text messages I'd queued up earlier to my friends were still in line, waiting to be sent. I turned to Katy to ask her if she could try her phone, when a scraping by the door made us spin around. Katy and I exchanged an alarmed glance.

I pulled out my sidearm.

Something or someone was just outside the cabin.

"Stay back," I whispered as I advanced toward the entrance.

Pushing the curtain aside, I peeked out of the front window, but there was no one.

The scraping sound came again.

Whoever it was, was right on the other side of the door.

Chapter Twenty-two

I turned the bolt and threw the door open.

"Freeze!"

But there was no one outside.

I swiveled my head, looking for the phantom door-scraper. That was when I heard the pitiful whine by the side of the cabin.

I lowered my weapon.

"Max?" came Katy's voice from behind me.

The dog wagged his tail, making snow fly in all directions. He was dusted in the white stuff, shivering, and leaning against the wall, seeking warmth.

"What happened to you, sweetie?" said Katy, pushing me aside. "Come in. This way. You'll catch hypothermia."

Max stepped up to the threshold and shook himself, showering us with icy pellets. He sniffed us, his tail wagging, like he was glad to have found friendly humans.

I scanned the area.

The clouds were low, and the sun was muted, its soft rays reflecting off the white cover on the ground, giving an eerie haze. Snow was still falling in soft, large balls of fluff, enveloping the cars, the cabins, and the lodge.

"Hey, Max," I said to the dog. "What did you want to show us?"

"Poor thing needs to warm up first," said Katy, coming over with a towel from the bathroom.

She crouched next to Max and wiped him down while he stood still, his eyes closed, his tail lowered.

I reached down and scratched his chin. He licked my fingers in return.

"Do you know where Mia is?" I said, wishing he could talk. "What about Rebeca?"

He wagged his tail in reply.

"If I was going to take a dog on a walk today, I'd put a coat on him," muttered Katy, as she rubbed him down.

"Max's a hardy pup," I said. "Probably grew up on the mountain."

Katy walked into the bathroom with the dirty, wet towel and returned with a plastic cup filled with water and a fresh towel. She flipped the towel on the dog's back and tied it loosely with one of Mia's trouser belts.

"What he needs are proper doggy boots," she said.

"We don't have time for boots," I said, turning to her. "We have to find the girls."

"What about the family? Shouldn't we tell them?"

"They want us to leave, remember? They might even chase us down the mountain."

"They'd listen once they see all this blood on the window, wouldn't they?"

"They didn't stop to help Mia when she fainted by the arch, did they? Besides, they could be involved in this, and I don't want to let them know we know."

"Let's just hope Nancy gets ahold of Officer Jensen soon," said Katy, a glum look on her face.

Nudging Max gently out of the door, we stepped outside and closed Mia's cabin behind us.

"Come on, Max," I said. "Lead the way."

After giving us a few puzzled looks, he turned around and started walking toward the woods. He kept his nose to the ground, but every once in a while glanced over his shoulder to make sure we were behind him.

Katy and I followed.

He seemed very sure of the direction to take. Max had been scraping at the door for good reason.

When we got to the tree line, I stopped and glanced back.

We were about thirty yards from the main building.

Yellow light seeped from the bay windows of the lodge that faced the woods. In contrast, the snow-topped cabins looked like they were hunkering down for the storm. Their windows were dark and silent. It was like no one was inside any of them.

Even Victoria's.

A short bark made me turn around.

Katy and Max had already crossed into the woods. I stepped over a rock and slipped in between the trees. Katy was peering around her, while Max stood on guard by her feet. He turned toward me when he heard me come, his head cocked to the side, as if to ask why I hadn't joined them.

I walked over.

It was unusually quiet in the woods. There were no animals scampering along the branches. There was no rustle of the leaves. It was like the entire forest was holding its breath.

"Keep going," I whispered to Max. "Find Mia and Rebeca."

As if he understood, Max got up and made a beeline through the trees.

Katy and I crept behind him, our eyes and ears on full alert. Once in a while, a sleet of snow or ice would slide off a tree branch, making us jump.

Pretty soon, the ground sloped down steeply, and we could hear the river raging in the gully below us.

Whatever Max wanted to show us, it had to be important. He didn't stop to sniff at the dry leaves poking out of the snow, or even glance at the wayward squirrel on a branch above us. He sloughed on, seemingly on a self-appointed mission.

"He's heading toward the cliff," said Katy in a hushed voice.

I kept scanning the area, listening to see if anyone was watching or following, but so far, the woods remained uncannily silent.

Though it was early afternoon, the canopy dimmed the sunlight, making it feel like twilight had fallen inside the forest. Maybe it was the surrounding darkness, but it felt particularly chilly in here, a chill that bit right into your bones. I was glad we had geared up.

We kept walking.

The roar of the river grew louder.

Suddenly Max barked.

"He found something," whispered Katy.

Chapter Twenty-three

Max was waiting for us by the edge of the escarpment.

When we got closer, he got up and started walking parallel to the gorge, his nose to the ground.

"Hold on!" I hollered, but he only picked up his pace.

"Someone cut the trees here," said Katy, pointing at the clearing up ahead. "There's a path."

"We're heading to the river," I said.

I had initially thought the only way down to the gully without getting killed was to rappel down the cliff face. I hoped we weren't going on a mad goose chase.

But Max had already disappeared. Every few minutes, an urgent bark came from farther on, like he was urging us to hurry.

"Who made this path, and for what?" said Katy as we stumbled down.

"On any normal mountain, I'd say this would be for hikers or cross-country skiers from the lodge," I said. "Maybe recreational sports fishers."

I pulled my phone out to check if it worked, but the signal bars remained resolutely red. We were entering even more desolate territory.

It took us fifteen minutes to get to the gully, walking carefully, taking care not to tumble down.

"I see him," said Katy finally, pointing.

We were at the bottom of the ravine. Max was by the river, about thirty feet from where the path ended and the rocky shore began.

Seeing us, he rushed our way, stumbling over the rocks.

"Be careful, Max," said Katy.

He whirled around and ran back toward the river, barking more enthusiastically than before.

"He found something," I said.

The light was brighter down in the valley compared to the woods. But that strange sense of foreboding I'd got ever since we came to Cloud Cabin Ski Lodge heightened even more. Whatever Max wanted to show us wouldn't be good news.

"Oh, my goodness," said Katy.

The dog was whirling around in a frenzy by the river.

That was when I noticed the body nestled in between the rocks. The upper torso was on the muddy bank while the rest lay in the water. It moved as the river rushed over its legs.

I stepped up to it, my heart in my mouth.

From behind me, I could hear Katy's tentative steps.

I stopped by a boulder and gawked.

It was a young woman.

Her face was deathly pale. Her eyes were closed, and her mouth was slightly open. She looked asleep, almost peaceful, lying in between those rocks and swaying in the shallow water.

But what caught my eyes was not her face. She was wearing a pink bridesmaid's gown, just like the ones Mia and Tiffany wore.

"Rebeca," whispered Katy, her hands on her face, like she couldn't bear to see the body. "She was in those photos."

I squatted next to the woman and felt for a pulse in her neck to confirm what my eyes already knew.

She was cold to the touch.

Cold, wet, and lifeless.

"This happened today," I said. "She couldn't have been wearing this dress any other day."

"That splash we heard, the thing Mia saw in the river," Katy said in a hushed voice. "It was her, wasn't it?"

"I'd bet every dollar someone pushed her over the edge."

"Murder," whispered Katy hoarsely. "Now Mia's gone too. What's going on in this godforsaken place?"

I stared at the dead woman, wishing I had answers.

"What's that thing on her leg?" said Katy, suddenly. "Who wears a humongous digital watch on their foot?"

I leaned across the boulder and squinted. Rebeca's pink gown had shredded from the force of the current, exposing her legs.

"It's an ankle monitor," I said.

"*An ankle monitor?*"

"It's what they put on prisoners, juvenile offenders, or people under house arrest."

Katy gasped. "What in the world was she wearing one for?"

"Don't know who put that on her, but something tells me she wasn't running from the authorities." I paused. "She was under some type of house arrest."

Katy gave a shudder. "Why would anyone do that?"

I glanced around. A remote river gully was a sad and lonely place to die. Rebeca's last minutes couldn't have been easy.

She'd probably tried to breathe but swallowed fistfuls of freezing water instead. She'd probably tried to call for help, maybe kicked and flailed in desperation, but got overtaken by the ruthless river.

A slow anger started to burn inside of me.

Where was Mia? The blood on her window ledge told me she had struggled, that she was a fighter.

Is she here too, half alive, hiding from whoever is after them? Or is she dead?

I stood up.

Leaving Katy to take pictures of Rebeca with Max by her side, I walked along the riverbed, calling out Mia's name.

Chandler's narcissistic personality alone hadn't been enough to persuade Victoria, but we had all the evidence to convince her to get away from her new in-laws now.

Their cagey answers, disregard for family members, that marriage certificate between a father and an adopted daughter all told me nasty things were going on here, things they didn't want found out.

And now we find a dead daughter.

I kept hiking until I came to the widest part of the valley. A quick check of my phone told me we were still disconnected from civilization.

There was no sign of another body or of Mia alive. If she was hiding, she should have spotted us, heard me, and come out by now.

I surveyed the area.

The town of Falcon Hills was several miles further down the mountain, but I couldn't say which way to head down. It would be easy to get lost among the trees.

There was only one thing to do now.

Chapter Twenty-four

I walked along the river back to Katy and Max.

"We need to return to the lodge ASAP," I said.

"We can't leave Rebeca here," said Katy. "She'll get washed out."

"We have to bring her up to the shore. I hate moving her, but we don't have a choice."

"What if I stay here with Max while you get help?"

I gave her an appreciative look. My best friend wasn't a fan of danger, murder, or dead bodies. She was being a sport, trying to do the right thing, despite her feelings.

I shook my head.

"I don't think it's a good idea to leave you by yourself here, even with Max," I said, looking down at the dog who was watching us, head cocked to the side like he was listening intently.

He had stopped his barking and whirling. He had accomplished his mission. It was up to us now to figure out what to do next.

"Besides, I don't know if I'll be able to get help with the phones down." I lowered my voice, though we were alone in the canyon. "We need to stick together right now. I don't trust anyone."

"David and Tetyana are hours by plane," said Katy, giving me a glum look. "And Jensen's still a rookie in a one-cop town—that's if Nancy gets a hold of him."

"He's better than nothing. He can get help from local counties like he did last time." I shook the snow from my hat. "But right now, we have to get back to the lodge."

"What if the person who pushed her is one of the Rupert family members?"

"I'm betting on that."

Katy shuddered and wrapped her arms around herself.

"Is there any way to go to Falcon Hills and get help?"

I looked at the river gushing by us, which seemed even more furious now that we had discovered the grisly secret it had held all along.

"We could follow the river, but it's hard to say where it winds through," I said. "If it cuts deeper into the woods and we get lost, that won't help anyone."

Katy pointed at the rock wall rising above us.

"What about walking down the main road?"

"It will take hours before we get anywhere near people, and we could freeze to death before that. We could take our car, but there's the risk of getting stuck halfway—"

I stopped and turned to Katy.

"Remember that Humvee with snow chains in the parking lot?"

"That gawdawful looking monster truck?"

"It's an older model, which means it doesn't come with complicated electronics."

Katy's eyes narrowed.

"I've hot-wired a car before," I said. "I could try it. It will be faster than taking our car down."

"We steal it?"

"She deserves answers," I said, pointing at Rebeca with my chin. "If someone pushed her in, Victoria's in bigger danger than I thought. Stealing is the least of my worries now."

I stepped up to Rebeca.

"Can you help me, Katy?"

Together, we hauled her body out of the water and onto the shore, trying not to scrape her damp skin against the jagged rocks.

Max watched us quietly, sitting on his hind legs by the river, patiently waiting for us.

Katy and I worked without talking.

If this was a murder, we were tampering with a crime scene, but I also didn't want the evidence to wash away in the swirling river and disappear for good.

But we weren't just moving evidence. Rebeca had been a living, breathing woman whose thoughts and fears had bled into the pages of her diary.

We knew her, even though we hadn't met her.

"I'm going to barf," said Katy, turning around once we were done. Her face was pale and crumpled like she was trying hard not to cry.

"We'll find who did this, Katy," I said.

"Why would anyone do something so horrible?"

"Maybe she saw something she shouldn't have. It's easy to remove a witness by pushing them off a cliff and blaming bad weather during a hike gone terribly wrong." I paused. "Except they didn't think it through, as she's in her bridesmaid's gown."

"I think this is all about Robert's sick life," said Katy. "Maybe she threatened to tell Victoria about his arrangement with Mia."

"Remember those photos of Robert kissing all the girls?" I said. "I have a funny feeling he had something going on with all of them."

"What do you mean?"

"He didn't adopt these girls. He married them."

"Four wives? That's nuts."

"Crazy, yeah, but legal in some places."

Katy let out a disgusted hiss. "This is New Hampshire, not Saudi Arabia."

But that would explain Barbara's attitude. I remembered these arrangements from my travels. The scheming, the in-fighting, and the miserable long faces. These family structures were all about power status for the man. The women were just chattel.

"He could be a cult leader behind that businessman facade," I said.

Katy threw her arms in the air.

"How come Victoria didn't see these people for what they are? There are so many red flags—"

Max stiffened.

Katy went silent.

"What is it?" I said, turning to him.

He was looking up, his eyes narrowed and sharp, his ears pointing forward, and his front leg twitching. I scanned the top of the cliff but couldn't see any movement. But something had alerted the dog.

Was someone watching us?

An icy shiver of terror ran down my back.

Suddenly, like he heard a secret whistle, Max darted away from us and dashed up the path.

I took my Glock out and pulled Katy behind the nearest tree.

"Someone's up there," whispered Katy.

"He's not barking," I said. "That means he knows who it is."

She shot me an alarmed look.

"We're sitting ducks here in the valley," I said. "We need to get back up."

"What if it's the person who pushed Rebeca over the cliff?"

"Good. It's time we found out who it was."

Chapter Twenty-five

Leaving Rebeca's body on the muddy banks, Katy and I scrambled up the hill.

"I wish I brought my Glock too," whispered Katy as we walked parallel to the path, shielded behind the trees. "Haven't trained for months, but I'd feel safer, and I could back you up."

"We came for a wedding," I whispered back. "We couldn't have guessed we'd find a cheating groom, a poisoned bride, and a dead bridesmaid at the bottom of the cliff of the wedding venue."

"You attract danger all the time," said Katy. "Why can't we just have a normal road trip for once?"

She was right.

I did attract the worst people. Being a private investigator meant I met the kind of people most folk would go out of their way to avoid. But this was my chosen vocation now.

Max barked once in the distance, in the same urgent tone as before.

"Maybe he found another dead body," said Katy with a shiver.

We progressed up the hill, stopping every few seconds to listen, but the woods kept their silence as if they were hiding a dark and ugly secret.

We stopped when we reached the top.

Max was nowhere to be seen.

I was about to take a step forward when Katy grabbed my arm.

"What if the killer's luring us in?" she whispered.

"Perfect," I said. "I want to know who it is. Don't you?"

Katy shrank away from me.

"Look, if they're one person, it will be two against one," I said. "Plus, we've fought worse before, remember?"

"We were teenagers," said Katy. "And it was so long ago."

"The muscle memory will come back once you get into it."

"I'd rather not get into it, in the first place."

"Come, we're heading toward the road," I said. "We can always turn back and return to the lodge."

The rustling sound of feet running came from nearby. Katy and I scooted behind a tree.

"Max," I said in relief, seeing the dog run up to us.

He scampered around, barking madly again.

"Have you found Mia?" Katy was asking the dog when I realized something.

We'd been here before.

My eyes swept the area.

We were at the exact spot Katy and I had stopped by on our way up. While the road curved around the mountain, taking longer to get to the lodge, we had hiked straight down, cutting time and distance drastically.

That was when I saw them.

The boot prints.

Prints on the ground, sheltered from the falling snow by a hanging branch of a pine tree.

"Don't move," I whispered to Katy, sidestepping the area to not disturb the markings.

There were two distinct sets of prints. One was of a large boot. The second was smaller but spaced far apart, like they had been running.

Did one of these belong to Mia? Or Rebeca? Or both?

Why did the small prints run toward the ravine? That would have been suicidal.

I walked along them. While the large boot prints came and went, the small footprints only went one way. Toward the ledge.

Behind me, Max barked. Urgently.

I stepped up to the edge and kneeled down. The river was crashing against the boulders, pushing furiously through the gully.

The forest grew to the edge of the cliff. If someone didn't know these woods, they could have easily walked right through and careened into the gorge below.

Max let out another bark.

"Hang on, boy," I said.

I leaned over and peered.

"Be careful," came Katy's voice.

The snow had been disturbed right at the ledge where the small prints stopped. I crouched next to them.

My blood chilled as I realized what I was looking at. There were hand marks on the ground. Someone had grabbed at the snow in desperation.

A futile exercise.

"Two people were here, one big and one small," I said. "The smaller one didn't go back."

Katy's eyes widened.

"This is where Rebeca was pushed," I said.

"Oh, my gosh," said Katy, bringing a hand to her mouth. "Remember that shadow in the woods—"

Max barked. He sounded annoyed, if dogs could be annoyed.

"Here, boy," I said, wishing I had treats on me. "Settle down."

He didn't come over. He whirled around impatiently in one spot, then, without a warning, dashed in between the trees, barking loudly.

"Hey, Max!" called out Katy.

I took pictures of the scene before the snow obliterated everything.

My next step was to return to the lodge and compare the boot prints to the shoes of the family members. I wanted to find out who had been near the edge of the cliff that day. But something made me propel along, as if pulled by the dog's incessant barking.

"He went that way," said Katy, pointing.

I gripped my gun tightly.
Were we going to find a dead Mia next?

125

Chapter Twenty-six

We stopped and stared at the derelict structure nestled among the trees, twenty yards in front of us.

"It's the shed," whispered Katy.

It stood solitary, silent, and dark.

Max was sitting at the threshold. He perked up as he saw us approach and twirled around before sitting back down, facing the door.

"Someone's inside," whispered Katy.

The curtains were drawn, and no light came through them.

Is Mia inside? Or someone else?

Is this a trap?

That was when I saw them again. I pointed at the prints on the grounds.

"Someone was here between the time we came and now," I said.

"Two people," said Katy, frowning. "All smudged though. Hard to say."

I scanned the area.

In between the trees, I spotted a long, white open space. We weren't too far from the road that curved up the mountain and ended at the ski lodge.

Katy started walking around, snapping photographs of the footprints. Leaving her to the job, I stepped toward the shed to see if any of the windows were open.

Max came running up, his nose bumping against my knee, as if urging me to go inside.

Taking care to not touch anything, I tiptoed up the stairs and stepped up to the porch. Max came and stood by my feet, wagging his tail in anticipation.

For one disorienting moment, I wondered if I should knock. I reached over and tried the doorknob. It didn't move.

I looked down at the dog. "Do you know who's inside, pup?" I whispered, wishing for the hundredth time that day he could talk.

I still had Robert's letter opener and the paper clip I used to break into Rebeca's cabin earlier, but they were useless. The lock was an electronic one with a number pad.

Someone had reinforced the entrance to this little shed in the woods. The only reason anyone would do that would be to keep something valuable inside. Or to stop something or someone from getting out.

"Hey," came Katy's voice.

I swung around to see her several yards away from me. She was on her knees, staring at something on the ground.

"Come, see this," she called out.

I stepped down and jogged toward her with Max at my heels.

"The hatch," I said, as I spotted the small wooden door we'd come across earlier. I had concealed it last time, but someone had pushed the snow aside. I stared at the steel ring handle, an intense urge to pull on it coming over me.

"Where's the burlap cover?" I said.

"I removed it. I cleared the snow too," said Katy, "but look closer. I spotted this when I was taking pics."

I peered at the small door, big enough for an adult to slip through. That was when I saw the hint of pink buried in the white stuff on one end. Katy reached over and pulled it out.

"Rebeca's dress," she said, swinging the piece of ripped cloth in front of my eyes. "She was here."

"Or Mia," I said. "Could have been Tiffany too. Whoever it was, they either got out through this hatch, or they were taken in from here."

Katy shook her head. "Why do I feel like we're at the mouth of a serial killer's lair?"

I bent down and pulled on the ring. It didn't move. I pocketed my gun and used both hands. This time, the door wobbled slightly.

"Help me?" I said, as I pulled on the ring.

Max bumped in between us to sniff at the door.

"We're busy," scolded Katy, pushing him away.

We spent a good minute trying to pull on the handle when I realized our mistake.

"Wait," I said. "Let go. Let me try another way."

As soon as she removed her hands, I turned the steel ring clockwise. The low click came as a surprise.

"That was easy," said Katy as I pulled the door and hauled it to the side, letting it hang open on its hinges.

We stared at the gaping hole in the ground, marked by the perfectly square opening.

"A dungeon in the woods," said Katy with a shiver.

Without any warning, the dog pushed in between us and jumped inside the hole.

"Max!" cried Katy.

"Wait!" I said, but he had vanished. I pushed my head in, but all I could hear were his paws clicking on a stone or concrete floor.

The air smelled fresh, here, like the hatch had been open recently. Either that or air was coming in from some place else.

"Get back here now, Max!" called out Katy.

The sound of his paws clicking on the floor continued. He was on a mission again.

"He's been here before," I said, fishing the flashlight from my pocket. "Otherwise, he wouldn't have run down like that."

I shone the light and Katy and I peered in.

A series of steps greeted our eyes. I shone the flashlight around, trying to gauge the size and space, but it was too dark to see further than the five steps right below us.

"Max!" I hollered.

No answer. Not even a small bark of acknowledgment.

I didn't know what was down there, but there was no way we could leave a dog like this. I scanned our surroundings, my heart beating fast. I felt the trees watching us. This time, I almost heard them say, *See, we told you.*

What had we got ourselves into?

"Do we leave it open and go?" said Katy.

"Mia's still missing," I said.

"You think she's in here?" said Katy, her eyes widening.

"She could have been brought here, or she ran away when she was attacked and is hiding in here."

"Do you think she's still alive?"

The urgency to find the injured girl was overcoming my fear of the unknown. There was only one way to find out.

I stepped into the hole and turned around to face my friend.

"Coming?" I said.

It took Katy a few seconds to decide.

I stepped down to give her space.

"Close it after you," I whispered. "If anyone's following us, we don't want to give away our position."

Katy lowered herself into the hole and closed the hatch over her head.

Chapter Twenty-seven

We were in a small underground passageway.

My flashlight was the only illumination.

Katy had turned her phone off to save battery power. My phone had one app turned on. Video recording. If anything happened down here, I wanted the world to know.

Space was tight, just enough for us to walk in single file. Like Katy, I had to bend my head to not hit the ceiling, too.

Whoever had carved this tunnel had gone to considerable lengths to make this walkable. While the walls were craggy and rough-hewn, like they had shoveled the dirt by hand, the makeshift floor had long wooden planks, some rotting, but better than dirt.

My claustrophobia had flared up the second Katy closed the hatch. My heart was beating fast, but this was no time for a panic attack. I had to focus.

"What *is* this place?" whispered Katy from behind me, a nervous tremor in her voice.

The crawlspace went straight for about fifty feet and curved at the end. There weren't any entrances inside other than the one we came from.

"Maybe this tunnel isn't connected to the shed at all," I said, shining my torch around. "Maybe it's a separate underground cave of some sort."

"Great. Makes me feel a whole bunch better."

"I'd say it's an escape hatch," I said.

"Escape from *what*?" said Katy.

"The opening is close to the road, and it was camouflaged when we stumbled on it. Seems like something you would build as a getaway."

"But what would they be getting away *from*?" said Katy, glued to my side. "Whatever it is, you realize we're walking right into it?"

"Max didn't seem too scared," I said.

"Maybe the serial killer has made friends with him," she grumbled. "Given him enough treats to lure women down."

"I don't think this is a random killer," I said. "Everything going on at this lodge has something to do with the Rupert family."

"A freaky, psycho family. Can't imagine how Victoria could have been so blind."

"Chandler played his cards well."

"If he's down here, I'll have a few good words for him," said Katy, her voice turning hard.

Something sharp jabbed at me from inside my pocket. I stopped, reached in, and pulled out the letter opener.

"What is it?" whispered Katy.

I passed it to her over my shoulder.

"It's a little blunt, but it can do double duty as a dagger."

"Better than nothing," mumbled Katy, taking it from me.

We continued our walk quietly, while I tried to not let my mind run away with morbid imaginings.

The sound of doggy paws clicking on the wooden floor was coming from farther down. Max hadn't yelped in pain or barked in surprise. Not yet, anyway. That was reassuring.

We were getting closer to the bend at the end of the tunnel. Suddenly, the dog's head popped out from around the curve.

Max bounded toward us. I bent down to pat his head.

"What have you got us into?" I whispered.

He licked my hand, then whirled around and scurried back down the passageway. He stopped once to glance over his shoulder as if to check we were following him. He barked, the sound echoing through the hollow space, startling Katy and me.

We had kept our movements as quiet as possible, but the dog was making no attempt to guard his silence. If there was someone at the end of this tunnel, they now knew we were here.

I swiveled the flashlight around, checking for stains along the wall or ripped cloth on the wood planks. If Mia had been brought inside or if she had dragged herself down here, there would have to be a few drops of blood, if the blood on her windowpane had been hers.

Max barked again. I could almost hear him say *hurry up, you two.*

Katy and I hastened our steps.

We stopped at the curve in the underground hallway and waited a few seconds before we walked further. My gut said the tunnel was empty, other than the dog and us, but we had to be prepared for anything.

Aiming my weapon forward and shining the flashlight, I stepped into the turn.

About thirty feet ahead of me was a small wooden door, the type you'd expect to see at the entrance to a cellar or basement. Low, rustic, and with a rusty door handle.

Max was sitting in front of it, his entire focus on it. He turned around as the light shone on him and wagged his tail, the same way he did at the entrance to the shed above.

Katy and I crept up to the door. Max got up as we approached. He twirled around, bumped us with his snout, and whined loudly.

"Settle down," I whispered, but it was useless. If someone was waiting to ambush us, they'd be primed now.

"I'm prepared," came Katy's voice from behind me. I looked over my shoulder to see her standing with a grim look on her face, her hand raised and that little dagger pointing over my head. I wasn't sure what good the letter opener would be, but we needed all the gumption in the world.

I turned around and reached over to the door handle. I pushed it down, expecting resistance, but to my surprise it opened easily, like the hinges had recently been oiled.

Before I could do anything, Max pushed in between my legs and jumped in. Whoever was inside was someone he knew, someone he trusted.

It was dark inside. I pointed the flashlight and peered in. A wall of clothes greeted us. A dozen women's dresses, shirts, and coats hung in a row on a wooden rod just above our heads.

"It's a wardrobe," whispered Katy.

I pushed the dresses aside and peeked in. We were in a small walk-in closet. On the floor were a half a dozen pairs of running shoes and hiking boots, lying neatly side by side.

The space wasn't larger than a kitchen pantry. A musty smell pervaded the closet, like it hadn't been aired for months.

Max was now standing with his back toward us, his attention on the other door in front of him, waiting for us to open it for him.

Taking care not to trip over the shoes, I stepped inside and huddled by the hanging dresses. Katy came after me, pushing the clothes all the way to the end to make space.

The folding double door in front of us was made of a light wood, but there were no cracks for light to come through. There was no way to say what was on the other side of this strange setup.

"Ready?" I whispered to Katy, but it was Max who replied. He scratched at the wood panel and whined impatiently.

I reached over and put pressure in the middle of the fold. The doors slid aside silently.

Max bounded out.

I shone the flashlight into the space.

"We're inside the shed," whispered Katy.

Chapter Twenty-eight

I recognized the curtains too.

I twirled the flashlight around the room.

"Mia!" cried Katy, pushing me aside and darting inside.

I lowered my weapon and holstered it.

Mia was lying on a cot.

She was on her back, with duct tape covering her mouth and her hands bound in front. She was still in her bridesmaid's dress, but her shoulder straps were cut like someone had tried to pull them off. Or she had ripped them during a fight.

Mia was convulsing.

That was when I realized there was no heat or light in this shed. Whoever had brought her here had left her to die.

Katy bent over her and put the letter opener to the ropes. I leaned over and pulled the duct tape off the girl's face, making her jerk her head in pain.

"Sorry," I said, drawing my hand back.

"This dang dagger's blunt like heck," grumbled Katy.

I walked across the tiny shed to where a portable stove sat unlit by a gas cannister on a counter. Through a small door by the kitchenette, I glimpsed a white ceramic sink and part of a toilet.

I pulled open the drawers under the counter, pushing the utensils aside until I found what I was looking for. I plucked the sharpest knife from the bottom drawer and hurried over to the bed. Katy snatched it from my hand and turned back to the ropes.

That was when I saw it.

On Mia's right foot was an ankle monitor, the same kind we'd seen on Rebeca. It had been concealed by her long gown all along. Someone had controlled these girls and was now attacking them.

Mia's face was a deathly hue and her eyes looked drained of all energy.

"We'll get you out, soon," I said to her as she turned to me, with tears in her eyes.

Saying a silent prayer to whatever gods could help young Mia, I stepped into the closet to grab the largest and warmest piece of cloth I could find.

When I returned, Mia was trembling all over. I placed the woolen shirt over her chest and tucked it around her shoulders. It wasn't a proper blanket, but it would have to do for now.

"What happened to you, hun?" I asked.

She turned her frightened eyes away but didn't say a word.

"Done!" cried Katy, pulling the ropes away and hurling them to the floor. She took Mia's hands and started rubbing them to keep her warm.

"You're going to be fine, sweetie. You're with us now. We'll get you out of here."

"Who did this to you, hun?" I said.

Mia didn't answer, but gave me that scared side glance again.

"She's in shock," said Katy, rubbing her shoulders to warm her up. "And she's got a fever."

I leaned over to touch Mia's forehead.

Katy was right. Her skin was blazing.

Mia wrapped her arms across her chest and shuddered.

"Give her space," said Katy.

As I stepped back from the bed, I bumped against something soft on the floor.

Max had taken position by the foot of the bed while we tended to Mia, his head lying forlornly in between his paws. It was like he knew we were trying to help her.

This dog deserves a medal.

I grabbed a soup bowl from the kitchen cabinet, filled it with water, and put it on the floor next to him. I watched him lap at the water, my mind buzzing a million miles a minute, trying to figure out what was going on here and how to get everyone out of here in the middle of a snowstorm.

I surveyed the space.

We were in a one-room studio. Other than the tiny toilet and mini kitchenette, the sparse space contained a bedside table and an uncomfortable-looking plastic chair. Along one wall was the closet we'd walked in through.

I scanned the room for a phone, a radio, anything to call for help, but there was nothing. This looked like a self-sustaining shed in the woods made for hunters or hikers.

Except it wasn't.

The tunnel that cut through the woods toward the road told me this was no ordinary cabin. The passageway that led to the back of the closet also told me whoever made it didn't want the entrance discovered.

I peeked out from behind the curtain. Outside was a beautiful Christmassy scene, but I knew that belied the dark goings-on at this lodge.

If I opened the curtains, we'd be able to see better, but I couldn't risk it. The door was locked, but whoever had the combination could spot us and come in at any time.

Mia groaned.

"What in heaven's name?" cried Katy.

I whirled around.

Katy had got Mia to sit up, exposing a large red stain on the sheets beneath her.

She had been bleeding.

I shone the flashlight behind her to see a long gash on her upper back. Someone had slashed her between her shoulders. That would explain the blood on her windowpane.

I ran to the bathroom and grabbed a towel. For the next ten minutes, Katy and I cleaned and dressed her wound.

Mia kept her eyes closed, but her face was scrunched in pain and her hand grasped Katy's arm tightly.

"Stay awake, hun," said Katy, as she worked on the makeshift bandage.

Mia nodded, her eyes still shut.

"We're going to get you help soon, okay, sweetie?" said Katy once we were done. "You don't have to talk. Just rest. Breathe."

I paced the room.

Our phones were still down. Rebeca's body lay in the gully below. Mia needed urgent medical attention. Victoria was in her cabin with Chandler, and Nancy and Jim were at the lodge.

I had to do something, and I had to do it fast. But if I wanted to get everyone out quickly, I needed to know who to trust and who to watch out for.

I turned to Mia.

"Hey, Mia, I need you to help us so we can help you, okay?"

Silence.

"Was it Chandler who did this to you?"

In response, Mia buried her head in Katy's shoulder and sobbed.

Chapter Twenty-nine

I squatted by the cot.

"Hey, Mia, if you tell me who did this to you, I can help the others before they get hurt too."

Mia lifted her head, wiped the tears from her cheek, and gave me a dazed look.

"Otherwise, more people could get hurt. Do you understand that?"

No answer.

It was time to try another tactic. Pushing aside the bloodied towels we used to clean her up, I sat at the edge of the cot.

"Is Robert your adopted father?"

She shook her head.

"Is he..." I swallowed hard. "Is Robert your husband?"

She looked down at the floor where Max was sitting. He saw her and wagged his tail, a pleasant thump on the hard wood floor.

Mia nodded.

"Can I ask how old you are? Eighteen?"

Without glancing up, she held up both her hands. She curled them into fists, then flashed them open, showing seven fingers.

Seventeen.

Katy closed her eyes in distaste.

"Are Rebeca and Tiffany also Robert's wives?" I said, keeping my voice as soft as I could.

She nodded.

"What about Barbara? She's his first wife, isn't she?"

Another imperceptible nod.

"Is Chandler the son of Barbara and Robert?"

She nodded, still not looking at either Katy or me, her eyes on Max. I wondered if she'd trust us if the dog hadn't been here.

"Who slashed you, honey?" I asked.

No answer.

"Was it Chandler?" said Katy.

My blood chilled at the thought of him being behind these grisly activities. We had left Victoria with him. Alone.

Mia shook her head.

Katy and I exchanged a surprised glance. I'd been so sure of that obnoxious, cheating man.

"Did Chandler ever try to hurt you?" I asked.

This time, Mia's answer was clear.

"N... no."

Relief flooded through me.

"It was Robert, wasn't it?" I said, narrowing my eyes.

Mia put her face in her head and started rocking.

"Did he do this because you were going to warn Victoria about your, er, family arrangement?"

She stopped rocking and turned a tearstained face at me.

"Y... yes."

She spoke so softly I barely heard her.

"What about Michael Brown? Did he ever threaten you?"

No answer, but silent tears were rolling down her cheeks.

"Oh, my goodness, sweetie," said Katy, wrapping her arm around her shoulders. "You've been through so much. My heart breaks for you."

Max got up, put his paws on the cot, and extended his snout toward her.

"R... R... Rebeca too," she said softly to Max.

A shiver went down my spine. Did Rebeca get killed for trying to expose the madness of her family? We hadn't told Mia that we'd found her body yet. The time for that news would come.

"Did Barbara ever threaten to hurt you or the other girls?"

Mia nodded.

"A... all the... the t... time."

Katy raised a brow.

"What about Tiffany?" I said. "Is she in danger too?"

No answer.

I sighed. I needed at least a few allies on my side when I returned to the lodge. "Can we trust her?"

Silence.

"Did you meet Tiffany and Rebeca at the Falcon Hills Psychiatric Institution?"

Mia looked up as if in surprise, like she hadn't expected for me to have heard of that place.

She nodded.

"How old were you when you were admitted, sweetie?" asked Katy.

She showed eight fingers. "After M... Mom and D... D... Dad died in a car crash." She stopped to take a breath.

"When did you come to the lodge?"

"L... later..." stammered Mia.

"What happened?"

"T... to... this sh... shed. H... b... brought m... me to... sh... shed....."

Katy looked away, like she was nauseous.

My stomach churned.

I didn't even want to imagine what might have happened in this haunted shed for years, with the rest of the family knowing what was going on. They had been silent witnesses to horrors no child should have ever gone through.

I jumped to my feet.

"You know that Humvee in the parking lot?" I said, turning to Katy.

"The truck you plan to hot-wire?"

"I'm going to go back up and bring it down here so we can get her to a doctor ASAP."

Katy's eyes widened.

"What about Victoria? Nancy and Jim?"

"I'm going to get them in the car without anyone knowing. If all else fails, I'll use firepower."

I paused.

"We're not too far from the road. If you can bundle her up and get her to the tree line in half an hour, I can come down to pick you up."

Mia's eyes flickered. She turned her head and reached out to me with her hand.

"N... no."

"Why, sweetie?" said Katy.

"B... be... be c... careful...," she whimpered.

"Don't worry," I said, pulling my weapon out of my pocket. "I won't let anyone hurt you or anyone else, okay? It's a promise."

She stared at my Glock for a few seconds and shivered. I quickly slipped my sidearm back inside my jacket, hoping I hadn't traumatized her further.

"Th... th... that won't h... help... you."

It was my turn to stare at Mia.

Why the heck not?

"What is it, honey?" said Katy, holding on to her shoulders. "What are you trying to tell us?"

"D... don't... go...," she said in a hoarse whisper. "Th... they... they're k... k... killing every... everyone...."

Before I could ask anything more, Max got up and growled.

He was on his hind legs, his ears pointed up, and his eyes on the door.

Katy pulled Mia in closer.

I stepped toward the window and lifted the curtain slightly and peeked out.

Two shadows were advancing toward the shed through the woods.

Chapter Thirty

"Get inside the tunnel," I hissed, without taking my eyes off the window.

"Who is it?" whispered Katy.

I watched the shadows approach the shed, a stream of sweat trickling down my back.

Every muscle in my body was tense. Goose bumps sprang up on my arms. I felt like a cat ready to pounce on their prey, except I didn't know who or what it was.

From behind me, I could hear Katy coaxing Mia to move and get inside the closet. Mia murmured something, then whimpered. She was in pain. I didn't dare move away from the window to help them.

The shadows became clearer.

It was Robert.

He had someone with him.

Nancy!

Robert was holding a gun to her head. Nancy's face was crumbled, her eyes screwed shut as if she expected a bullet to smash through her brains at any moment.

I felt a roar in my ears as my adrenaline spiked and my blood pumped furiously.

Something serious must have happened at the lodge for him to haul Nancy over like this.

My stomach flipped.

Is Victoria alive? Is Jim okay?

Behind me, Mia was still whimpering. Max's paws clicked against the hardwood floor as he paced up and down, agitated. He sensed the danger.

"Mia," Katy was pleading in a whisper. "Hold on to my shoulder."

Robert was walking up the steps, pulling Nancy along by one arm.

"Please, Mia," whispered Katy urgently.

Robert was on the porch now.

I took position in front of the door, my weapon at the ready.

Soon, I heard the electronic pings of him punching numbers into the lock, like a phone being dialed.

My mind whirled.

Do I shoot him as soon as he enters? Will he shoot Nancy first?

The sound of a loud thud behind made me jerk up, but I didn't turn. Someone had stumbled to the ground. Mia cried out. Max barked. Katy hushed him.

But it was too late.

The pinging sound on the lock stopped. Robert had heard them.

He knew someone other than Mia was here now, someone who'd brought the dog inside.

I cursed under my breath.

"Oh, my goodness, Mia," came Katy's voice, urgent, terrified. More stumbling from behind me, then the sound of something dragging along the floor.

I kept my eyes forward, praying for Nancy. I could feel the dark energy on the other side of the door.

Robert was going to be prepared now. There was only one thing to do. Surprise him before he surprised me.

I leaped toward the door and yanked it open.

"Freeze!" I shouted, thrusting my gun at Robert's head.

Nancy screamed.

Max let out a volley of barks.

I lunged toward Nancy, but Robert had the upper hand.

He pressed the muzzle of his gun against her forehead so hard, she bent over from the pressure.

"I'll shoot!" he shouted.

I stopped in mid-step, my sidearm still aimed at his head.

We glared at each other for what felt like an eternity. This was as close to checkmate as I'd get.

"What the hell are you doing in my shed?" growled Robert, finally.

"Seems like you've been hiding some sick secrets," I growled back, not wavering in my stance or my gaze.

I wanted badly to talk to Nancy, to tell her she was going to be all right, to help me help her, but she was quaking like a leaf in the wind.

"Let her go," I said to Robert. "Nancy has done nothing to you."

"Like hell I will," he said, pushing the gun even harder on her temple. "You bitches come here interfering with my plans."

Robert's transformation from smart businessman to the hideous psychopath was astounding, even after what Mia had told us. He was a real-life Jekyll and Hyde.

"Please don't," cried Nancy, as she stood hunched over, her face turned away, cowering in terror. "Please don't shoot me."

A red-hot flash of anger spiraled up my spine, but I had to remain calm. One false move and Nancy could die. It didn't matter that I subdued this man if my friend lost her life or got hurt during my attempt.

My eyes shifted to his revolver. It was the vintage piece I'd seen in his office. For a moment, I wondered if he was bluffing.

Does that even work?

Nancy turned to her captor, her face a picture of horror.

"Please, please, sir, don't kill me... please..."

My heart fell to hear her beg for her life. I wanted nothing more than to smash this sick man's face before I finished him for good. I gritted my teeth, only one thought swirling through my mind at hurricane-force speed.

Today, I'm going to kill a man.

"What do you want from her?" I snarled. "She came to help with your son's wedding. Leave her out of your dirty games."

"You think I'm stupid?" snapped Robert. "Let me inside, you witch."

"Not until you tell me what the hell is going on," I snarled back.

Robert cocked the gun. "Fine. Have it your way."

"No!" cried Nancy. "Please... I didn't do anything. It was Chandler who—"

"Shut up, bitch!"

"Hey!" I shouted.

Max barked, whirling around my feet. I hoped to goodness Katy and Mia were safely out of the way. But I kept my eyes on Robert.

"You pull that trigger," I said, "and I promise you, I'll lodge a bullet right between your eyes in one hot second. She dies. You die too."

"Is that how you want to play?" said Robert with a raspy, hollow laugh.

My heart skipped a beat. He was calling my bluff.

I took a deep breath to settle myself. All I needed was to get into the best position to shoot this man without hurting Nancy, but in the meantime, I had to keep him talking.

"What do you want?" I said.

"Wouldn't you want to know?"

Behind me, Mia was sobbing loudly.

Max kept turning around and around, his paws clicking on the wood, his whines increasing in intensity. He was confused. His mistress was in distress and his master was hell-bent mad.

"You want a fight?" I said. "Let everyone go. Then you and me can duke it out."

"I'd love some hand-to-hand combat with you," smirked Robert.

My stomach churned.

"You don't know what I'm capable of," I said, unsmiling.

"I'd love to find out."

"Let the others go and you will."

Robert laughed out loud.

"You two-bit girls come from New York like hotshots. Who do you think you are?"

"Someone who's not afraid to take you on, Robert Rupert."

Chapter Thirty-one

My muzzle was ten inches from Robert's head, but his caustic smirk widened.

While I was sweating bullets, struggling to talk him out of killing my friend, he was enjoying the banter.

Behind me, Katy was whispering something urgent to Mia. I prayed they were by the closet, close enough to slip through and escape if a shootout began.

Robert's eyes bored into mine, that ugly jeer on his face taunting me. He knew he had the upper hand. If devils wandered this planet, I was staring at one right now.

"What are you trying to prove, holding a gun to an innocent woman's head?" I said.

"It's too late to ask that question," he snarled. "Should have thought of that before you drove all the way here."

"We came for a friend's wedding. How could—"

I stopped as my mind cleared. Victoria's hasty marriage had nothing to do with love, and everything to do with money.

"This is about her property, isn't it?" I said. "You want Cedar Cottage and all that prime land."

Robert narrowed his eyes.

"You're trying to get your dirty hands on Victoria's estate."

The smirk turned into a scowl.

Bingo.

"How's business these days?" I said, keeping my voice casual, suppressing the urge to grab him by the neck and smash that Adam's apple.

But if he was deranged enough to kill Rebeca and slash Mia, he wouldn't think twice of shooting Nancy, a woman he just met.

Nancy stood slumped over, her shoulders drawn in and her face toward the floor, like she was trying to make herself as small as possible.

"The new ski franchise has taken away most of your customers, I hear," I said. "You shoveled a ton of cash into upgrading your resort and buying all that machinery. You're deep in the red, aren't you, Robert?"

"That's none of your damn business."

"It becomes my business when you mess with my friends."

An anguished wail came from behind me.

Mia.

Why isn't she in the closet already?

Though Robert's presence grated on every nerve of my body, I had to keep him talking.

"You sent Chandler to Cedar Cottage to seduce Victoria. Then you arranged this phony wedding, so you'd own her property by proxy. Are you looking for more land to expand your resort? Or did you plan to sell Cedar Cottage to the highest bidder to pay your debts?"

"What the hell are you talking about?" he growled.

His face had turned a light purple, and his eyes wavered. He was nervous, and he was losing focus. From the corner of my eye, I saw his latch on Nancy loosen.

"Chandler doesn't love Victoria," I said. "So why on earth were you planning to hold another wedding in Paris?"

I badly wanted to double-check my phone.

My cell was snug inside my pant pocket, which meant there would be no video, but this audio alone would be priceless. It would be all I needed to nail this man. If it was still on.

"Because even with the new family connection," I continued, "you weren't sure you could talk Victoria into handing over her estate to you, am I right?"

His scowl deepened.

"I don't believe a second wedding has been planned," I said. "That's a sham too—"

"They're not going to Paris!"

I jerked around, startled.

Nancy had lifted her chin and was staring at me, a small fire glowing in her eyes.

"What do you mean, Nancy?" I said.

"Shut up." Robert snarled at her.

"Hey," I shouted at him. "Watch your mouth."

"Yeah? What are you going to do about it?"

"I found tickets," cried Nancy, despite Robert's furious glare. "They're going to Lebanon."

She was still scared, but a sliver of anger was growing inside of her. *Good.*

I turned to Robert.

"Lebanon, eh? What were you planning to do there?"

He didn't answer, but he frowned. Nancy was telling the truth. She'd opened another door to his scheme, and he didn't like that one bit.

"It's none of your damn business what I do with my family."

A chill went through me as I realized what he'd been hatching all along.

"How were you going to get rid of Victoria?" I said, my voice hardening. I took a step closer. I could almost touch his temple with the muzzle of my gun.

"Were you planning for her to be lost at sea? Stranded in the desert? A quick and dirty accident in the Middle East where the police aren't trained, fast, or straight as they are here. They wouldn't give a hoot what happened to a woman, a foreign one at that, and will believe anything you say."

Robert gnashed his teeth.

"Then you and the family will return home, spend some time in public mourning before you scoop Victoria's property into your own portfolio. You'll return a richer man than now."

"Shut up!"

"I swear if even one hair of Victoria or Jim's heads has been harmed, you will pay. I will make your last moments so miserable you will wish I killed you with one bullet to the head."

The sound of feet dragging came from behind me. I crossed my fingers, hoping Katy had finally got Mia to move.

"I know what happened to Rebeca," I said, keeping my eyes on Robert. "We found her body at the bottom of the gully. You pushed her over. You murdered her."

An ear-splitting shriek reverberated from inside the shed.

Chapter Thirty-two

"**S**he deserved to die!" yelled Robert.

"So, you admit it?" I said, keeping my eyes steady. Mia let out another shriek.

"You... you... k... k... *killed*... R... Rebeca?"

"Katy, get her in the tunnel," I said, not looking back.

"She won't move!" cried Katy in an exasperated voice.

"You... s... s... said... if I t... tell Vic... Victoria, you... you'll kill... me...," Mia stuttered, her garbled voice rising.

"Shut up, woman!" Robert shouted, spittle flying from his mouth.

"Y... you k... killed R... Rebeca! H... how... c... could... you?" Mia's voice was rising to a fever pitch.

"You don't like the truth being spelled-out, do you?" I said, observing Robert carefully. "We know more about your nasty games than you think."

He glowered.

"You adopted three girls from the mental institution. You abused them and played mind games, even marrying them in sham weddings to tighten your leash and keep them quiet. People like you should be locked up for life."

Robert's face tightened. He bared his teeth. "You bitch!"

I didn't flinch.

His eyes flitted from me to Mia behind me.

"What you didn't bank on was the girls were smarter and braver than you thought," I said, glaring at him. "They decided to speak up and that must have been infuriating. Infuriating enough to kill them?"

"Shut your mouth!"

"How old were the girls when you supposedly adopted them?"

No answer, but if his eyes could kill, I would have turned to cinders.

Mia's raspy voice came from behind me.

"I... I... was t... twelve...."

The fury I'd been trying to contain all along rushed up my spine and threatened to explode in my head. I pressed my weapon to his temple.

"You're a dead man," I said, between clenched teeth.

That was when Robert pushed Nancy in front of him.

I whipped around her, but he dove to the floor, his arm wrapped around her neck.

Nancy shrieked and flailed.

I aimed at Robert's torso, then his legs, then his head, but Nancy was thrashing violently.

"Let her go, you scumbag," I shouted, as I tried to get a good aim.

The rotten wood on the railing broke in two. Robert and Nancy toppled off the porch and rolled on the icy ground.

Nancy was fighting back like an angry mountain lioness, but that wasn't helping me.

I jumped down after them.

Suddenly, Robert released her. Nancy sprang up and jumped toward me.

"Move!" I yelled, pushing her away.

Instead, she flung her arms around my neck and held on tight, weeping. I turned, but Robert had already vanished to the other side of the shed.

I pulled Nancy back against the wall, knowing he could easily fire at either of us, at any second.

"Get down," I said to Nancy. "Please. Now."

She clung to me.

I aimed my weapon at the corner of the wall and pulled the trigger.

Nancy jumped three feet high.

The sound of someone scrambling came from the other side of the shed. Pushing Nancy behind me, I stepped toward the corner, my weapon aimed forward.

He had disappeared.

"Robert!" I shouted. "You won't get away with this."

Silence.

I scanned the woods, keeping cover by the wall. My eyes darted back and forth, trying to ignore the chaos that had erupted behind me.

Max was barking nonstop. Nancy was crying nearby, and Mia wailed.

What are they all doing outside?

"Mia!" Katy was shouting. "Get back in here!"

I kept my eyes on the woods.

That was when I spotted the glint of something behind a tree. I aimed and pulled the trigger. It was a shot in the dark, but I wanted him to know I wasn't playing nice.

"I'll show you what happens when you interfere with my family!" Robert's roar reverberated through the woods.

A shot echoed through the cold air.

"Down!" I screamed, as I slammed to the ground and covered my head.

The bullet ricocheted over me and crashed through the shed's window, splintering it to bits.

Someone screamed.

I spun around to see Katy hunkering by the doorway.

Mia was clutching her chest and leaning against the porch like she was about to plunge over the railing. Nancy sat crouched under the shattered window, staring at me with sheer terror in her eyes.

"Katy!" I shouted. "Get them inside now!"

I whirled back around, but that short distraction was all Robert had needed.

I scanned the grounds, trying to find any clues that would give away his position, but there was nothing to see and the only sound I could hear was the roar of my blood pounding in my ear.

There.

I caught his shadow behind a tree about thirty feet away.

Just as I put my finger on the trigger, Max shot by my legs, and ran barking toward the clump of trees.

"Max, get back here!" I shouted, bracing for another shot. Robert was just the type of man to shoot a dog.

Max's barking got louder. Then the shadow moved. He was taking off.

That was when the second shot rang out.

"Down!" I screamed as I dove to the ground again.

I was about to jump up and race after Robert when Katy's panicked voice came from behind me.

"Asha!"

I whirled around.

"She's hit!"

My stomach fell.

I leaped back up the stairs toward where Katy stood by the doorway.

Katy was leaning over Mia, holding her head up, trying to talk to her. Mia's eyes were half closed and her mouth half open. A dark red stain was spreading on the front of her dress.

Robert's bullet had got her.

The blotch of blood on the wall told me she had been standing when she got hit, before she slithered to the floor.

Robert could have shot any of us. But he had aimed at her.

Mia moved her hand toward me, like she was trying to tell me something. Then, she gurgled and her head lolled back against Katy's shoulder.

Katy looked up at me, her eyes filled with tears.

Fury swirled inside of me.

A whimper made me turn.

Nancy!

She was squatting under the window, covered in broken glass, rocking back and forth with her hands over her head.

"Oh, my lord, oh, my lord."

I darted over.

"You okay, hun?" I said, scrutinizing her for bullet wounds.

She peered at me through her fingers. She was in shock. Her face was cut, but she was otherwise okay. I pulled her away from the window and picked the large glass pieces off of her hair.

"We need to go in *now*!" I said, spinning around to Katy.

I helped her carry Mia inside, unsure what more damage we were doing to the girl by moving her, but we had no choice.

"Keep your heads below the window, everyone, in case he shoots again," I said, pushing Nancy inside before slamming the door shut and bolting it.

Katy leaned against the cot, holding Mia's head in her lap. Mia's chest was spasming and the stain of blood on her dress was growing larger by the second.

Keeping a low profile, I dashed into the bathroom for more towels. All I knew was we had to stop the bleeding.

"Here," I said, dashing back to hand the towels to Katy. "It probably hit a main artery—"

Katy shook her head and gave me a sorrowful look.

"She's gone," she said in a trembling voice. "It's too late."

Chapter Thirty-three

Mia's hands lay limp on the floor.

Her eyes were slightly open but glazed, like a thin, gray film was covering her eyeballs.

I reached over and felt for a pulse on her wrist and bowed my head.

"He's killing them, one by one," said Katy, through her tears.

I fell back on my haunches, feeling numb with defeat. If I'd acted faster, she would have been alive.

Katy covered her with a blanket. She wiped her eyes and turned away as if she couldn't bear to look at her anymore.

Nancy was sitting on the floor, leaning against the wall, her shocked eyes on Mia's shrouded outline. While Katy and I had had our share of gun battles and had seen dead bodies, this was all too new for her.

I hated to leave Mia on the cold floor of the shed, but there was nothing more we could do. Her body was now evidence, evidence I hoped would soon incriminate Robert Rupert and put him where he belonged.

In prison for life.

"We can't stay," I said, straightening up and shuffling over to the kitchenette on my haunches. "We're sitting ducks in here."

When I'd been rooting for a tool to cut Mia's ropes earlier, I'd noticed something else. A large hunting knife was too unwieldy to work through knots wrapped around delicate wrists, but it would make a perfect weapon.

I pulled it out and turned to Katy who was crouching by the cot, hugging herself.

Her eyes widened as I handed the knife to her. At least she had trained years ago, but Nancy was another story. I picked a smaller kitchen knife and passed it to her.

Nancy looked at it tentatively.

"What do you want me to do with this?" she said, a slight tremor in her voice.

I put a hand on her shoulder.

"It's better than nothing," I said. "Just follow instructions and you'll be fine. Stay strong, okay?"

She nodded, but she clutched the utensil so tightly her knuckles turned white.

I inspected my weapon.

I had fired at least two shots, which meant I should have thirteen rounds left, at the least twelve.

I was glad I'd brought my Glock. My only regret was I hadn't brought extra cartridges, my trusty Tanto knife, and a few bulletproof vests for all my friends and Mia.

Then again, I hadn't expected a friend's wedding to turn into a bloodbath on the mountain.

I checked to see if my video app had remained on. It was. There was still no cellular reception, but my battery was draining.

I turned to my two friends.

"Keep your weapons and cells handy at all times. My phone's got twenty minutes tops. Katy, turn on your audio in fifteen, just in case."

She nodded.

I turned to Nancy. "Keep your phone turned off until we need it."

"But mine's still in the dining-hall," she said in a trembling voice. "That's where I was when he got me."

"What exactly happened?" I said, squatting by her.

"Robert came to the kitchen and said he wanted me to bring in canapes to the dining room. He said Jim was busy with the photographs, so I did...."

Nancy wrapped her arms around her shoulders and shuddered visibly.

Her adrenaline was diminishing, and with only one woolen layer between her skin and the chilly air rushing through the cracked window, she was going to freeze.

Katy spun around and shuffled toward the open closet.

"Here," she said, plucking a jacket and throwing it at Nancy. "Might be a bit small, but it'll keep you warm."

She rustled up a pair of thick socks and boots from the back of the closet as well. Nancy took the socks gratefully and pulled them on.

"Was Tiffany there?" I asked as Nancy laced her boots.

"She was sitting at the table looking bored. She was munching on grapes but didn't say much."

Katy raised her eyes at me.

"She's his next target, isn't she?"

"Something tells me," I said, "she's not the type to give away family secrets to just anyone."

"What do you mean?"

"It's a hunch, but I get the feeling she'll only talk for a price, and that should save her." I paused and shook my head. "But she could be dead right now for all I know."

I turned to Nancy.

"How did Robert nab you?"

"I went to put the cheese plate on the buffet table when I saw it."

"Saw what?"

She dropped her voice and leaned forward, though there was no one to overhear us.

"A brown envelope tucked under a vase. I don't know what came over me. I'm not a snoop, but it had Victoria's name on it, so I couldn't help it."

Was it the same envelope that had passed hands between Robert and Michael?

"Did you open it?" I asked.

She nodded and lowered her voice to a whisper.

"That's where I saw the tickets to Lebanon. There was also a printout of a hotel address in Beirut. At first, I couldn't figure out why they weren't going to Paris."

I frowned. "Lebanon doesn't have an extradition treaty with the US. That's probably why they were heading there."

"Extradition... what?" said Katy.

"If you commit a crime and want to hide overseas till things cool down, some countries are better than others. The US can't force them to hand you over and bring you to justice here. It's not a guarantee, but a good bet."

"My goodness," said Katy. "They planned it well."

"If officials in those countries are more likely to take bribes, you have even a better chance of getting off scot free."

"Sounds exactly like what that corrupt Robert Rupert would do."

"That's not the only thing I found," said Nancy, her eyes narrowing. "I saw the marriage license and an insurance policy."

"Life insurance?" I said, recalling the hushed voices I'd overheard in the office. "On Victoria?"

Nancy nodded.

"Her will was in there too."

The puzzle was coming together. Robert had been planning Victoria's death all along. They'd had their ducks lined up until Mia and Rebeca rebelled and Katy and I arrived at the lodge.

My eyes flitted to Mia's lifeless body. She and Rebeca had paid the ultimate price for speaking up.

"I was so shocked," Nancy was saying. "I didn't even see Robert come over to the buffet table."

Her words were tumbling out fast. Katy leaned over and put a hand on her arm.

"Slow down, hun."

"I didn't have time to warn Jim. I couldn't even call out to him. Robert was holding a gun to my stomach. He told me to walk fast, or he'd shoot me first, then Jim."

Her arms moved jerkily as she told us the story.

"He was mad because I opened the envelope. He pushed me out of the patio door before anyone could see and brought me here."

Nancy clutched my arm, a pained expression on her face.

"I didn't know what he was going to do to me. When I saw you here, I was so relieved. I knew you'd do something. You'll get Jim and Victoria out safe, right?"

Her face was so earnest, I didn't have the heart to tell her about the fears crowding my mind. Jim could very well be in trouble. But it was Victoria I was most worried about.

I got to my feet and stepped away from the window.

"Time to go back to the lodge—"

That was when a bloodcurdling scream came from the woods, stopping me in mid-sentence.

Chapter Thirty-four

Max started barking in the distance.

Then, just as he started, his yapping receded like he was chasing someone or running away from something.

Katy, Nancy, and I stared at each other.

The screaming had cut off so abruptly, it made my blood chill. Nancy's face had turned completely white.

"What was that?" whispered Katy.

I straightened up halfway and slipped the curtain aside with the muzzle of my gun. Outside, snow was falling thicker and faster, already covering Robert and Max's footprints, but there was nothing to see.

Where did that scream come from?

Who was it?

It had been so startling I hadn't even registered if it had been a woman or a man. Whoever it had been, they had sounded terrified.

"It was a man," whispered Katy. "That was definitely a man."

My mind whirred.

Robert?

Chandler?

Michael?

Please don't let it be Jim.

"It wasn't Jim," said Nancy, as if reading my mind. "I'd recognize him. It wasn't him." She sounded more hopeful than sure, but I nodded.

I leaned closer to the window and peered through the woods.

The trees had fallen silent again. There were no signs of the birds or squirrels we'd seen on our way down to the valley below.

I could feel an ominous energy around us. It was like the trees were watching us, whispering to each other, trying to guess which one of us would live through the day.

"I don't like this," I said, turning to the others. "Robert could be waiting for us behind those trees. We'll be targets as soon as we open the door."

"What about the hatch?" said Katy.

"Exactly what I was thinking too," I said. "But there's a risk he knows about it. We also didn't cover up the entrance after we got inside."

"That would have been impossible," said Katy. Her jaw tensed. "If he's there waiting for us, it'll be three of us against one man."

I looked at her, then Nancy.

"I saw Michael with Robert in his office. I couldn't hear them, but they looked like they'd just done a good business deal. That's where I saw the brown envelope. All to say, we need to stay alert for any of them to be out there."

"Are you saying they're *all* in this together?" said Katy.

"Maybe even Barbara. I'm sure they all knew they were heading to Lebanon and not Paris."

Nancy took a sharp breath in.

"Do you think they're going to hunt us down?" she whispered.

"Chandler and Robert might, but maybe not the others. Someone has to monitor Victoria."

"God, I hope she's okay," said Katy.

"If they want to get their hands on Cedar Cottage without too many questions asked," I said, "they'll have to make it look like an accident. As long as they're on US soil, I'd say Victoria has a fighting chance."

"Thank goodness."

"They'll be controlling her and lying to her, though. Maybe that's Chandler's job." I paused. "But things could have changed now Mia and Rebeca are dead and Robert found us here."

My friends exchanged an alarmed look.

"If I were them," I said, "I'd be adjusting plans pronto, and that could mean drastic action."

Nancy's face turned even paler.

"Like what?"

"Just keep your eyes and ears open," I said to her. "We'll find Jim and Victoria and we'll get through this. I promise."

I turned to Katy.

"You know the drill?"

Katy sat straighter and clutched her knife. "I'll be right behind you and ready."

My old friend was returning.

Mia's tragic death had affected her the most. She was the one who'd held the girl as she took her last breath, and that would unsettle anyone. Katy wouldn't forget this nightmare for a long time.

None of us would.

"And Jim? What about him?" said Nancy, her face flushing and her eyes getting fiery again. "If anything happened to him, I wouldn't know what to do. They'd better not have... I'll, I'll show them."

"That's the spirit," I said. "Let's go, ladies. Keep quiet and stay close."

I got on my knees to keep my head below the level of the window and shuffled toward the closet door. I stepped inside, shining my flashlight in front, and kicked open the small wooden door at the back.

The tunnel looked even more depressing than before.

"All clear," I said, gesturing to my friends to follow me.

It was a relief to walk upright, even though it was cold and dreary in the underground passageway. We moved in single file, with Nancy sandwiched in between Katy and me. My flashlight gave the only illumination as we trudged along.

I stopped and put an arm out when we got to the end of the tunnel, where the steps to the hatch door began.

"What do we—?" started Nancy.

"Shh…" I said, turning to her. "We don't know who's out there."

We waited by the steps, huddled together, our ears cocked, alert to any sounds from above. After two minutes, I gave my friends the signal.

"Here goes nothing," I whispered as I handed the flashlight to Katy and stepped up toward the hatch door.

I put my hand on the handle and pushed it, my Glock at the ready.

It took several tries before I could thrust the door open. I shoved it an inch, bracing for a gunshot, a surprised yell, running footsteps, or even barks.

But it was eerily quiet outside.

Keeping my gun aimed at the slit, I pushed the hatch slowly, inch by inch, stopping every few seconds to listen, ignoring the door's weight on my arm and shoulders. But the only sound I could hear was my heart pounding against my ribs like a jackhammer at a construction site.

It felt like an eternity before I opened the hatch all the way.

My eyes darted in all directions, but there was nobody in the vicinity. I wondered where Max was.

After a three-hundred-and-sixty-degree scan of the area, I hauled myself out and checked behind the closest trees, before helping Nancy and Katy out of the hole.

"Where to?" whispered Katy.

"This way." I pointed.

The three of us moved stealthily. We crept from tree to tree, pausing and listening before moving, watching each other's backs. A plan was slowly forming in the back of my head.

Our destination was the ski lodge.

Our targets were Robert and Chandler first, then Barbara and Michael.

We were deep in the woods, but a pale-yellow light shimmered farther away, in between the trees. It appeared and disappeared as the branches swayed back and forth to the light wind. The lodge wasn't far, but I didn't know what would be awaiting us.

We'd just stepped up to a large fir tree by a clearing when Nancy cried out.

"Oh!" she said, clutching Katy's shoulder, forgetting her promise to stay silent.

"Who's that?" whispered Katy, her eyes widening.

A body was lying under an oak tree, only fifty feet from us.

Chapter Thirty-five

Katy and Nancy huddled closer together.

Is this a trap?

"Watch my back," I whispered to my friends.

I stepped toward the prone body, shielding myself behind the trees, staying as quiet as possible. I could feel Katy and Nancy's reassuring presence, glad they were with me.

I crept closer.

It was a man.

Robert.

This could be a ruse. I wouldn't put it past him.

But he was lying in a position only a circus contortionist would be capable of. His neck was inclined at an uncomfortable angle and his knees had been turned completely the wrong way.

Did he trip on a root and fall?

It would have to have been one heck of a tumble for him to end up like this.

Robert didn't stir.

All the hairs on my neck were standing up now.

Next to his arm was a club, a brown polished baton, not the kind you'd come across in the middle of the woods. It looked familiar.

It was when I got to fifteen feet from him, I realized he wasn't playing. Someone had bashed Robert's head in.

After a quick scan around, I stepped out from behind the tree line.

I stared at the lifeless body.

How did this happen?

The polished stick next to him was a baseball bat, the one signed by the Fisher Cats I saw on his office wall only hours ago. The bloodstains and hair stuck on the large end of the bat explained his crooked knees and his battered head.

Someone had been waiting for him among the trees and had pounced on him. Robert's face looked like something out of a brutal, surreal painting. Whoever had killed him had killed in fury.

My stomach churned. It was a good thing I hadn't eaten much that day or I'd have vomited it all out.

I stepped back and took a deep breath to calm my nerves and take stock.

For the past hour, only one goal had occupied my mind.

Robert Rupert had been an evil man. I'd been plotting to prove his guilt, to make sure he got thrown behind bars for the rest of his life. I'd even pulled the trigger when he'd shot Mia, and would have gladly seen him fall to the ground, screaming.

Still, to see him dead so suddenly was disturbing. Someone had wanted him to pay for his sins, or someone had had a quarrel with him serious enough to justify murder. This meant only one thing.

Another killer was roaming the lodge.

If I'd thought things had been bizarre here, they had taken an even stranger turn.

I searched the area for Robert's revolver, but it was missing. Nancy and Katy had been silent so far and I hadn't seen a shadow in the clearing, but my gut tightened even more.

I pulled my phone out and snapped a few pictures in case the killer returned and moved him. Stepping gingerly around the body, I picked up the bat from the top end and melted into the trees.

This was a major crime scene and the baseball bat was evidence, but I also knew that after you killed once, it was easy to kill again.

We were alone here to fend for ourselves.

I scurried back through the woods toward my friends, relieved to see them still crouching behind the tree, their worried eyes on me.

"Robert," I said, lifting up the bat to show them my find. "Beaten to death."

Nancy gasped.

"I know who would do this," said Katy with a grim look.

"Who?" I said.

"Barbara."

I raised an eyebrow.

"She was the fourth wheel, sidelined by three young wives," said Katy. "I could see her killing him. I think she murdered Rebeca too. She's just the type."

"I think it's Tiffany," said Nancy. "She's so cold, almost like a robot. I can picture her smashing up a man and not caring one bit."

"For revenge?" I said.

She nodded.

"But Tiffany's a petite woman while Robert was a big-boned man," I said. "Whoever did this has major upper-body strength."

"If you're angry enough, anything is possible," said Nancy, screwing her eyes.

"Good point."

I extended the bat toward her. "Backup weapon. We need to use all we've got."

She drew back in disgust.

"What's that on it?"

"Try to ignore the red splatter and, er, the hair."

She took it with the tip of her fingers, making a face. I turned around for one last glance at Robert's body when Katy let out another gasp.

"Hey, who has long blonde hair?" she said, pointing at a clump at the thick end of the bat I hadn't noticed before.

"Barbara," whispered Nancy. "Tiffany too."

"How did that get there—" I stopped.

A rustle was coming from somewhere in the woods.

"Someone's heading this way," said Katy in a hushed whisper.

I aimed my Glock in the direction of the sound. Nancy held up her bat. Katy took a fighting stance with her butcher knife.

We waited, not breathing.

The rustle got closer. My heart raced.

Is it the killer?

But it didn't sound human.

It wasn't.

"Max?" whispered Katy in a shocked voice.

We stared at the dog as he bounded up to us.

He got on his hind legs and gave Katy's hand a lick. He sniffed at the baseball bat suspiciously, then turned to me, his tongue lolling.

"Do you know who did this, Max?" I said, patting his head.

He twirled around, as if he couldn't have been happier to have found us.

"Once this is over, we need to get him away from this wacky place and find him a new home," said Katy.

As if in agreement, Max barked loudly, making a flock of birds take off to the skies from the tree above us.

I was about to shush him when I heard someone call out.

Max perked his ears and stood still for a second. Then, he dashed through the woods back in the direction he came from.

"Max!" called the mysterious voice again, faint and in the distance.

It was a woman.

Who else is in the woods?

Chapter Thirty-six

"Detour," I whispered to my friends.

I turned around and headed back into the woods.

There were only three women in the lodge other than us. That voice had to be Tiffany, Barbara, or Victoria, but it had been too far and too faint to make out clearly.

"It can't be Victoria," whispered Katy, sounding more hopeful than anything. "What would she be doing out here?"

We crept quietly, staying covertly behind the shadows of the trees. Soon, we heard the river gushing below, not too far from us.

We hadn't heard a peep from Max again, and the woman had turned silent. It was hard to know if we were heading toward her, or away.

The rush of the river got louder.

We stepped up to the last few trees that stood between the ravine and the woods.

Katy clutched my arm.

I turned my head to look at what she was pointing at.

"Who's that?" whispered Nancy, peering through the trees.

We stared at the hazy silhouette of a lone woman by the cliff, a few hundred feet from us. She was hunched, her face turned toward the gorge. Next to her was the shadow of a small head with pointy ears.

"Whoever it is," I whispered, "it's someone from the lodge, or Max wouldn't be sitting so quietly like that."

The woman was staring into the open void, her back to us. It was like she was waiting for something. Or someone.

Rebeca's body by the river shores below flashed across my mind.

I shivered.

Was someone luring these women to the bluff and pushing them over?

I turned to my friends.

"That's not Victoria," I whispered.

"It can't be Barbara either," whispered Katy. "She's bigger and rounder."

"Could be Tiffany," I said.

"She was in her bridesmaid's dress, drinking wine at the dinner table last time I saw her," said Nancy. "This woman's in pants."

"She had time to change," I said.

Max turned in our direction.

He either sensed or smelled us. We drew back hurriedly, but the woman didn't move. That was when I noticed she was holding on to the dog's collar.

Does she know we're here?

Katy turned to us, her eyes opened wide as if she'd just thought of something.

"What if it's someone else altogether?" she whispered.

"Rebeca and Mia are dead," I said. "That leaves—"

Katy shook her head impatiently.

"What if there are people at the lodge we haven't met yet?"

"Impossible."

"We didn't check all the cabins, did we? They were dark and closed so we assumed they were empty."

"Maybe there are more sheds in the woods," said Nancy, with a shudder. "Maybe Robert kept other girls."

A chill went down my spine.

More captives? More secrets?

I gazed at the silhouette in the distance, bent down like she was saying something to Max.

I had been so sure Robert had been behind everything, but while he had hedged and reacted in fury, he hadn't confessed to anything.

"There's another possibility," I said. "What if neither Robert nor Barbara killed Rebeca?"

"Robert said Rebeca deserved to die," said Katy.

"He didn't say he did the deed."

"But he killed Mia right in front of our eyes," said Nancy.

"I held the gun, so I was the biggest threat. If I were him, I'd have shot me. I think he tried, but he was a lousy shot." I paused. "The thing is, we can't forget there's another killer on the grounds."

Katy pointed at the woman by the edge of the cliff.

"Are you saying the killer lured her up here?"

"Or she's the one," I said.

Katy and Nancy gasped out loud.

"I think it's time to go over and talk to her," I said.

"Are you crazy? I'm not walking up to a murderer," said Nancy, giving me a dark look.

"Three of us against one of her," I said. "Plus, we're armed. Keep watch and stay alert."

It took us a good ten minutes to creep through the woods, staying parallel to the ravine. Max worried me the most. It would take him seconds to give away our position. As soon as the thought crossed my mind, he perked up, turned around and let out a bark.

We stopped in our tracks.

The dog whirled, furiously wagging his tail. The woman spun around and stared.

"Tiffany," said Nancy in a hushed voice.

Gone was the beautifully done updo and wedding makeup. Her bottle blonde hair fell carelessly around her shoulders. She had changed into blue jeans and a red plaid lumber jacket, dressed for the outdoors, unlike Rebeca or Mia had been.

She was very close to the ledge. One foot back, and she'd plummet into the canyon below.

Holstering my weapon, I stepped out from behind the tree, ignoring Nancy's warning hand on my shoulder.

"Hello, Tiffany," I called out.

She stared at me like I was an alien, like she had never seen me before.

Does she know what happened to Rebeca? Is she out here looking for Mia?

Tiffany no longer looked like the snotty, mean girl more concerned with her nails than anything else. Her back was hunched, her shoulders up, and her hands were curled into fists.

It was a defensive position.

"Hey, you okay?" I called out, keeping my voice casual but not getting any closer.

She didn't speak.

I wondered what I must have looked like, emerging from the forest the way I did.

Is she scared of me? Or is this something else?

From behind me, I heard a rustle, and soon Nancy and Katy stepped out and flanked me.

Tiffany's eyes widened.

She took a step back and teetered at the ledge.

Chapter Thirty-seven

"**W**atch out!" screamed Nancy.

I leaped forward and grabbed Tiffany by the arm. Her right foot had slipped over the ledge, but I held on. Katy sprang toward her and snatched her by the shoulder.

Together, we held on tight.

To my relief, Tiffany brought her foot back and stepped away from the edge. She squinted at us under her eyelashes, a wary expression on her face.

Strange.

We tried to stop her from a sure death and she suspects us?

Max gave us a confused look and whined.

I didn't let Tiffany go. She could step back at a moment's notice and take all of us down with her.

Now that I was closer, I could see her focus wasn't steady.

"What were you doing here?" I said.

Tiffany didn't reply.

"You must be cold," said Katy with a small smile. "Have you been out here for long?"

She stirred and shook herself, like she'd just woken up from a trance.

Her eyes fell on the baseball bat Nancy was carrying. She gave a startled cry and pulled back as she spotted the bloodstain.

"Careful," I said, tightening my hold on her.

But Tiffany wasn't listening to me, her full attention on the wooden weapon.

"Where did you find that?" she said, her voice reedy and thin.

"I, er, found this in the woods," said Nancy, slipping it behind her to hide the telltale splotch of dark red. "Think it belongs in Robert's office. Strange it was out here, isn't it?"

Tiffany stared at her, like she didn't believe her.

"Come," I said, nudging her away from the edge. "Let's go back to the lodge and pour ourselves a nice cup of hot chocolate, shall we?"

To my surprise, Tiffany turned to me and reached out with her hand, like a kid.

I let go of her arm and took her hand. She grasped mine so tightly, I winced. Despite her petite frame, this woman was strong.

Robert's mangled head came to mind.

Gripping her by the hand, I ushered her toward Nancy, who had retreated to the tree line. Max whirled around our feet, like he was happy we had all come together finally.

I wondered how flawed his doggy instincts were. Wouldn't he be more guarded around someone who had taken a life? Then again, Tiffany was part of his home pack, miles ahead of him in the family hierarchy.

We were the outsiders.

"What were you doing out here by yourself?" I asked, keeping my tone casual.

"It was... getting a little hot inside. I needed fresh air," she said in a small voice, not at all like the dismissive huffs we'd heard from her at the wedding.

"Is that right?"

No one in their right mind would have walked to the edge of a ravine, deep in the woods, just to get fresh air. A quick stroll in the garden would have been enough. She wasn't telling the truth.

"I guess a good stroll in the woods always helps to clear your head, doesn't it?" said Katy with an amiable smile.

Tiffany gave her a dazed look, but didn't answer.

Max was making a beeline back to the lodge, followed by Nancy. I realized we were trailing them blindly, but we were about to make a big mistake.

That path would take us close to Robert's body.

"Hey, Nancy," I called out. "This way. Snowdrifts are too high on that side."

Nancy turned around. I steered Tiffany away from the path. We were going to take the longer route, but she didn't protest. She held on to my hand, stumbling along like she wasn't really there, but lost in another world.

My mind was buzzing.

Am I holding the hand of a cold-blooded murderer?

Did Tiffany kill Robert in a flurry of vengeance, then decide to end her life, driven by guilt? If she was the killer, wouldn't she have put up a fight, not meekly come with us like this?

None of this answered who killed Rebeca. Had it been Robert after all?

We walked in awkward silence. While I held on to her, my other hand was in my pocket, ready to bring out my Glock in half a second.

It was mid-afternoon, and we still had daylight, but the events of the day cast a dark spell around us.

With every step toward the lodge, the heavier my heart felt.

I wanted to dash over to make sure Victoria and Jim were safe, but Tiffany was clutching our arms like her life depended on it.

Her eyes were so glazed, I wondered if she'd taken some medication or drugs. Either way, the girl floundered like she couldn't move more than a few steps without our help.

It was peculiar how quickly the self-centered and aloof bridesmaid had turned into a mess of blubbering nerves.

Or was this all an act?

Something was wrong with Tiffany, but she wasn't a killer. She was barely present.

"Where were the others when you left the lodge to go on your walk?" I asked.

She mumbled in a low voice. I leaned in close but couldn't make out any words.

"Is there anything you want to share, Tiffany?" I said. "Did you see anything? Hear anything?"

More mumbling. Suddenly, she pulled her hand away from Katy and covered her mouth. We stopped as she made gagging sounds.

As Katy and I held her, she bent over, her body shuddering. She sounded like she was about to vomit but nothing came out.

"Last night's dinner effecting you too, hun?" said Katy, her brow furrowed.

Tiffany straightened up and wiped her mouth with the back of her hand. "The wine made me sick... that's why I came outside."

The missing rat poison under the kitchen sink flashed to mind.

Jim had poured the wine for the table. While the wedding party had drunk the alcohol, Katy, Nancy, Jim and I had stuck to water. Victoria had been too sick to eat or drink.

I kicked myself for getting diverted by the anonymous messages and for not staying in the hall and watching her more closely. She had sworn off eating all day to settle her stomach, but I now wondered if anything had been added to her glasses.

The feeling that something bad had happened at the lodge was getting stronger and stronger.

"Did you see Victoria before you left?" I tried again.

Tiffany stumbled and lurched forward. We caught her just in time, but she kept her face to the ground, her loose hair falling over her, obscuring her expression.

"We got you," said Katy, rubbing the girl's arm.

I looked up ahead.

Max had disappeared, but Nancy was powering on, propelled by her desire to see Jim, I imagined. She hadn't even noticed us slow down. My sense of urgency was growing too.

"Can you walk faster?" I said.

Tiffany shook her head.

It took us longer than expected to get out of the trees and onto the open grounds. The lights at the main chalet were all on, but my gut was giving me warning flags. I didn't have time for a stroll.

I scrutinized Tiffany quietly. She was pale. Maybe she wasn't lying about feeling sick after all. She was shorter and smaller than Katy and unarmed. Katy was carrying her butcher knife with her.

I turned to my friend. "Hey, can you stay with her?"

Katy nodded.

I jogged toward Nancy, who was plowing on, oblivious to the cold, her jacket flapping with every step.

"I'm so scared for Jim," she said as I caught up to her.

We marched silently through the snow, now several inches deep.

I was scared too.

For Jim. And especially for Victoria.

Chapter Thirty-eight

Nancy and I stopped when we got to the path that wound its way toward the main building.

It forked to the right, leading to the parking lot, and to the left toward the cabins and the lodge.

"Footprints," said Nancy, pointing at the fresh snow on the ground.

"They're coming from the lodge," I said, wiping the snowflakes from my eyelashes.

I squinted at the parking lot. Our car was exactly where I left it. So were the others. But the footprints headed that way.

"Come," I said, motioning to Nancy.

We followed the prints along the parked vehicles.

I crouched low by each car, in case someone was hiding underneath. It was a remote possibility, but with all the events of the day, I didn't want to take any chances.

"They were going to the Humvee," said Nancy, pointing at the oversized all-wheel drive I'd been planning to hot-wire. I wondered if someone else had got the same idea.

"Stay back," I said, holding my Glock out.

I stepped up to the vehicle. There was no one inside. I walked around, trying the doors and the trunk, but everything was locked.

I plucked my flashlight from my pocket and shone it around. The back seat of the vehicle was filled with duffle bags and backpacks.

Nancy sidled up to me and peered inside.

"Whose ride is this?" I asked.

"Chandler's, I thought," she said. "Just the kind of obnoxious car he's likely to drive."

"Was this packed when you saw it last?"

"Didn't notice to be honest."

"Looks like someone's ready for a trip," I said.

"They're heading to the airport tomorrow, remember?" said Nancy.

I flipped on the stronger switch on my flashlight and shone it around again. The two front seats were clear but if we were going to use this as our getaway car, we'd have to empty it first.

"This looks more like what you'd take on a road trip than on an international flight."

I spun around to see how much progress Katy was making with Tiffany.

They had stopped halfway across the grounds. Tiffany was bent over, looking like she was gagging again, with Katy holding on to her. Max had returned and was circling them, sniffing around as usual.

It would take ages for them to get here.

I turned to Nancy.

"Our first job is to get Victoria and Jim out of the lodge and into this car without alerting the others."

"How do we do that?"

"We'll figure it out," I said, taking her by the arm and ushering her back to the pathway.

Our first stop was Victoria's cabin. We hastened toward it.

The image of Chandler slamming the door on our faces sprang to mind, making me grit my teeth.

He'll be feeling the muzzle of my gun on his pretty face soon.

I stepped up to the cabin door, reached over to the doorknob, and turned it, expecting it to be locked. But the door opened. I slammed it wide.

"Victoria?" I called out as I stomped inside, my heart in my mouth.

Nancy gasped out loud.

I surveyed the mess, a swirl of horror rising in me.

"What happened here?" cried Nancy.

"Someone trashed the room."

A quick check in the closet and ensuite bathroom told me we were alone in the cabin.

Nancy turned to me, her eyes bulging. "What's going on, Asha?"

Were they searching for something? What were they looking for? Who was it?

"Jim," stammered Nancy, her breath coming fast and shallow. "Did something happen to... oh my—"

"To the lodge," I said, pointing at the door, and nudging her outside. "We have to move fast."

A quick glance over my shoulder told me Katy was still stumbling through the snow with Tiffany hanging on to her.

"Let's go," I said.

Pulling Nancy along, I raced toward the main building.

I stopped by the front entrance. Nancy gave me a scared look. I didn't know who could be waiting for us inside, but she wasn't in the proper frame of mind to back me up.

Leaving her at the bottom of the steps to keep watch, I walked up, staying as close to the wall as possible.

I peeked through the entrance. The corridor was empty, and the building was eerily quiet. It seemed like no one was inside the lodge at all.

I gestured for Nancy to come up.

"Do you hear anything?" I whispered when she reached the doorway.

She cocked her head to the side, then shook her head.

"Exactly," I said. "There was music and voices in the dining-hall before. So, where did everyone go?"

Nancy's face turned white.

"Jim!" she said, turning toward the kitchen.

I grabbed her by the arm.

"There's a killer roaming around," I whispered. "We'll take this step at a time."

She froze in place.

I counted the occupants at the lodge in my mind. Robert, Mia, and Rebeca were dead. Tiffany was with Katy. That left Barbara, Michael, and Jim. And Chandler and Victoria, who had vanished from their cabin.

We stayed by the entrance for another minute until I was sure there was no one nearby. Then I tiptoed toward the dining-hall entrance and peered in.

A ghostly scene greeted my eyes.

It was like everyone had got up and left in the middle of the party. Half-drunk wineglasses and half-eaten plates sat on the table next to unfolded napkins and dirty cutlery. The music had been shut off, and the patio doors remained closed.

What happened here? Did someone take them all?

Nancy tugged at my arm.

"Jim," she whispered hoarsely.

I nodded.

We crept along the corridor toward the kitchen.

I put my ear on the door when we got to it, but no noise came from inside.

I turned the knob slowly and pushed the door open, expecting to feel the resistance of Nancy's dish towel under the door. To my surprise, it slid open easily.

Someone had removed the rag at the bottom of the door.

Nancy pushed me aside and walked in. She turned around, her eyes wide open, her hands shaking.

The kitchen was in the exact state it had been when I left.

"Where is he?" she said, whirling around. "What happened to him?"

I closed the door and started my search with the walk-in pantry, seeking clues, anything that would tell us what had happened at the lodge. Nancy watched me by the kitchen table, looking like every fiber in her was trembling, as if she was expecting the worst.

It was after I'd scoured the room, I realized the only place I hadn't checked was the corner Nancy was standing.

I walked up to her. That was when I noticed the piece of paper tucked under a stack of recipe books at the end of the table. I didn't recall seeing it before. I leaned over and plucked it out.

"What is it?" said Nancy.

I unfolded the paper and read the note.

Nancy,

Victoria's really sick. Going to town to get the doctor. Be back soon,

Jim. XXX

Chapter Thirty-nine

Nancy's eyes welled up in tears.

"What in the world was he thinking?" she said in a trembling voice. "Our little two-seater is never going to make it down the mountain. That's practically suicide."

"But your car was in the parking lot," I said, narrowing my eyes. "Buried under the snow."

"So, he didn't go? Where's he then?"

I looked at the note again.

"Is this Jim's handwriting?" I said.

She took a sharp breath in and grasped my arm, pulling the paper closer to her. She squinted at the letter for a few seconds.

"It's his. I'm sure it's his."

I held the paper to the light, but there were no secret etchings or messages. It was a simple note written in plain blue ink. I'd noticed the blue ballpoint lying on the stack of recipe books.

It was easy to assume Jim had scrawled this hasty note before leaving or trying to leave the lodge, but my spider senses were tingling.

"He'd never leave Victoria in danger alone," I said, more to myself than her.

"Something's happened to him," said Nancy, almost hyperventilating. "Where *is* he? Maybe the killer's got... got him too? Oh, my go—"

"Highly unlikely," I said quickly before her imagination ran farther. "The killer is going after the Rupert family. This is personal. Jim and you have nothing to do with them, so he should be safe. Besides, Jim's resourceful. He won't let anything happen."

Footsteps came from the corridor.

I whirled around.

"Stay back," I whispered, stuffing the note in my pocket and stepping toward the entrance. I opened the door, my gun aimed forward.

It was Katy, carrying the butcher knife.

She was alone.

I poked my head out and gestured for her to come inside. She scurried over with a relieved look on her face. I pulled her inside and shut the door.

"What happened to Tiffany?" I said.

"Too sick to walk," she said, placing her weapon on the table, and plopping down on a chair with a weary sigh. "She wanted to go to her cabin, so I left her there with Max."

I raised a brow. Being alone in their cabins was exactly how Rebeca and Mia got abducted and eventually killed.

"I made sure she bolted the door," said Katy, seeing my face. "I even checked the window to make sure it was locked, and I told her to not open the door until the police got here."

I nodded. "Maybe that's best. We can't move fast with her tagging along."

"She didn't want me to hang around, anyway. Got a little cross when I said I could stay with her."

"Did you see Victoria's cabin on your way here?" I asked.

Katy gave me a puzzled look.

"Someone turned her room upside down like they were looking for something," said Nancy.

"Where's Victoria?" said Katy, her voice higher than normal.

I gave her a grim look. "We'll find her. I promise."

"What about Jim?" said Katy, whirling around.

"He's gone too!" wailed Nancy.

"This place is insane," said Katy, putting her head in her hands. "It's like we're stuck in a nightmare that gets darker and darker. When are we going to wake up—"

"Hey, slow down, Katy," I said. "We got this. We'll figure this out one step at a time."

"I just wish I knew who we were up against," said Katy, giving me a miserable look. "We don't even know who the psycho murderer is."

"Don't assume it's a crazed killer. This looks more like a calculated plan to me. That's even more danger—"

I stopped as a look of alarm spread across Katy's and Nancy's faces.

"We have work to do, girls," I said. "Our first job is to check all the cabins and rooms, starting with this building."

I looked from Nancy to Katy and back. Action was the cure to unfettered fear, even if it was temporary.

Katy picked up her knife and took a deep breath in.

"I'm ready."

I looked at Nancy.

She straightened and nodded, but I could see the apprehension in her eyes.

"My gut says Victoria and Jim are in the lodge somewhere, but alive. The faster we find them, the sooner we can get out of this place."

After checking the corridor, I led my friends out of the kitchen and into the dining-hall. While Katy kept watch by the doorway, Nancy and I searched the room.

"Check for hidden doorways, hiding places, everything," I said as I walked over to the buffet table in the corner.

The brown envelope Nancy had rooted through had vanished.

Who had it now? Michael? Chandler? Or was it Barbara?

Something told me that item was the linchpin to everything that was going on here.

After searching all corners, I stepped up to the glass doors that led to the back, where the wedding ceremony had taken place. They were shut but not locked. The only footsteps I could see in the snow were from the main patio door leading toward the woods. They were faint and getting fainter by the minute.

"That's where he took me," whispered Nancy, coming over.

"What were the others doing?" I asked.

"Sitting around the table. The music was playing, and the fire was roaring. No one noticed Robert push me out. He covered the gun with his jacket, but I felt it jab on my waist."

"Was everyone here?"

"Except for Victoria and Chandler. They were in their cabin. That's what I thought."

"What about Jim?"

Nancy's face scrunched up like she was about to cry.

"He was by the fireplace, taking photos of Barbara. She was being fussy and making him retake it over and over. That's the last time I saw him."

"Next stop, Robert's office," I said, pulling on her arm.

The three of us slipped back into the corridor. Keeping our eyes and ears open, we crept toward Robert's office.

Though the place was eerily silent, I couldn't shake the feeling someone was watching us. A quick glance around me and up at the ceiling told me there were no cameras in this place. No visible ones, anyway.

The deathly quiet bothered me.

While I'd told my friends we'd find Jim and Victoria alive, I was beginning to think I was fooling myself.

Chapter Forty

Katy stepped up to the wall where the baseball bat had hung that morning.

She pointed to the bat Nancy had in her hands.

"Someone came in here and took this to bash Robert's head in. Who would do such a thing?"

"Someone who couldn't find a better weapon," I said, walking over to the desk. "That's good news for us."

I opened the third drawer to see the spot where Robert had stored his revolver. It was gone.

I looked up at my friends, who were staring at the space on the wall, a mix of shock and disgusted expressions on their faces.

"Start searching, guys," I said. "Spread across the room and check everything."

We worked swiftly, going through the drawers, the cabinets, even opening Robert's cigar and liquor collection to see if there was anything there that would give us the whereabouts of Jim and Victoria. Or the identity of the killer.

I was hunting for one more thing. The brown envelope that had changed hands between Michael and Robert. I was sure the killer had it or they were after it, too.

"Look what I found," called out Katy.

I spun around.

"The envelope?" I said.

Katy was pulling out a square wooden box from the bottom drawer of Robert's liquor cabinet. I scooted over just as she opened it.

"It was tucked all the way in the back," she said as she pried the lid open.

A soft sponge foam lined the box. Nestled inside was a cardboard pack of bullets and an antique revolver, exactly like the one Robert had on him.

Katy plucked the revolver out.

"Another gun?" said Nancy. "Looks old."

"Better than a baseball bat any day," said Katy as she slipped the bullets out of their box. She slid them into the revolver's chamber, one by one. "I'll feel so much safer with this."

I frowned as I watched her load the gun.

"So there were two sidearms in this lodge, and Robert had one," I said, trying to piece things together. "Whoever took the bat didn't know there was an extra revolver with ammunition hidden in here. Who could that be?"

"Chandler would have known," said Katy, looking up from her task. "He was the apple of his father's eye, after all. I'm sure they shared everything."

"Barbara could have known," I said. "If we found it here, she would have figured it out too. She looks like the type who always ferrets things out."

"The creepy Michael dude wouldn't have known," said Katy matter-of-factly. "He doesn't live here."

Was it Michael who was creating all this havoc then?

Nancy stepped toward us and placed the bloodied bat on the cabinet. Then she picked up the cleaver Katy had been carrying with her and turned to us with a dark expression on her face.

"I don't care who it is," she said, clutching the knife close to her chest, her eyes flashing. "I swear if anything has happened to Jim, I'll... I'll... Don't stop me."

I nodded somberly. I couldn't blame her. I'd probably do the same if it was David. I just hoped we'd find Jim alive before Nancy butchered anyone.

But I was glad to see her fighting spirit come alive again. That was exactly what we needed as we prepared to battle an unknown killer.

After finding nothing else, we left the office and crept along the corridor toward the back of the lodge. We were in the section of the building we hadn't been in before. These were Robert and Barbara's private quarters.

"Empty," said Katy as we passed a small guestroom with a bed and nothing else. That left only one room at the end of the passageway with a large double door which was closed.

"The master bedroom?" said Nancy as we approached it.

I stepped up to the door and leaned my ear against it.

There was silence on the other side, but my gut was screaming. It was telling me there was something in there, something I wasn't sure I wanted to see.

I touched the doorknob. It turned effortlessly. That was too easy.

Is someone waiting for us inside?

My stomach tightened.

Gripping my gun, I pushed the door open and jumped in, shouting, "Hands up!"

My eyes fell on the queen bed, and I froze.

My gut warnings had been right.

There was someone in the room.

"Come in and close the door," I said quietly to my friends.

Nancy crossed herself as she stepped up to me. Katy came in, stared at the body on the bed, then turned away, like she was about to throw up.

Someone had beaten Barbara to a pulp.

Just like her husband.

Her legs and arms were splayed out at hideous angles, like the attacker had jumped on her in a wicked frenzy. Her beautiful blonde hair that had been done up perfectly now lay across the sheets in a mangled mess of yellow and red. But her face was the most stomach churning, a mutilation of flesh, bones, and blood.

I shuddered.

What happened here?

"The baseball bat," whispered Nancy. "They hit her first, then went after Robert in the woods. That's how the long blonde hairs got on it."

Barbara was still in her mother-of-the-groom gown and the three-strand pearl necklace I'd seen her wearing when we first met. She even had one of her silver kitten heels on. The other lay on its side, on the floor.

I reached down to check her pulse.

"She's not cold yet," I said with a grimace. "She died in the past hour."

Either Barbara had come to her bedroom to lie down and someone had followed her in without her knowing or they had pushed her in here and beaten her viciously.

Nancy covered her mouth with her hand and shook her head. "Why kill them? I didn't like them, but how could anyone do something like this...?" She trailed off.

"The good news is this narrows down the killer," I said.

Nancy and Katy looked at me in alarm.

"It's Chandler or Michael," I said. "Or they're in this together."

Chapter Forty-one

Nancy stood by the windows, keeping an eye out for anyone approaching from the grounds.

Katy kept watch by the master bedroom door, her eyes on the corridor. I searched the room, working furiously.

At first, nothing seemed amiss. Except for Barbara's battered body.

Robert and Barbara's designer clothes were hung neatly in their closet, and their shoes were lined in a row at the bottom. A vanity table across the bed held a plethora of expensive lipstick and high-end powder compacts next to a couple of premium perfume bottles.

A bookshelf stood in a corner and by it was a comfy red leather chair. Exactly what I would expect to find in the master bedroom of a wealthy couple's ski lodge.

After a quick check to make sure Nancy and Katy were still on watch, I stepped up to the bedside table, keeping my eyes averted. I had already taken pictures of Barbara's body to hand them to the authorities, and my stomach was barely holding it together.

I hadn't particularly liked Barbara, and I had practically detested Robert after discovering his sick fetishes. Still, stumbling across their viciously damaged bodies had made me nauseous.

A clean shot with a bullet would have sufficed. If the killer hadn't had a gun, one strategically placed blow to the back of the head would have done the job. That would have been easier to stomach than these grisly finds.

But it told me one thing. Whatever Barbara and Robert had done to the killer had to have been heinous. This was personal.

Barbara was an enigma to me.

She'd stayed in a fake marriage to a bigamist who had been abusing young girls. She'd even signed their adoption papers as a co-parent. The hospital would have never handed orphaned children into the custody of a single, middle-aged man. She had to have known what was going on.

Whether it was Stockholm syndrome, sheer terror, or willful blindness, Barbara was an accomplice who'd protected the perpetrator of a foul crime.

But there was another reason for her to do what she did, one I suspected was closer to the truth. She did it selfishly to protect her lavish lifestyle, her personal reputation, and her standing in her influential social circles.

So, why was she killed now?

Did Robert attack her before heading off to the woods and getting killed himself? I'd have suspected the three girls, but two of them had been brutally murdered, and the third could now barely walk.

I pulled the top drawer of the bedside table open.

A small earring caught on the lip of the drawer fell to the floor with a clink. The stone twinkled at me. I picked it up and held it to the light.

Nancy turned and raised her eyebrows.

"That's huge," she said, staring at the translucent jewel dangling from my fingers. I hadn't seen a diamond earring this big either.

"That probably cost tens of thousands," said Katy, turning around to see my discovery.

I resumed my search.

I pulled out a silver jewelry box tucked in the corner and flipped it open, expecting to find the second of the pair of earrings. But it was empty.

That was when I noticed the velvet lining inside had been ripped apart, like someone tore at it to find something underneath.

I pulled out the remaining boxes. They were all empty. I opened the second drawer. More empty boxes.

A single emerald ring sat at the bottom of the third drawer, like it had dropped through the cracks.

Was I barking up the wrong tree? Was this a jewelry robbery gone bad?

I signaled to my friends to come and look.

"What's all this?" said Katy, peering at the empty boxes lying open on the floor.

"Just when I think I've figured out what's going on, I find someone stole all their jewelry," I said.

"But this was more than a robbery," said Nancy.

Katy bent over to pick a silver box up when we heard the barking outside.

I whipped around with my gun aimed at the door.

"Max," I said. "He's found something."

"That dog has a million lives," mumbled Katy as we stepped up to the double doors.

I peeked out, my Glock at the ready, and scanned the corridor. The hallway was empty, but the barks were getting louder.

I kicked the door open just as Max came rushing inside the lodge, barking his head off.

Seeing me, he dashed along the corridor toward the master bedroom, his frenzied barks echoing off the walls.

"Hey," came Nancy's warning voice from behind me. "I smell smoke."

"Me too," said Katy.

I sniffed the air. They were right.

As if he knew we'd got the message, Max whirled around and skedaddled back toward the entrance.

The smell was stronger now.

I spun around to my friends. "Get out! Now!"

The three of us dashed out of the master bedroom and ran helter-skelter down the corridor, following Max's barking.

I crashed through the main entrance and froze on the top step.
My heart stopped as I realized what was happening.

195

Chapter Forty-two

The three cabins in the back were burning.

Max was going berserk, yapping hysterically.

I didn't have time to think. I leaped down the steps and dashed along the pathway, desperately looking for a hose, a tap, water, anything to douse the fire.

The cabins closest to the lodge, the ones occupied by Victoria and the girls, were untouched. It was those farthest away that were burning. The ones with the darkened windows. The ones I had assumed to be empty.

Maybe Katy was right.

Maybe Robert had kept more women in these cabins. Maybe he'd threatened them to keep quiet until the wedding was over and the guests had departed.

I ran up to the first cabin on fire and clasped the door handle. I pulled back with a yelp. Even with my winter gloves on, I felt the heat of the steel handle.

"Get a log!" I yelled to Katy, who had come racing toward me. "We have to break down the doors!"

I scurried around to see if I could spot anyone through the windows. The curtains inside were in flames.

I remembered the red fire extinguisher near the bathroom door inside Victoria's cabin. I'd spotted one in Rebeca's and Mia's cabins too. If anyone was stuck inside, they had at least something to protect themselves, though temporarily.

"Gas!" shouted Nancy from somewhere nearby.

I smelled the gas too.

Log cabins didn't burn in the middle of the winter, out of the blue. Someone had doused the walls with gasoline before igniting the fire.

I scuttled around the cabins, trying in vain to listen for screams, yells, or cries for help, but all I could hear was Max's mad barking as he ran in circles, threatening to trip me up.

Whoever set these structures ablaze had planned it well.

The doors had been doused with gasoline, too. Breaking through the thick wooden panels would be a herculean task and even if we cracked them open, anyone walking out through those doorways would burn.

What do we do?

Is anyone inside?

"Found one!"

I turned around to see Katy and Nancy dragging a snow-dusted wooden log from the parking lot. I scampered over and grabbed one end.

"The back window!" I hollered as I ran toward the closest cabin, pulling my friends along with me. When we got to the back, I aimed the front of our battering ram at the middle glass pane.

"In three!" I hollered over the crackling.

"One, two, three!"

The log rammed into the glass, splintering it into smithereens.

"Anyone inside?" I yelled as I dropped the log and rushed up to the broken window. Katy, the tallest among us, pushed me aside to look in.

"Empty!" she shouted.

"Next one!" I hollered over the dog's howls.

The three of us picked up the log and darted to the next cabin to smash the back window.

With the insides in complete darkness, it was difficult to see if anyone was standing by the windows and getting showered by the broken glass, but we had to take the chance. Getting them out alive was worth a few cuts or scratches.

It was when we smashed the window of the third cabin, we heard the frightened yells.

"Someone's inside!" cried Katy.

"Get a chair!" I shouted. "A ladder!"

Katy dropped her side of the log and ran back up the pathway.

"We'll get you out!" I hollered, turning back to the broken window.

The cry for help came from inside the cabin again.

It was a man.

"Jim!" screamed Nancy suddenly, dropping the log and rushing toward the window.

"Get back!" I shouted, leaping forward, grabbing her by the arm, and pulling her away.

Nancy tore from one end of the cabin to the other in panic. "Jim! Jim!" she shrieked. "Someone help! Get him out of there!"

The yell from inside came again, and a shadow crossed the window. Then another.

There were two people inside.

"Nancy!" I screamed. "Pick up the log! Help me!"

She ran over, sweat and tears streaming down her face, and pulled her end up again.

"Now!" I yelled. "All your power!"

We ran toward the window, aiming at the bottom. The glass shattered into pieces. I turned my face away as the splinters rained down on me.

"Jim!" Nancy screamed from behind me. "Get out!"

"Again!" I hollered and rushed toward the window to create a larger opening.

"Here!" came Katy's voice from behind me.

I spun around to see her running toward us with a wooden chair.

Jim's frightened face popped out from the other side of the broken window, but he jumped back, throwing a hand up to shield his face. The heat from the flames was increasing. We had to get them out before they burned to a crisp.

Jim popped his head out again. He looked drenched. Thank goodness. That meant the fire sprinklers had kicked in.

I grabbed the chair and positioned it next to the wall under the broken window. I got on the chair and lifted my arm to shield my face from the heat.

Where did he go?

"Jim!" I yelled. "Get out now!"

"Victoria!" shouted Katy, pointing at the window and jumping up and down next to me.

Victoria's pale face appeared through the broken glass.

Her movements were sluggish. She was wobbling like she was trying to find her footing. That was when I realized Jim was trying to get her up on a table or something.

"Get out!" I hollered. The flames were almost enveloping the cabin now. They had little time.

"Victoria! Jump!" shouted Katy.

Either Jim pushed her, or she came out of her own volition. One second Victoria was staring at me through the broken glass, and the next, her body hurtled out of the window and smashed on top of me.

We slammed to the ground, together.

A searing pain rushed through my head.

I blinked, but all I could see were stars.

Through the hazy gray smoke, I saw Katy and Nancy grab Victoria and drag her to the side. Ignoring the stabbing pains on my sides, I sprang to my feet and pulled the chair upright.

"Jim!" I shouted. "Your turn!"

He didn't have to be asked twice, and he didn't need help. He jumped out and fell with a crash on the chair, tipping it over.

He tumbled to the ground on his knees. He clutched at the snow and coughed, a rough, hacking sound. Nancy rushed up to him.

"I'll get water!" shouted Katy as she dashed toward the parking lot.

I turned to Victoria who was on all fours on the ground, vomiting. Her hair was stuck to her scalp, soaked from the sprinklers. Her chest was heaving and her entire body was shaking.

She was still in her wedding gown, now torn, stained, and blackened. Soapy foam from the fire extinguisher caked her shoulders. She needed water, but I had a more urgent task at hand.

I turned back to the two remaining cabins on fire. Something told me there were others inside these burning buildings.

I ran over to the nearest cabin. I was twenty feet from it when the roof caved in with a thundering roar. All four walls came crashing down.

I jumped back and covered my head as dust, ash, and splinters rained on me.

Chapter Forty-three

"Come back!" screeched a voice from behind me.

I whirled around.

Victoria was holding a hand up. I stepped up to her. She snatched my leg and tried to pull me close.

"It's okay, hun," I said, kneeling by her. "I won't leave you. You're going to be fine."

She turned to me with an agonized expression on her face. She opened her mouth to say something, then closed it again.

"Talk to me," I said, leaning forward. "What happened?"

She let her hand fall to the ground, breathing heavily.

"Chandler," she said in a hoarse voice. "He went to the lodge. Please... please... find him."

I had been hedging too long, and it had only got her into more danger. It was time to ask her a few straight questions.

"Victoria, did Chandler start this fire?"

She took a raspy breath in and pulled on my arm.

"Help him. Find him!"

"Water!" shouted Katy, crashing next to us with a plastic bottle she'd dug out of our car. She twisted the cap. "Here, sweetie," she said, holding it to Victoria's lips. "This will do you a world of good."

Victoria took one sip, then doubled over, and threw up again. Katy held her hair back while she eliminated whatever poison was eating into her.

"Good job," Katy was saying. "Let it all out. You'll feel so much better after this."

I surveyed the scene around us. It was a like a fighter jet had bombed the lodge.

We had shattered the windows of all the cabins on fire, but I had seen no one else inside and hadn't heard any more shouts for help.

I wondered if there were others lying on the floor, smothered by the smoke, incapacitated. But other than calling for a fire truck, there was little more I could do now.

Jim and Nancy were standing huddled against a tree, catching their breaths, hugging each other, with tears running down their soot-stained faces. Max sat by their feet, as if he knew of their pain.

I stepped up to them and gave Jim a once-over to make sure he wasn't burned or cut. Other than a few bruises and looking terrified and wet, he didn't appear hurt on the outside.

"Hey Jim, how did you two end up in that cabin?" I asked.

"Got a note," he said, his voice quivering. "Said to come here, ASAP."

"Where were you?"

"In the kitchen."

"I thought you were in the dining-hall the whole time."

"Barbara told me to bring another bottle of wine. I was rooting around in the wine cooler when someone slipped that note under the kitchen door."

"Did you see who it was?"

He shivered, pulled Nancy in closer, and shook his head.

"What did it say?"

"It was from Victoria," said Jim, as Nancy buried her head in his chest. "Said she was really sick and had moved to the last cabin for some space and quiet. The note said it was urgent and for me to go get the doctor from town."

Nancy and I locked eyes momentarily. That explained the letter we found in the kitchen.

"Where's the note you got?" I said to Jim.

He gave me a wistful look. "Probably burned to nothing now."

I turned around to look at Victoria, who was leaning against Katy, hyperventilating. She shook her head when she saw me look.

"I didn't... I didn't send anything...."

She swallowed hard.

"Breathe, sweetie," said Katy, rubbing her arm. "Breathe."

"How did you get here?" I said to her. "This isn't your cabin."

"Barbara," said Victoria, barely getting out the name.

"Why on earth would she bring you here?" I asked, frowning.

"She... she came to my cabin... said Mia was looking for me...." Victoria spoke haltingly in a raspy voice, struggling to get her words out.

"Mia?" gasped Katy.

I shot her a warning look.

Jim and Victoria had had enough shock as it was. Telling them how that girl died would only terrify them even more.

"But Mia's cabin is a couple down from yours, isn't it?" I said.

"Barbara said Mia had moved to the end unit," replied Victoria.

"Really?"

"She said it was urgent. Told me to hurry. Something about sorting things out before we left for Paris."

"Where was Chandler all this time?"

"Barbara said Robert wanted to see him about the trip.... Some last-minute things, so he left right away." Victoria's face scrunched again.

"Please, find Chandler. He went to the lodge. He doesn't know... please find him."

I looked away, swallowing the words that came to my throat.

"Victoria," I said, keeping my voice firm, "didn't you think it strange that Mia had moved to another cabin?"

Victoria shook her head.

"I wasn't thinking... I didn't.... Barbara told me to go and stay till Mia came, but Mia never came."

That was because someone had taken her to the shed in the woods, tied her up, and left her to bleed to death.

"The note I got said it was urgent too," said Jim. "I thought Victoria was in trouble so I didn't ask too many questions. I just came here and knocked."

"You must have figured out right away it was a ruse."

Jim nodded forlornly.

"Someone must have been watching us, because as soon as I went inside, the door slammed shut and someone locked it."

"Did you see who it was?" I asked.

Jim and Victoria shook their heads.

"We banged on the door and shouted, but they'd locked everything down," said Jim. "The windows, doors. Couldn't open anything from the inside. It was weird. Not like the other cabins."

"Who's doing all this? Why?" cried Victoria, tears streaming down her face.

I shook my head. I wished I knew too. Just when I thought I'd figured things out, matters seemed to take another grotesque twist.

"Find Chandler, please," cried Victoria.

Katy pulled her in close. "It's okay, honey. We'll figure this out."

I looked around me.

The last three cabins were now completely enveloped in flames, but the fire wasn't spreading as far as I had expected. The falling snow and the cool temperatures were helping.

"Time to get the heck out of here," I said. "We'll call for help as soon as we get a signal. Worst case, we'll drive straight to the Falcon Hills station and talk to Jensen."

"How do we get down?" said Jim. "My car is useless. What about your rental?"

"I have a better idea," I said. "A Humvee with snow chains—"

A crash made me whirl around.

The roof of the second cabin on fire was crumbling. Max jumped up and raced around the structure, barking.

"Get back here!" shouted Katy, but the dog didn't seem to hear her.

He whined loudly. Something was keeping him near the burning structure.

Someone's inside!

"Max!" I yelled. "Get away from there!"

I ran up to the dog and grabbed him by the collar. The roof had partly crashed down. The heat was stronger on this side, but that didn't seem to affect Max one bit.

He sat on his hind legs, refusing to budge, staring at the crumbling cabin like he was expecting someone to emerge from the flames.

What's he looking at?

Leaving him where he was, I stepped toward the cabin.

The weight of the roof had buckled the wooden door, breaking it in half. The wood panels were barely hanging on their hinges, but I could see inside now. The fire was licking the walls, casting a dark and eerie red glow on the wreck.

That was when I saw it.

I staggered back, realizing what Max had been trying to tell us.

In the darkened hallway by the bathroom was a charred body.

Chapter Forty-four

R*ebeca.*

Her body was inches from the broken door. If she had been a foot closer to the entrance, her head would have been crushed under the collapsed roof.

Shielding my eyes with my arm, I stepped closer, ignoring the scorching heat.

"Hey!" I hollered over the crackling and the crashing. "Anyone still in there?"

The fire extinguisher was still in place. Unused. If anyone had been alive, struggling to get out, they would have used it. They would have at least ripped it off the wall.

Rebeca must have been alone.

I stared at her body, lying among the flames. Someone had brought her up from the riverbed and plunked her inside before setting the cabin ablaze.

She had been dead when we'd found her by the river. There was nothing I could have done for her then, and there was nothing I could do for her now.

I glanced back. Max was staring at the cabin, whining.

Poor dog.

I turned back and peered inside, wondering if I should risk running in and dragging Rebeca out. That was when I saw the second body on the floor, by the bed.

Mia.

Half her body was under the bed in the darkest corner of the room. No wonder we hadn't seen either of them when we smashed the back window in.

The flames flickered and danced around the broken door, as if they were taunting me to pass through. The fire would soon devour the entire structure, and Mia's and Rebeca's deaths would be reduced to nothing but ashes.

Something bitter came into my mouth.

I turned away and looked up at the sky, struggling to contain my tears.

Gray plumes roiled and rolled angrily from the smoldering buildings. They rose high and mingled with the billowing clouds until it was hard to say which part was smoke and which part was vapor.

This fire wasn't an accident. Someone was trying to destroy the evidence of these brutal killings.

I hadn't checked the third cabin yet, but the fire had already ravaged it to the ground. The only way to spot a body in there would be by a forensics team.

Until then, I'd thought Robert would be lying in the woods or had been thrown into the gorge for the river to suck him away. But now, I wondered if he was in the third cabin, getting cremated in the most unholy manner.

I was about to step toward the last cabin when I realized something was amiss.

My heart jumped to my mouth.

Where did everyone go?

I swiveled around, looking for my friends and for one harrowing moment, I was sure the killer had got them all.

Why did I leave them alone?

"Asha!"

I spun around.

"We're here!"

Katy was waving to me from the parking lot. A flood of relief washed over me as I saw them by our car. I dashed over with Max at my heels.

Nancy was grabbing a blanket from the trunk, and Victoria was getting into the back seat, visibly shivering.

"I brought them here," said Katy, helping Nancy unroll the blanket, "before the whole place blows up."

"That won't happen because we interrupted the arsonist. That's why only the last three cabins went up in flames." I paused. "I found Rebeca and Mia."

Everyone snapped their heads my way. Victoria took in a sharp breath.

"Mia?" said Jim, looking up. "Is she dead too?"

"Someone brought their bodies and stuck them inside the cabins before setting them on fire," I said.

"Who's doing all these crazy things?" said Jim.

"What a nightmare," said Nancy. "It never ends."

I looked at the raggedy crowd huddled by my car. My friends were safe, but I'd failed to prevent the deaths of two innocent women. And there was one more person I was overlooking.

Tiffany.

How could I have forgotten her?

A rush of guilt hurled through my head.

Was she still inside her cabin, too scared to come out, or did the killer already trap her?

"Tiffany's the next target. We have to get her out before they get her too."

Katy's face turned pale. "I left her all by herself—"

"Show me her cabin," I said to her, and turned to the others. "Get in and lock the door. No matter what, don't come out."

I turned around and jogged back to the path with Katy by my side.

"Be careful," I heard Nancy call out from behind us.

We raced up the path.

"This one!" said Katy, pointing at the cabin next to Victoria's. The arsonist hadn't got to it yet. I darted toward it and rattled the doorknob. The door was locked.

I banged on the door, shouting Tiffany's name.

No answer.

Please be alive.

"Jimmy the lock," said Katy.

My hands were shaking and my adrenaline was sky high. I couldn't trust my fingers to be nimble with a key lock right now. Instead of the paper clip, I pulled out my Glock.

Katy stepped back in alarm.

"No time," I said.

I fired a shot directly at the lock. Then another. The gunfire echoed through the grounds.

"The killer will hear you," whispered Katy, panic in her voice.

"Let them come," I said between clenched teeth. "I have a few rounds with their name on it."

"Asha—"

"Help me, Katy," I said, positioning myself by the door. "Throw all your weight."

Katy reluctantly stepped beside me, but she knew what to do.

We slammed against the door.

Once.

Twice.

The lock rattled loose, but it wasn't enough to open.

"One more time," I said.

We tried again with more force.

Three times lucky. The door swung open. We fell inside and crashed to the floor.

I sprang to my feet, my gun at the ready.

Katy and I stood shoulder to shoulder by the entrance, staring at the empty room.

"Where did she go?" said Katy, her brow furrowed. "I put her to bed and even tucked her in."

The window was closed and latched tight. The sheets were ruffled, and a pillow lay on the floor, like Tiffany had jumped out of bed in a hurry and walked out.

"So, that's how Max got out," I said, frowning.

"The killer took her," whispered Katy, putting her hands to her face.

My gut sent me a warning flag.

Something was wrong with this picture.

Chapter Forty-five

I stepped out of the cabin.

"I don't like this," I said, gripping my weapon tightly.

Katy grabbed my shoulder.

"Did you see that?" she whispered, pointing at the lodge.

I pushed her behind the wall of the cabin. I'd caught the movement from the side of my eyes too.

"Someone's inside," I whispered.

"Who do you think—"

"Stay completely still," I said with a finger to my lips.

I inched toward the edge of the wall and peeked out.

The shadow crossed the main entrance again. They were in the corridor, heading from the kitchen. They passed by too quickly for me to distinguish who it would have been.

"Stay here," I said.

Crouching low, I scooted over to Victoria's cabin.

"Who is it?" whispered Katy as she darted up to me.

I glared at her.

"Didn't I tell you to stay put?"

"I'm not leaving you to fight the killer alone."

She rummaged in her jacket pocket and hauled Robert's antique pistol out. "Besides, I have this now."

"We don't even know if it works."

"It's polished," she said, holding it up. "Robert's the type of guy who'd service his gun collection."

"Get back in the car."

"No."

I turned around with a sigh. Keeping my head below the level of the windows, I dashed over to the lodge and stopped by the main entrance, shielding myself behind the stairs.

Within seconds, Katy was next to me, breathing down my neck. Behind us, the smell of fire and smoke was heavy.

I hoped Nancy, Jim, and Victoria had remembered to lock themselves in. I hated to leave them alone with no protection, but there were only so many places I could be at once.

A surprised yell came from inside the lodge.

The hair on the back of my neck sprang up.

Katy clutched my arm.

We drew back and crouched low by the steps.

"No!" shrieked the voice from somewhere inside the building. "Why are you doing this to me?"

It was a man, and he sounded terrified.

"Michael," whispered Katy. "Sounds like he's being tortured."

I scooted up the steps, my gun aimed forward.

The corridor was empty. The commotion was coming from the dining-hall.

I hid in the shadows by the front door with Katy huddled behind me, listening, trying to pinpoint the voices, the number of people, and their positions inside the dining room.

The smell of gasoline wafted our way. It was stronger here than anywhere else.

The arsonist was here.

Michael screamed again. His terrified voice echoed through the lodge, sounding more like an inhuman banshee gone mad.

I swallowed feelings of terror threatening to overcome me.

"I'm so sorry," he blubbered. "Don't do this to me. Please, I beg of you. Let me go."

I'd only heard him speak briefly when Robert introduced him to us just before the wedding. I had missed both the ceremony and his talk during lunch, but I remembered his smug voice. It had been the voice of a man who knew the prominence he held in this family.

It was a very different Michael we were hearing now, pleading for his life.

Whoever was with him hadn't said a word. There were no sounds of a weapon being used, or even a struggle. It was difficult to say how many were with Michael or if they were armed.

If they outnumbered us, our only advantage would be the element of surprise.

Michael shrieked again.

I slipped toward the dining-hall entrance and hunkered by the doorway before tilting my head to the side.

My jaw dropped.

It was Michael all right.

He was seated on the floor in between the patio doors and the fireplace. His legs were tied with rope and his hands were bound behind his back. Tears streamed down his cheeks and his chest was heaving.

Hovering over him was Tiffany.

Katy stepped up to me and gasped.

The fireplace was roaring—I could feel its heat even from here. The grate was open, and the flames were licking the iron frame. Gas.

I narrowed my eyes. The puzzle was coming together.

Tiffany had bewildered me from the start. Her erratic behavior at the luncheon and then in the woods had been inconsistent.

"She said she couldn't walk," whispered Katy. "I had to help her get into bed."

"An act."

"Why?"

"Revenge."

"But why Rebeca and Mia?" said Katy, frowning.

That was my remaining question, too.

"Did you see any weapons in her cabin?" I whispered.

Katy shook her head. "I didn't look. She was so weak, I didn't think—"

Another agonized screech came from Michael, followed by the sound of liquid sloshing. The smell of gasoline got even stronger.

Tiffany's eyes were fixated on Michael as she poured the toxic liquid out of the red can, dousing his head, shoulders, and body, creating a flammable pool around him. But her posture was casual, almost nonchalant, like she was watering a houseplant.

I wasn't sure which was more shocking: learning it had been Tiffany all along, or knowing the vicious methods she'd employed to eliminate her family members, one after the other.

I doubted Tiffany, Rebeca, or Mia were diagnosed with a legitimate mental illness to warrant their stay at the mental institution. Other than the trauma they'd suffered at the hands of this household, they looked like intelligent young women. Their only misfortune was to have been in the wrong place at the wrong time.

But they had grown up, strengthened in confidence, and refused to accept their fate. Rebeca and Mia had yearned to speak up and warn Victoria, but Tiffany had different plans.

What Robert hadn't realized was he had adopted his own killer.

Michael struggled to move away from Tiffany, but he slithered on the slippery surface. He rocked back and forth violently, gasping for air in vain.

I peeked inside and scanned the dining-hall from one corner to the next. There was no one else in there other than the screaming Michael and the silent Tiffany.

A shiver went through me as I realized we'd have to search for Chandler soon. Or his body, to be more precise.

The hardwood floor glistened, but it wasn't water. Tiffany had crisscrossed the room, scattering the gas all over the place. One flick of a match and the entire lodge would be ablaze.

When the can was empty, Tiffany hurled it out of the open patio doors. I knew what was to come next. I turned back to Katy and mouthed *now*.

We jumped into the room shouting, "stop!"

Michael jerked his head up, and Tiffany jumped.

But she had a head start.

In her right hand was a cigarette lighter.

Chapter Forty-six

Tiffany glowered, her eyes burning fire.

Katy and I froze in position, our weapons aimed at her.

Michael still had a chance, but it was a slim one. If she flicked on that lighter, he was done for. We would all be.

I struggled to breathe as the potent smell of gasoline invaded my nose. My heart pounded inside my chest like it was about to burst, but I kept my gaze and hands steady.

"Hello, Tiffany," I said, keeping my voice level, though what I really wanted to do was scream at her to stop. "Why don't you put that down?"

"Why should I?" she snarled. Gone was the scared and sickly young woman. The pouty and dismissive mean-girl persona had returned.

"Don't you think you've done enough?" I said.

She stared back at me with those same dazed eyes I'd seen before. I wondered if I'd been wrong. Maybe she was battling a severe illness. Either that, or she had drugged herself. Or someone had drugged her.

"Why did you even come?" said Tiffany, sneering our way. "Why didn't you go back after the ceremony like you were supposed to?"

"Like we were supposed to?" spluttered Katy. "So you could ruin Victoria's life?"

Tiffany growled. Her hand moved down an inch.

"Don't do it," I said in a quiet voice. "You've created enough damage to have nightmares for the rest of your life."

To my surprise, she laughed, a high-pitched, hyena-like laughter. She's so gone, I thought, a smidgen of compassion rising in me for her. "You've gone through a lot, Tiffany. Whatever you—"

"Shut your mouth!" she screamed, her eyes flashing in anger.

Tiffany stepped closer to Michael, her arm extended toward his head. It would take one second for Tiffany to decide Michael's fate.

My finger was on the trigger, but I didn't want to kill this woman. Also, I had no idea what a bullet in this environment would do.

"What have you got against Michael?" I said. "He's not even family."

My words seemed to only enrage her more. Her hand moved down, almost touching the top of Michael's head.

"Don't!" I shouted.

Her finger slid against the switch on the lighter.

"No!" screamed Katy.

Michael threw himself on the floor, screeching in horror.

The lighter clicked, but didn't turn on.

Sweat streamed down my back. My entire body felt numb. Thank goodness for those annoying contraptions. They usually never worked on the first try, but she was playing Russian roulette.

"What do you want, Tiffany?" I said. "Maybe we can help you."

A leer broke across her face, but she didn't click the lighter again.

Michael was now lying on the floor, his eyes bulging and his face red. He was gasping for air, smothered in that flammable liquid. If he didn't get burned to death, he would die inhaling those lethal fumes.

"Please talk to us. Tell us why you are doing this," I said, wishing I knew more about her so I could convince her to stop what she was doing.

Another worry was gnawing at me. While my boots were good for traction on snow and ice, they were useless on a floor doused with gasoline. One wrong step and Katy and I could slide down the slippery floor and end up next to Michael.

I kept my eyes on Tiffany.

"If these people did bad things to you, there are other ways to make them pay. You're just hurting yourself."

The sneer widened, but she didn't speak.

Is she taunting us?

That was when I realized what she could be up to.

Tiffany was on a suicide mission.

Her plan was to kill Michael, all of us, and herself. We were in the middle of nowhere, with no connection to civilization. By the time anyone found our charred bodies, it would be too late.

I had to keep her talking until we figured out how we would get out of this nightmare.

"Tiffany, we understand why you wanted Robert and Barbara dead. Hey, I might have done it myself if I were—"

"I didn't kill them!"

It was my turn to jerk back in surprise.

I stared at her. Her outburst had been so strong, I could have sworn it was the truth.

"Then who?" said Katy. "Who killed them?"

Tiffany's scowl turned uglier, but she didn't speak. I looked down at Michael.

"Was it you?" I said.

He groaned in reply.

I turned to Tiffany.

"Was it Chandler?"

"To hell with you!" she shouted, her face flushing. "Everything was going fine until Victoria invited you. Barbara said you wouldn't come all the way up here, but you had to show up, didn't you?"

There was so much venom in her voice, it made my blood curdle.

"Can you at least tell us what's going on?" I said, taking a small step forward, not changing my aim.

"Come closer and I burn him," she snarled.

I stopped.

Tiffany stood quietly, her eyes our way, but not really looking at us. I wondered what was going through her muddled head.

I'd never met someone on the verge of suicide. That faraway look and her slumped posture signaled that she had given up. But there was a deadly fire in her belly that would take us all out with her.

Katy took a cautious step forward.

Tiffany glared.

"Hey, honey," said Katy. "I'm sorry for everything that happened to you. I'm also so sorry for Rebeca and Mia—"

Tiffany snapped her head back and let out a strange howl.

"Don't you dare talk about them!" she shrieked. "Rebeca and Mia didn't deserve any of that!"

Katy had touched a raw wound.

"Can you tell us what happened to them?" I asked.

In response, Tiffany hissed like a rattlesnake, one about to recoil and jump on its prey. Then, without a warning, her arm jerked sideways. She bent down, flipped the lighter on, inches from Michael's hair.

Michael screamed in terror and pushed away, but it was too late. His gasoline-soaked hair instantly caught on fire.

Tiffany jumped back, a horrified expression on her face, like she hadn't realized the inevitable outcome of her action.

Michael writhed in agony on the floor, his excruciating screams deafening us.

I spun around and seized the tablecloth off the dining table. Plates, glasses, and wedding flower vases mashed to the ground. I threw the heavy tablecloth over Michael. He struggled, but I held it down.

Using her knife, Katy slashed the curtains and threw them over his body. It took a minute for the flames to subside and for Michael to stop screaming.

I pulled the curtains and tablecloth away to find a singed Michael underneath, convulsing like he was having an epileptic fit.

He was alive, at least.

"Watch him!" I hollered to Katy and jumped to my feet.

I whirled around.

The patio door was wide open. Snow flurries landed softly on the fuel-soaked hardwood floor, transforming into instant puddles of water.

In between the puddles were small footprints that led outside.
Tiffany had disappeared.

Chapter Forty-seven

"First-aid kit!" I yelled. "Check the kitchen!"

Katy dashed out of the dining-hall.

I scanned the room for something to help us move Michael away from the pool of gasoline he was drowning in.

His shirt had been burned through, showing ugly charred marks on his skin. His right arm was splotchy with black and white patches.

He was gurgling, struggling to breathe. His face was as pale as a ghost and his arms lay limp by his sides, no longer flailing.

I scrambled across the hall.

What we needed was a stretcher that wouldn't hurt him any more than he already was. If we didn't treat him immediately, those burns would seep in through his skin and into his organs, and that would be the end.

"Found it!" cried Katy, rushing back inside.

Using the tablecloth and ripped curtains, we half carried and half dragged Michael away from the toxic pool.

He screamed every inch of the way, but we had no choice. If he hadn't been too weak to struggle, we'd have had a battle on our hands. But every one of his agonizing cries made me shudder in horror, knowing this could have been us too.

"This is good," I said, when we got close to the doorway.

We laid him on the ground. Katy ripped open the first-aid kit and pulled out a compress and a packet of moist gauze. I loosened the man's belt and ripped his shirt, trying not to retch at the sight of the burned, leathery skin.

While Katy and I had first-aid training, we were no paramedics. What the man needed was medical attention at a burn unit in a hospital.

Katy placed a soft gauze on his stomach. He let out a piercing scream that rang in my ear and hit every nerve in my body. She worked fast, but I could see she was trying to hold her emotions in check.

Michael could have been complicit in the abuse of those young women. He was a creep, the kind of man I'd cross the street if I saw coming my way. Still, it was hard to see a human being suffer like this.

"We need to get him and all of us out of this place," I said, turning to Katy.

She nodded, but didn't look up.

"Tiffany will do anything to bury us. And we haven't seen Chandler—"

A gunshot blasted from outside, making Katy and I both jump.

I leaped to my feet and spun around.

"Who was that?" Katy whispered in a horrified voice.

"Stay here," I said, grabbing my Glock from the floor. I picked up Katy's revolver and placed it by her side.

"The others," she said, her hand on her heart. "Do you think Tiffany shot... Nancy and Victoria, they were alone..." She trailed off.

"That was just one shot," I said, putting a hand on her shoulder. "Could have been just a warning. Stay put. I'll go check."

With a dazed look, she turned back to her patient.

I crept out of the dining-hall and into the corridor.

I looked to my right where the main bedroom was located, where Barbara's bashed body still lay. With a shudder, I turned toward the main entrance.

It was quiet now, but that shot had come from outside.

Why fire a single shot? Was it Tiffany? Was it someone else? Did Tiffany shoot herself?

She hadn't been carrying a gun when we saw her last. I'd found the unlit cigarette lighter on the floor by the patio doors, but other than that, she had been unarmed.

My stomach lurched at the thought of anything having happened to my friends. I'd told them to stay in the car with the doors locked.

Did they get out for some reason? Why were they so quiet?

I stepped onto the pathway, my eyes sweeping the grounds.

The cabins at the end were now smoldering, shrouded by a hazy gray smoke.

After a quick scan to make sure no one was watching me, I darted toward the closest cabin and slammed against the wall.

I waited for a second, listening.

There was a commotion by the parking lot now.

I scampered over to the next cabin, my heart beating fast. I moved from cabin to cabin, but quickly ran out of hiding spots. I had wanted to take Tiffany or whoever fired that shot by surprise, but I had no choice.

Suddenly, the roar of an engine came from the parking lot. That didn't sound like our car.

The image of packed bags in the back of the Humvee flashed to mind.

Someone was getting away.

Chandler's absence bothered me.

Was he dead or alive? Who killed Robert and Barbara? Is Katy tending to a murderer right now?

The engine revved and coughed as it battled with the cold air. Someone was trying to warm it up, fast.

I had been so sure Tiffany had been suicidal. Had she been planning for an escape all along?

I gritted my teeth.

If she'd hurt one hair of my friends, I wasn't going to let her get away.

I leaped from behind the cabin and made a beeline to the parking lot, pushing away the worries of finding a grisly scene in our car.

Please be alive.

I was thirty feet from our car when I saw the shadow move from behind the Porsche.

"Stop or I shoot!" I shouted.

Chapter Forty-eight

"It's us!" cried Victoria, popping her head out from behind the Porsche.

"Don't shoot!" came Nancy's panicked voice.

I scanned behind them to see if anyone was targeting them.

The Humvee was at the end of the parking lot, but it was pointed away from us. The engine whined and spluttered. Exhaust was coming out of its tail pipes.

My pulse quickened as a dark shadow moved by the driver's side window. Someone or some people were moving around inside, but I couldn't see much with the vehicle cloaked in snow.

Keeping low, I scampered over to the Porsche. Nancy and Victoria were crouching behind it, clutching each other.

"What happened?" I said, scanning them from top to toe, looking for bullet wounds, blood.

"Jim," cried Nancy, her eyes welling with tears. "He... he g... got hit."

"Where?" I said, swiveling my head. "Where is he?"

"In the car," stammered Victoria. "It's his shoulder. He... We came to look for you."

I dashed over to our car, momentarily registering the cracked window in the back and the shattered glass on the ground.

"Jim!" I said, pulling the back door open.

He gave me a bewildered look, like he didn't recognize me, still in shock. Max was sitting by him, his head in Jim's lap.

The blanket covering Jim's right shoulder was soaked in blood. The girls had tried to stem the bleeding. I reached over and pulled it aside to examine the wound.

"I've... never... been shot before," he said in a weak voice.

"Flesh wound," I said, looking at his ashen face. "It grazed you badly, but it's only a graze. You'll survive, Jim."

A rustle nearby made me turn. Victoria and Nancy had scuttled over and were huddling behind our car, their faces white and eyes wide in shock.

"He'll be fine," I said.

"Thank goodness," said Nancy, a hand over her heaving chest.

"Did you see her?" I said.

"Who?" said Victoria, her brow furrowed.

"Tiffany."

Nancy and Victoria exchanged a puzzled glance and shook their heads.

"Did you see the shooter?"

Victoria pointed at the cracked window. "The snow was piled up in the back, we couldn't see a thing."

"We stayed in and locked the doors like you told us to," said Nancy.

"I only knew when Max barked and Jim yelled," said Victoria.

Nancy shook her head. "One minute we were sitting quietly, then it was like the world blew up."

"I got hit because I was in the back seat," said Jim. "Glad it was me and not the ladies."

I leaned over and squeezed his hand.

"We need to dress your wound," I said. "It could get infected. Katy's got a first-aid kit inside—"

The Humvee engine revved again.

I jerked my head up.

"It's Tiffany, I'm sure," I said, motioning Nancy and Victoria to crouch lower. "She's the one who started the fire. She tried to burn the lodge down, starting with Michael."

"Michael?" said Victoria, frowning.

I turned to her.

"The others are all dead," I said. "Except for Chandler. We haven't found him yet."

Victoria sank to the ground at the mention of her husband's name.

Seeing her face, I just couldn't get myself to tell her there were only two possibilities now. He was the next victim, most probably lying dead somewhere on the lodge grounds, or he was part of this murder racket.

The Humvee roared. It was ready to roll.

"Head back to the lodge," I said, turning to Nancy and Victoria. "Just be aware Michael is in the dining-hall and he's burned badly."

They stared at me, speechless.

"Was he inside the cabins too?" said Victoria, her lips quivering.

I didn't have time to explain.

With another roar, the Humvee moved from its spot. From over the tops of the other cars, I could see it wobble over a snowdrift as it pulled out of the parking lot.

"Asha!"

I whirled around.

It was Katy.

Motioning to the others to stay low, I scooted toward the pathway.

She was running down the path, her revolver in hand, but her face stricken. I stepped out in front of her. With a look of relief, Katy rushed toward me and clutched my arm.

"He's gone," she said, panting.

"Michael?"

"Stopped breathing. He...." She paused and looked away. "I checked his pulse, but it wasn't there. I did everything I could."

"I know you did," I said. "We have bigger issues to worry about right now."

She glanced around her, a wild look on her face.

"Where's everyone?"

The Humvee revved loudly as it tried to navigate a high snowbank.

"Who's that?" said Katy.

"Tiffany," I said. "I think."

I pulled Katy by the arm toward our car.

I opened the door to see our friends huddled in the back seat now, with Max lying on their laps, frightened expressions on everyone's faces. They looked like refugees who'd escaped a war zone, except we were in the middle of New Hampshire's White Mountains.

All I wanted was to take them back to town, and give them a place to rest from this ordeal. But the vehicle I'd been banking on was now gone, and the one I had wouldn't make it down in these conditions.

"Jim!" said Katy, seeing the bloodied towel. "What happened?"

He shot her a weak smile. "They tried to get me, but they didn't."

I turned to Katy.

"Can you take everyone to the lodge?" I said. "Get the first-aid kit and make sure Jim's wound is cleaned and dressed."

"What about you?" she said, her eyes widening.

I turned to look at the disappearing back of the Humvee. It was moving slower than I'd expected, as it plowed through a foot of fresh snow.

I turned to my friends.

"I have a killer to catch."

Chapter Forty-nine

"**A**re you out of your mind?" said Katy.

"How are you going after her in this?" said Nancy, pointing at the ice and snow on the ground. "That Humvee had tires the size of a house."

"Which is perfect," I said. "All I have to do is follow its tracks."

"Why don't we all get in, then?" said Katy. "We can get out of this place."

"No! We have to find Chandler first!" cried Victoria, reaching out and clutching Katy's arm. "I'm not leaving without him."

I shook my head and looked away. I felt bad for her.

"The tracks will make it easier, but it's still dangerous terrain," I said. "It will get dark soon and the last thing I want is for us to get into a wreck halfway down the mountain." I paused. "If she ambushes me, I'd rather tackle her on my own."

"She shot my man," said Nancy, sitting up. "I'm coming with you."

"I'm not taking you on a wild goose chase," I said. "I promise you when I get her, I'll make sure she will regret her decision to shoot at Jim, okay?"

"You plan to go after that crazy woman by yourself?" Katy spluttered. "She'll roll down the mountain and take you down with her."

I looked at each of my friends.

"Please stay in Victoria's cabin. Dress Jim's wounds. Stay put till I come back. And for all things holy, don't light a match or a candle anywhere near this place."

"You're going to leave us here with all these dead bodies?" stammered Jim.

"It's not the dead I'm worried about. It's the ones who are still alive I'd be watching out for."

"But Chandler?" cried Victoria again. "I want to know where he is. We have to find him."

I looked at her anguished face, wondering if I should tell her what I thought I spotted inside the Humvee.

"We can't risk our lives looking for him right now," I said.

"But—"

"Unless you want all of us to end up dead too."

That stopped her.

She looked away, tears streaming down her face.

Victoria didn't know the real reason I was after that Humvee. She had more to lose than she knew. I'd seen enough clues to know she'd be constantly looking over her shoulder for the rest of her life if we didn't stop that vehicle.

But if she knew what I suspected, I'd be dragging everyone into a heartbreaking conversation, which would only waste precious time. Time we didn't have.

Jim shook his head.

"What if you don't come back?"

"The snow will stop soon. The resort crew will head this way tomorrow morning to clear the road."

I gestured to the vehicle next to ours.

"You'll find the keys to the Mercedes in Robert's desk. Second drawer on the right. This has snow tires and will be good to go once the road is cleared."

"That's not what I meant," said Jim, giving me a stern look. "What if something happens to *you*?"

"I'll figure it out."

"Well, you're not going alone," said Katy with a huff. "You can't drive in this weather and pay attention to a killer at the same time."

My friends stared at me, as if daring me to protest.

I turned around. The Humvee had already disappeared down the driveway.

"Deal," I said. "Katy, you're with me."

It was a somber group that trudged up the path to Victoria's cabin.

After making sure Jim's wounds were dressed and they had locked themselves safely inside the cabin, Katy and I walked back to our SUV.

Robert's pistol was now with Nancy. Though none of them were trained, I couldn't in good conscience take both weapons with us. My only hope was Victoria wouldn't break her promise and go roaming around the grounds in search of Chandler after we left.

I stared at the broken shards lying near the rear tires of our vehicle.

Tiffany had aimed right at the middle of the windscreen. If Jim had placed his head just a few inches to the right, he'd be dead now.

She should have known there were people inside. Or she had been betting on it.

To shoot at the back of an innocent person who'd done you no harm took a special dark heart. Tiffany was more vicious than I'd first thought.

Thanking the angels that had been protecting Jim, I jumped into the driver's seat. Katy slipped into the passenger side and slammed the door shut.

I turned the key, praying the engine wouldn't be too cold to start. To my relief, it came to life.

"What's your master plan?" said Katy. "Shoot at her tires? If we stop her, then what? Make a citizen's arrest?"

"Improvise," I said, as I eased in between the snowdrifts. "And watch each other's backs."

Warming up the car before rolling would have been the right thing to do, but I wasn't sure how much of a head start Tiffany had. I powered forward, pursuing the path she had carved with her heavy-duty wheels. It was like following another skier down a cross-country ski path.

Visibility was low, and the road was tight. It curved dangerously around the mountain, never too far from the gully below. The biggest danger was black ice, ice I'd never be able to see that could put our car into an instant tailspin and right into that river.

"Why don't we just let her go?" said Katy, as I took a sharp corner, praying we wouldn't spin out of control. "She had a horrific past. She wanted revenge, and she got it. She's now going to live with this forever. This has nothing to do with us."

"I could never sleep if I let a killer get away," I said, not taking my eyes off the road.

The car hit something. I pushed on the gas, making it jump. Katy and I whiplashed forward, but the car kept rolling.

"She's insane," said Katy. "We are too, racing down an icy mountain like this."

I turned to my friend.

"Buckle up, Katy. This is going to be a roller-coaster ride."

Chapter Fifty

"Why did Tiffany try to kill Michael?" said Katy.

"He spearheaded the fake marriages. Probably goaded the girls into signing the documents, pretending it was real to keep them quiet," I said. "He was a witness to the abuse, that's for sure."

She let out a heavy sigh.

"It's a horrible thing to say, but, aside from Rebeca and Mia, the others deserved everything that happened to them."

I gave my friend a side glance.

"Don't you think it strange we didn't find the brown envelope?"

"What does that have to do with anything?"

"Everything," I said. "I'd bet you it's tucked in the back of that Humvee together with Barbara's jewels."

Katy gave me a quizzical look.

"How much would you bet she'll be visiting a pawnshop soon?" I said. "Then, she'll run off overseas where she can lie low for a while."

"Lebanon?"

"That was Robert's idea. But her plan might be someplace closer, somewhere south."

Katy let out a low whistle.

"So what happened here is one killer, Tiffany, is double crossing the first killer, Robert."

"I'm still trying to piece things together, but I think her plan was to get rid of everyone, burn the evidence, and claim everything for herself."

"She'll never get away with this. Forensics will find evidence. All that gasoline confirms it was arson."

I didn't answer, my focus on the road.

The descent was steep. Too steep.

Snow was still falling steadily, piling high on either side, creating deep drifts that could swallow a human whole. I grasped the wheel tighter. Drivers had died in better conditions than this.

"We'll never catch up," said Katy, peering through the windshield as the wipers pushed the snow away, making squeaky noises with every turn.

"She'll be heading to the airport after the pawnshop," I said. "Her plan is to get away before anyone discovers the carnage at the top of the mountain."

"The road crew will find out first thing in the morning," said Katy. "That gives her ten to twelve hours, tops."

"Jensen will need to rustle up a team from the nearby counties. They'll sniff around, need to get forensics up to identify the remains, and confirm who's missing, all that before alerting the border guards."

"She could drive to Canada, fly out from there, and disappear by then," said Katy with a huff.

"Can you check for cell reception?" I said. "We should catch a signal as we get down in elevation. Call Jensen and let him know what to expect."

Katy scrambled to pull her phone out of her pocket.

"Here's mine," I said, taking a hand off the wheel to fish my cell out.

That was bad timing.

"Watch out!" cried Katy.

The turns were hard to see with everything a blinding white. We were at a sharp switchback. I dropped the phone, grabbed the wheel with both hands, and eased off the gas.

But I took the curve faster than I should have.

The car fishtailed.

Katy grabbed the door handle.

The dashboard lit up in red. The vehicle stability assist light blinked ominously.

I pumped the brakes. The car straightened, the tires making a hair-raising grinding sound underneath us, but I had no traction anymore.

We were heading down fast along the Humvee's tracks. The crunching of the snow against the undercarriage sounded like our vehicle would break apart any minute.

"I see her!" cried Katy.

The Humvee was less than a hundred yards ahead of us. Through the snowfall, I could see the faint outline of its back lights.

My heart hammered as I pressed the brakes, but the car gathered speed, instead of slowing down. We were on a steep incline, and it was going to take a lot more to stop the car's momentum.

"Can she see us?" whispered Katy, crouching low in her seat.

I had turned my headlights off, but I didn't have the heart or the time to tell her hiding in our seats wouldn't stop Tiffany from noticing a six-thousand-pound vehicle come thundering behind her. I had to stop the car before we got any closer.

I pumped the brakes even harder.

"We're going to crash!" cried Katy.

Ahead of us, the Humvee roared, like it was trying to jump over an obstruction.

"Snowbank!" shouted Katy.

I steered a hard right.

Katy and I whiplashed as the car shuddered to a stop, the front of the vehicle jamming under a pile of snow.

I took my shaking hands off the wheel. We were stuck, but we were now shielded from Tiffany. If we had fishtailed in the opposite direction, we would have crashed through those trees and ended up in the gully by now.

Katy was clutching the seat so tight, her knuckles were as white as the snow outside.

I rolled my window down and listened in.

The Humvee hadn't stopped revving. If Tiffany's focus had been on getting her vehicle over the barrier, there was the chance she missed us. The falling snow had been a godsend, a camouflage I hadn't expected.

"Let's give her a head start, then drive to town. First thing we'll do is let Jensen know what's going on. They have the right equipment to chase her to the airport."

"That's if we survive this killer diamond run first."

I unbuckled myself, scrambled to the back seat, and rolled down a window. That was when I spotted the head on the passenger side. I recognized that profile.

"She's not alone," I said.

"*What?*" said Katy, whirling around.

While I watched, the Humvee let out a deafening roar and jumped over the bank. Within seconds, it sped away and disappeared from view.

I withdrew and pulled the window up, not the most useful endeavor with a bullet hole in the back.

"Chandler," I said. "I thought I saw him in the parking lot, but I know for sure now."

"Oh, my gosh," whispered Katy. "He's alive."

Chapter Fifty-one

"I thought she killed him," said Katy in a hushed voice.

"They were in this together all along," I said. "Tiffany couldn't have done all that by herself."

"So, Chandler killed his own father and mother," said Katy. "Why?"

"If they were abusing the girls, what's not to say they were abusing him too?"

"My goodness."

"I'm guessing here, but it may have had more to do with Chandler's relationship with Tiffany."

"But he was with Victoria, for goodness's sake."

"It was Robert's plan to get him to marry Victoria so he could grab her estate. It was a fake marriage, but Tiffany and Chandler had grander plans and if you ask me, they were in love. Could have been for a long time."

"*Natural Born Killers,*" said Katy, shaking her head. "I'm going to throw up."

I felt the same. They had pulled the wool over our eyes more than once, pretending to be who they weren't.

Katy jabbed my arm. "What about Rebeca and Mia? Why did they have to go?"

"Robert wanted them dead for trying to expose their weird family arrangement," I said as the puzzle came together in my head. "If Victoria ever got wind of that, she'd never agree to marry Chandler. Maybe Victoria's marriage was a trigger for them. It woke them up."

"Poor girls. They were conditioned from childhood. They weren't even allowed to leave the lodge," said Katy. "It's like those baby elephants they tie to a stalk in circuses. They won't run away even after they're grown up and can uproot the whole thing in a second."

"Robert probably went hopping mad when he learned their plans. Victoria pulling out of the wedding would mess up his scheme and he'd get exposed to serious criminal charges. Bigamy, child abuse, kidnapping, forceful confinement, sexual assault of minors, and who knows what else? He couldn't have that."

"So, he killed them."

"Tiffany was the crafty one. She used what was going on to her advantage, but she had a partner in crime."

"Now we know who Chandler kissed behind the hedge," said Katy, with a disgusted hiss. "This family is so twisted, my head's spinning."

"It's sad Victoria refused to see any of it. There were so many red flags. I felt it the second we met Barbara and Chandler. Something was off."

"Me too, but that girl let love blind her. The jewels, the insurance papers, the will, and the fire to burn everything down. It all makes sense now."

"I have a feeling they weren't going to use the spare gasoline. We messed up their plans, so they acted rashly. I bet you they would have used that kindling by the lodge to make it look like a natural fire tragedy."

"Jim said he saw Tiffany by the fireplace with a pile of matches."

I nodded. "Without the gas, forensics would take longer to figure out what happened at the chalet."

Katy turned to me. "But who sent those texts to you?"

I stared out the window for a moment.

"I wish I knew."

"Could have been Mia or Rebeca trying to warn us," said Katy.

"Rebeca was dead by the time we arrived. It could have been Mia, but it's just not something she would do."

"Couldn't have been Barbara, could it?"

I shook my head and sighed. "Those messages are the biggest mystery to me."

"So, what do we do now?"

I put the car in reverse.

"Hold on to your seat belt, because we're going after Bonnie and Clyde."

It took me five minutes to extricate the car from the snowbank and get us back on the road. The only thought swirling in my brain was the prospect of getting a cell signal closer to Falcon Hills. We needed backup.

We drove silently, alert to any sound or sight of the Humvee.

"Hey, there's the detour to the ravine," said Katy, sitting up and pointing out my window. "That's where we almost crashed into the river."

I glanced to the side.

Cloud Cabin Ski Lodge.

The ominous sign was still there.

"We were the last to arrive at the wedding," I said. "I wouldn't put it past Chandler to move that sign deliberately to mislead us."

"He wanted to murder us," said Katy in a grim voice. "No one would have been here to even hear us smash into the gully."

The road straightened as we descended. I could now see about a mile ahead. I crept at a snail's pace, keeping a sharp eye. Chandler and Tiffany wouldn't take our presence nicely.

"I see them!" cried Katy, jumping in her seat.

She was right. The Hummer had stopped in the middle of the road, about a hundred yards ahead. It was struggling to get through another snowdrift.

I eased off the gas, so we wouldn't crash like last time. I rolled the window down and listened. The Humvee was revving madly just like before.

I scanned our surroundings.

Other than the sound of the engine roaring below, the woods and the mountain were silent. It was like everything had come to a standstill, waiting for the other shoe to drop.

Both Tiffany and Chandler were unpredictable. We couldn't take any chances.

For all I knew, this could be a diversion. They could be pretending to be stranded while either of them could have got out of their vehicle and were waiting along the road to ambush us.

The Humvee roared again.

While we watched, the window on the passenger side of the Humvee rolled down and Chandler's head popped out.

That was when the gunshot rang out.

"Down!" I screamed, grabbing Katy and pulling her into the footwell.

Chapter Fifty-two

I spun the wheel sharply to the right and rammed our car into the nearest snowbank.

We came to a complete stop behind a four-foot wall of snow.

I peered over the wheel and through the windshield. The bullet had missed us by a mile. We were safe behind the drift, but we couldn't stay here forever.

"Do something!" cried Katy, looking up from the footwell, her face flushed. "Shoot their tires, their windows, anything before he kills us!"

"He's too far away. He was shooting blindly and so will we." I narrowed my eyes. "We need to recon before we take action."

"Recon?" said Katy, gesturing wildly in my face. "We need to shoot back, that's what!"

"Stealth and surprise are better weapons than a Glock."

"They saw us!"

"Yes, but they don't know what we'll do next," I said. "They could both be armed and trust me, we don't want a shootout on the mountain."

Katy shot me an angry look.

"We won't let them get away," I said. "What we need to do now is outsmart them, not outgun them."

I opened my door and stepped out.

"Stay close and keep your head below the snowbank."

"Next time we pack our Kevlar vests," grumbled Katy as she slipped out on her side.

"We came for a wedding, remember?" I replied as I shut the door gently. "This way."

I clambered up the snowbank and peeked over it.

The Humvee's tires were turning, the engine roaring like an angry mountain lion. Tiffany was pushing the gas pedal to its limit. They must have been truly grounded or they would have disappeared by now, especially after firing at us.

I surveyed the road and the woods, watching for movement, a glint of a weapon, but there was no one outside the vehicle, at least that I could see.

A shiver went through me. It was a good thing we'd changed into our outdoor gear before we left. It would get dark soon and the temperatures would drop even more.

"I see him," whispered Katy, hunkered behind the snowbank. "Chandler's in the car, on the passenger side."

"Follow me," I whispered, as I scampered around her and stepped toward the tree line, staying shielded behind the snowbanks.

The woods were thicker down here. The trees huddled close on both sides of the road. Beyond that was the gully. I could hear the river rushing below, now that the sound of my heart pounding in my ears had subsided.

"I smell diesel," said Katy, sniffing the air.

"Hurry," I said. "Once they jump that drift, they'll be going down fast."

We crept along, parallel to the road, keeping behind the trees. We were getting deeper into the woods, but descending. The sound of the Humvee got closer and closer.

A car door banged shut. Katy jumped and clutched my arm. I peered through the branches.

We were fifty feet from the Humvee now.

Chandler was standing outside the vehicle, a shovel in his hands. As we watched, he started digging the snow from around the wheels.

We slowed our pace as we weaved through the trees, trying not to crunch the snow under our boots.

"Try again!" shouted Chandler, waving at the driver's side window.

The Humvee revved, but the wheels still spun. The weight of the heavy-duty vehicle meant it was only digging itself further into the ground.

Perfect.

The snow was still falling, softer now. But if it didn't let up, the parking lot at the ski lodge would be buried by morning. I prayed our friends were keeping safe.

I surveyed the area and put a hand out to stop Katy from going further.

She turned and gasped.

"Look!" she said, pointing down.

I'd seen it. At the foot of the mountain, nestled among the Coniferous forest far below us, were the twinkling yellow lights of a small town.

A white church spire rose from the middle of the quaint buildings. It looked so peaceful down there, like a magical town from a fairy tale.

"Falcon Hills," I whispered.

It was a relief to glimpse civilization again.

"That's a long way down," said Katy. "It will take us forever to walk."

Suddenly, the sound of the shoveling stopped.

I turned around and peeked through the tree trunks.

Chandler was staring into the woods.

I pulled Katy by her arm and stepped behind the nearest tree. The car stopped revving and an eerie silence descended on us.

Katy and I stood frozen in place, not breathing.

I peeked out from behind the trunk.

Tiffany was leaning across the seats and peering out the passenger side window.

Did she hear us?

Impossible.

I had made sure we had stayed away from hearing distance, and we'd been stealthy as spies.

Why are they staring this way?

244

Chapter Fifty-three

Just as quickly as Chandler had stopped working, he got back to his job.

Soon, the sound of his steel shovel scraping against the ice echoed through the woods again.

I gestured for Katy to follow me. We had to get to higher ground.

"Did he see us?" whispered Katy, once we were farther up the slope, away from the road.

"He sensed us," I whispered back. "I don't like it. It means we don't have much time."

I glanced at the town below us, trying to think of the best strategy.

Tiffany and Chandler wouldn't hesitate to kill us in an instant. They'd killed before. All they had to do afterward was to roll our car and our bodies over the cliff like it was an accident. Given the road conditions and the weather, it would make a believable story.

But I wasn't ready to die that day.

A nervous gasp from Katy made me turn. She was staring down at her phone.

"A signal," she whispered, excitement in her voice. "We got a signal."

I pulled my cell out of my pocket. Mine was still in the red.

"Call nine-one-one," I whispered.

"Comes in and out," she said, punching numbers on her screen.

"Keep trying."

I stepped toward the edge of the slope, trying to think.

Stealth and surprise. That was what we needed. We would have to walk over to the road without alerting Chandler and Tiffany and take them unawares.

Then what?

Tie them up and take them to town, where Officer Jensen could charge and book them.

For that to work, we'd have to use their vehicle for the trip. If the Humvee was having trouble with the snowdrifts, there wasn't much hope for my smaller SUV.

But that meant we'd have to wait till they finished digging their vehicle out. Get them to do the hard work. By then, they'd be exhausted, maybe even dispirited for having lost so much time.

That would be perfect timing to take them down.

"Shoot."

I turned around to see Katy's disappointed face.

"Red again," she whispered, brandishing her phone toward me.

I looked around us. We were a hundred yards from the road. But, if we turned westward and walked down the slope, we would be closer to Falcon Hills.

"We're still several miles from town, but if you can get closer, you might catch a signal from a cell tower."

Katy's eyes lit up.

"Let's go," she said, brushing past me.

"I'm staying on watch," I whispered back.

"I'm not leaving you here."

"Try the phone as soon as you get a signal."

"Asha—"

"Don't worry about me," I said, showing her my Glock. "Get as far away as you can, so they can't hear you."

Katy let out a resigned sigh.

"Be back in five." She gave me a stern look. "Don't do anything crazy."

"I'll wait for you before I do anything rash," I said with a small smile. "I'll stay behind the trees. Promise."

Katy stepped gingerly over a root jutting from the snow and walked away from me. I watched her as she weaved in between the trees, treading carefully, her eyes glued to her phone.

I waited until she disappeared from sight. Then I turned back and crept toward the road.

Tiffany was out of the car now, helping Chandler dig their vehicle out with a smaller shovel. I watched them silently as they worked fast, without speaking. I could feel their sense of urgency.

They were going to be here for another fifteen minutes at least.

If Katy could alert the authorities, we would have backup in half an hour.

I watched the couple as they worked furiously, heads down, hands a blur. It didn't take me long to see the telltale bulge of sidearms under both their jackets.

They had been prepared. At least, until we spoiled their plans.

I scanned the Humvee. There didn't seem to be anyone else inside, nothing else other than their packed bags.

I was wondering if we'd find rope to tie them up among their luggage when a shrill cry for help came from behind me.

Katy!

I sprang up and whirled around, my gun at the ready, my eyes darting back and forth through the trees.

Katy yelled again.

I was just about to dash through the woods when Katy hurtled through two massive fir trees on her back and stumbled onto the road.

She landed twenty yards in front of the Humvee.

Chapter Fifty-four

"Hey!" Chandler yelled, spinning around, startled.

I sprang through the trees toward the road, but Tiffany had snapped her sidearm out.

She aimed her gun at Katy.

I stopped in my tracks, my heart sinking.

"Hands up!" shouted Tiffany, stalking over to my friend.

Katy was lying on her back, a shocked expression on her face. She must have slipped on ice, and before she knew it, plunged through the woods.

"I said, hands up!" Tiffany screamed. "Stay down! Don't move!"

The snotty Tiffany we'd met at the wedding and the sickly Tiffany we'd escorted through the woods to the lodge had all been an act. I was now seeing the real person behind the persona she'd cultivated over the years just to survive that mad family.

She marched over to Katy, her voice loud and angry, reverberating through the road. Katy lay awkwardly on the ground, her chest heaving, her hands slanted upward.

I gritted my teeth and clutched my gun tighter.

You hurt her and I'll put a bullet through your head.

The way Katy was lying told me she had hurt herself during the fall. Her hands were empty. Her phone must have fallen somewhere in the woods.

"Get up," snarled Tiffany, kicking Katy's leg.

Katy pulled back with a grimace.

I stepped closer to the road, my weapon aimed at Tiffany's head.

Chandler walked up, staring at Katy like he couldn't believe his eyes. The handle of his black gun jutted from under the jacket.

I turned my weapon on him.

If I shot him, that could distract Tiffany. I could shoot her, but either scenario could also trigger her to fire her weapon at Katy. I couldn't chance it.

I stepped closer.

"Where the heck did she come from?" spluttered Chandler.

"I told you I heard something," snapped Tiffany, keeping her steely eyes on my friend.

Chandler turned to Katy and gestured wildly.

"You were following us, you bitch!"

Katy flinched but didn't speak.

I cursed under my breath. He was too close to Katy for me to get him now.

"Get up," growled Tiffany, kicking Katy in the thigh again. "And no sudden moves."

Katy got to her knees slowly, her hands in the air.

Think girl, think.

I could surprise them now, but these two didn't fool around. One wrong move and Katy could end up dead. Whatever I did, I couldn't signal my presence. The quieter I remained, the better my chances were of rescuing my friend without her getting hurt.

"You alone?" barked Tiffany. "Where's your buddy, what's-her-name?"

Katy got to her feet shakily. Her pants were ripped from that tumble through the woods.

"Answer me!"

Katy shook her head as if she was unable to speak.

She didn't need to pretend. Having a gun aimed at your head after an accidental tumble through ice, snow, and roots would make anyone mute with shock.

Chandler stared at her, his eyes bulging, like he couldn't believe what had just happened.

"What were you doing on the mountain?" he said. "Were you driving that car?"

Katy nodded.

"Where are the others?"

"Up... up... at the lodge."

Tiffany raised an eyebrow. "They sent you down alone to chase after us?"

"I wasn't after you," said Katy.

"What the hell were you doing on the road?"

"They're hurt. I'm going to town to get help."

Atta girl. Stay strong, my friend, I prayed as I watched her. *I'll get you out soon, Katy.*

I scanned the area around me.

There.

A black stone jutted out from the snow. I bent down and pried it out as quietly as I could and slipped it into my pocket.

When I looked up, Tiffany was stepping around Katy, scrutinizing her from head to toe, a dark scowl on her face. She reached over and flipped Katy's jacket to check for weapons, then patted her down.

So far, Katy had kept her face away from the woods.

Thank you, I breathed.

Chandler stepped up to Katy, his face inches from hers.

"You're lying," he said. "If you were going to get help, why weren't you in the car? What were you doing up there?"

"Please don't shoot," said Katy in a shaky voice. "I told you, I was going to town to get help. They all got burned badly. They need a doctor."

"You interfering witches! Everything was going as planned until you came along." Chandler gestured wildly, almost hitting her in the face.

My shoulders tensed.

You touch her, and I'll shoot you in the face, you scumbag.

Chandler let out a frustrated yell and kicked at something on the ground. He turned to Tiffany, his face red.

"This messes things up now, doesn't it? Like it hasn't already? This is all your fault."

"I told you to stop them from coming up to the lodge," Tiffany yelled back, without moving her aim at my friend.

"You think I didn't try?" shouted Chandler right back.

"This is all *your* stupid bride's fault. They're her friends!" screamed Tiffany, almost frothing at the mouth.

"She's not my bride!"

"It's your problem! You take care of it!"

They were getting unhinged. And that wasn't a good thing.

I aimed my gun first at Chandler, then at Tiffany, but they were both too close to Katy. I clenched my teeth, badly wanting to shout to her, to tell her to move away. Just two steps back would do, but she was staring at the arguing couple with an increasing look of alarm.

"So what do we do with her?" said Chandler, throwing his hands in the air. "We're not leaving her here to tattle on us."

Tiffany didn't adjust her aim or her gaze.

"Get the rope," she said.

"What?" said Chandler, staring at her.

"I said, get the rope," replied Tiffany, her voice rising. "In the backseat. Now!"

Chandler stomped back to the vehicle. I turned on him, but he had walked to the other side of the car. The windows were all up and it would be tricky to get a good aim on him.

Shoot.

He opened the back door and pulled out a roll of yellow utility rope. He slammed the door shut and turned around to join Tiffany.

Now.

I kept my aim on Chandler.

Suddenly, I noticed eyes on me.

Tiffany had turned her face toward the woods, her eyes boring through the trees in my direction, like she had X-ray vision.

I pulled back.

Then, as if she knew I was watching, she pressed the muzzle against Katy's head, her eyes still my way. Katy tilted her head from the pressure and grimaced.

"Tie her up," said Tiffany as Chandler walked up to them.

He stepped behind Katy and pulled her arms to her back. Katy didn't protest. She didn't even look my way. But Tiffany did.

I stayed behind the tree, gritting my teeth.

Tiffany was a lot smarter than I'd thought. She was probably the mastermind behind this entire operation from the start.

"March," she barked at Katy. "Forward!"

Katy didn't budge.

Chandler put a hand on her back and pushed her forward, making her stumble.

"That way," said Tiffany, pointing toward the woods on the other side of the road.

I knew what they were about to do.

The ravine was only a few yards from here.

Chapter Fifty-five

Chandler and Tiffany flanked Katy.

Their boots crunched on the snow as they marched toward the trees.

Tiffany kept her gun aimed at Katy's head and didn't even glance behind. Her tight grip on my friend's arm and the unwavering weapon to her head told me she meant business.

I waited for them to get closer to the tree line before I slipped out and crept toward the Humvee. Chandler or Tiffany could turn around at any moment and see me by their vehicle. I crouched low by the passenger door, raised my head, and peeked through the windows.

They were crossing into the woods.

I was about to step away when something caught my eye.

The brown envelope.

It was lying on the passenger seat. It had to be the same one I had seen in Robert's hands only hours ago. The envelope that almost got Nancy killed.

I reached over and pulled at the door handle. It clicked open. I cringed at the noise, but a quick glance up told me no one had heard. They were no longer within hearing distance.

I pulled the door open, snatched the envelope, and stuffed it inside my jacket. Underneath it was a phone. Was it Chandler's or Tiffany's? Barbara's earlier words in the dining-hall flitted to mind.

We keep the tech stuff away from the lodge. We come here to disconnect from all that.

I grabbed the cell and slipped it into my pant pocket.

I scanned the interior, looking for anything else. Wedged in between the front seats was a stainless-steel flask. Perfect. Better than my rock. I picked it up and stuffed it in the other side of my jacket and zipped up.

I was dying to open the envelope and read the contents, but I didn't have time. Tiffany, Chandler, and Katy had already disappeared from view.

I scrambled around the car, my heart racing.

After a quick scan of the area, I dashed into the tree line several yards from where the others had entered. I could hear them stomping through the woods.

I weaved among the trees parallel to them, treading quietly in the direction I expected them to be heading.

It was dark in the woods. The clouds and snow had never let up all day, but there had been enough daylight. But nightfall came early on wintry days in these parts, and soon it would be difficult to see.

I scurried over to the edge, my heart in my mouth.

From between the tree trunks, I caught sight of their silhouettes. Katy looked limp and vulnerable, sandwiched in between the couple.

They were ten feet from the precipice.

A fiery flame of rage rushed up my spine. If they thought they were going to push Katy over the ravine to her death, they thought wrong.

I darted to the next tree. I stayed shielded, but my eyes narrowed on my target.

It was now or never.

I reached into my jacket pocket, pulled the rock out and threw it, aiming it a few feet away from Chandler. He whirled around. I pulled the flask out. It wasn't a hand grenade, but it was the next best thing. I hurled it at his head.

The flask hit him with a thump and fell to the ground. Chandler jumped high with a frightened yelp. He spun around, his eyes wide in shock.

I drew back, but kept my weapon aimed at them.

From my hiding spot, I watched Chandler swirl around jerkily, his eyes bulging, like he was on the verge of a panic attack.

"Who's that?" he shouted. "Who's out there? Come out or I'll shoot you!"

You'll have to see me first.

"What happened?" said Tiffany, snapping around, frowning.

Chandler pointed at the stainless steel bottle, which was rolling down the slope toward the cliff. Tiffany's eyes widened.

"Someone got in our car!" she cried.

She glanced up, her eyes narrowed and steely.

I was glad twilight was falling around us now. On a bright sunny day, they could have caught the glint of my gun or my shadow by the tree.

I swallowed hard, willing my nerves to settle down, to wait for the right time.

Tiffany hadn't taken the muzzle off Katy's head and hadn't moved away from my friend.

Katy stirred.

Though her hands were still bound, and a gun was pointing at her, she lifted her head up and straightened her shoulders. She glanced around discreetly, a determined expression crossing her face.

Atta girl, I said to myself. *Hang tight.*

I waited quietly as her captors scanned the area, nervous flickers on their faces.

They hadn't pinpointed my location yet, but I couldn't stay hidden for long. I was banking on one thing. As long as I kept them on their toes, they wouldn't take Katy to the edge of the cliff.

Tiffany was my primary target, but I didn't know how fast her trigger finger was. She had surprised me more than once, and I wasn't about to risk Katy's life.

"Who are you?" screamed Chandler, his voice high pitched. He pointed his gun frantically this way and that.

I had no qualms about killing either of them. They were both murderers, just like I was. Except my goal had been to eliminate evil, and it had been a long time ago when I had no choice but my life or theirs.

But I wasn't about to take another life, given the choice. And I had the choice today.

I took a deep breath in and aimed my weapon at Chandler's knee.

"Come out, you coward," he screeched. "Come out and fight like a man!"

I pulled the trigger.

Chandler fell to the ground with a hideous yell. He clutched his knee and flailed, howling in pain.

My focus shifted to Tiffany.

She had flinched when Chandler fell, but she had composed herself quickly. She knew my position now.

She was staring my way so hard, I could feel her eyes penetrate the tree trunk like laser beams cutting through steel.

She pulled Katy by the arm and took a step back.

Then another.

My heart jumped to my mouth.

The cliff was only a few feet behind them.

Was she going to jump with Katy?

When she had the cigarette lighter over the gas-soaked Michael, I had been sure she was suicidal. That was until she made her daring escapade down the mountain. Then, I thought her a smart criminal mind who could plot her way out of anything.

But now, I was no longer sure.

I could hear the river thundering in the gully below, sounding more menacing than ever.

Chapter Fifty-six

"**S**top! You're surrounded!"

My voice echoed through the woods, and for an instant, drowned Chandler's screams.

"Help me!" wailed Chandler, writhing on the ground, but Tiffany didn't even glance at him.

"We have people and equipment down at the gully, waiting for you," I hollered. "You want to jump? Go right ahead."

Even from where I was, I saw Tiffany's eyes flicker.

Did she believe my bluff?

"We know why you're doing this," I yelled from behind the tree. "The world will know what you two have been up to soon—"

I stopped as a faint sound came from the distance. A strange rumble. But just as I heard it, it vanished, and soon Chandler's painful howls were all I could hear.

I wasn't sure if that had been my over-extended imagination or my nerve-wracked brain playing tricks on me.

"I'm not afraid of you, you little witch!"

I turned my attention back to Tiffany. She had positioned Katy strategically in front of her and was screeching my way.

Not good.

"I'm not alone, Tiffany," I shouted back, my heart thumping loudly. "You thought we were just two chicks from New York coming to the wedding. You don't know what my real job is, do you?"

She didn't reply.

"Did you really think we'd let you get away with your mad scheme?"

Silence.

"You and Chandler got greedy, didn't you? You learned from Robert that wealth was power. You wanted his business and Victoria's estate. All of it for yourselves."

I peeked out. Instead of her calm exterior, she was now pursing her lips and jutting her chin out, her face a picture of fury.

I was dancing a dangerous dance. I needed her destabilized enough to get her focus away from Katy, but not so much that she'd do something dangerous.

"You goaded Rebeca and Mia to tell Victoria the truth about the family. When Robert found out what they were up to, he was furious. But was he mad enough to kill them, or did you push him to do the deed?"

Tiffany's face tightened, and her eyes turned black as coal.

I was hitting on a few hard truths.

"It was you who plotted for Chandler to marry Victoria too, didn't you? You were the mastermind behind all this."

Silence.

"No need to answer. Besides, once Chandler starts talking, you'll be finished."

Tiffany's cold eyes flitted briefly over to Chandler, who was crying in pain, tears and sweat streaming down his face. Her lips pulled back in distaste.

I had been feeling my way through the story, but her face and voice were telling me everything. She may have been a victim once, but she wasn't one now.

"Help me! Do something!" howled Chandler.

My mind spun. There was one thing Katy could do to make it easier for me, but it was a risky move.

From somewhere on the mountain, I heard the rumbling again. My heart leaped.

A vehicle.

I couldn't say if it was climbing up or heading down, but hope rose in me.

Did Katy call the authorities before she tumbled down?

The sound of the engine came and went, but it was getting closer.

Was it the turns on the mountain that made it fade in and out?

Tiffany cocked her head and stood straighter, like she was preparing for something. My heart sank.

Did she have an accomplice? A friend no one knew about?

"More backup!" I yelled out, my fingers crossed. "Like I said, you have no way out."

Tiffany was still behind Katy, but I aimed my weapon at her head and held my breath, watching her like a hawk. All I needed was for her to move just one foot in either direction.

Chandler's screams had subsided. He was now sobbing uncontrollably, pleading in between raspy breaths for someone to save him.

Tiffany's eyes kept darting back and forth.

The sound of the vehicle was below us. They were coming up from town.

Was it Officer Jensen? Or was it someone coming to aid Tiffany?

If it was the latter, I was running out of time.

My gut screamed. I had to act now.

"Katy!" I shouted. "Duck!"

Katy threw herself to the ground.

I pulled the trigger.

Tiffany jumped back with a shriek. She whipped her weapon my way and fired.

I pulled back quickly. Something blasted loudly next to my ear. She hit the trunk.

Before I could do anything, she turned around and shot at Katy.

Katy yelped.

"Katy!" I screamed, leaping out from behind the tree.

Tiffany whirled around and plunged into the woods.

I fired.

Missed.

"Help!"

I swiveled around to see Katy rolling toward the cliff, her hands bound behind her.

"Asha!" she yelled, kicking madly.

I dove and landed on her back just as she was about to plummet into the void.

Using all my force, I pulled her away from the ledge. Katy helped by pushing with her feet. I stepped toward the nearest tree and grabbed the trunk with one arm while I held on to my friend with the other.

There we sat for a second, hyperventilating like mad, staring at the abyss in front of us.

But we didn't have time to recover.

I pulled Katy around the tree and leaned her against the trunk. Making sure she was secure, I reached behind her and untied the rope. Chandler had done a fast job, so it wasn't too difficult to remove the knots.

Chandler was curled into a fetal position, only a few feet from us. The red stain on his pant leg had spread even more. He was losing blood fast, and with it, consciousness.

The sound of the engine was getting louder. Still muffled, but closer.

I threw the rope aside, grabbed Katy by the shoulders, and pulled her to her feet. She stood up shakily. I glanced over her. No wounds or blood. Tiffany had missed.

"You didn't get hit," I said, squeezing her by the shoulders. "Did you call the police?"

She shook her head. "I was trying to get a better signal when I fell."

I swallowed hard.

Whoever was coming this way would stop when they saw the Humvee. That meant one of two things. Reinforcement, or a bigger battle than I imagined.

Chapter Fifty-seven

I crashed through the woods and back onto the road.

The Humvee roared to life.

I dashed out of the tree line just as Tiffany pushed on the accelerator, making the vehicle lurch over the snowdrift. But she pressed too hard and too fast.

The Humvee spun around.

"Hey!" I shouted, jumping out of the way just in time.

Tiffany stared at me through the windshield.

I pointed my weapon at her.

"Get out of the car," I shouted.

She didn't budge from her seat. Something in her eyes told me she would run over me in a heartbeat.

I scrambled around toward the passenger door. It wasn't locked, not even fully closed, just like I'd left it after I snagged the brown envelope. She mustn't have even noticed the door in her rush to escape.

I leaped inside, aiming my sidearm at her head.

"Stop the car and get out," I snarled.

She whipped her gun at me.

The Humvee purred. The key was in the ignition and the engine was still running, but it was like the world had stopped.

Our eyes bored into each other, dark and angry, our weapons aimed at each other's temples. Her face was flushed, and her hand was clenching her weapon tightly. I held my breath, every muscle in my body tensed to the hilt, expecting to hear a blast from her sidearm.

"Where are you running off to?" I said.

She didn't answer.

The rumbling came in the distance again. It was louder and clearer. More than one vehicle was coming up the mountain.

My stomach flipped.

Could these be police cruisers and emergency vehicles from town? Officer Jensen and his team? Who else would be coming up in these conditions?

Someone must have alerted them.

I couldn't say for sure, but something told me Tiffany didn't know either.

"You hear that?" I said. "The only way you're leaving this mountain is in handcuffs or in a body bag."

Tiffany didn't blink.

"Your choice," I said. "You can get out of the car and cooperate with me, or get manhandled by a SWAT team who will be happy to have your head."

She didn't make a move, just stared right at me, the muzzle of her gun inches from my head.

I wondered how long we were going to sit here, glowering at each other.

I had to try another tactic.

"Tiffany," I said, softening my voice. "I'm sorry about what you went through as a kid. Whatever Robert or his family did to you, it was wrong. You deserved a better childhood."

Tiffany's eyes flickered, but only for an instant. Then her frown deepened, but she didn't take her eyes off me.

My ears stayed alert, hoping against hope to hear a siren soon. *Please let it be the police.*

"You went through hell as a little girl. Rebeca and Mia too."

I paused, wondering if my next words would rile her up or break her down.

"But did Rebeca and Mia need to die?"

"I didn't kill them," she whispered.

Her voice was soft, like that of a child. A frightened child.

I cocked a brow.

"Who killed Rebeca? Tell me."

No answer.

"Was it Chandler?"

Tiffany stared.

"Or was it Robert?"

She blinked.

I quickly scanned the area behind her. There was no sign of Katy. If I knew her, she was ripping up Chandler's shirt and bandaging his knee to stop the bleeding. I hoped to goodness I hadn't misjudged Chandler.

But I was stuck here with a gun pointing in between my eyes.

"Tiffany," I said, trying to think of how to get that muzzle away from my face. "This means you still have a chance. Put that down and let's figure this out together."

She bit her lip but remained silent.

"You don't know this, but Katy and I didn't have the suburban dream childhoods either," I said. "We had a real rough time when we were kids. All the adults who were supposed to protect us let us down, but we learned to create a different life for ourselves. You're young. You have your entire life in front of you. You still have time."

"Time for what?"

"Any judge or jury who hears your story would understand and give it consideration."

Her eyes darkened.

"I'm not going to jail," she said.

"That's not what I said. What I meant was this is not the end for you."

"Why don't you shoot me right now?"

I jerked my head back in surprise. Her voice had been soft, but her eyes were steely. For one moment, I wondered if she was playing with me.

Either Tiffany had been so brutalized as a child to the point she didn't know right from wrong, or she was in full control of her senses and had the mind of a master manipulator.

"I don't want to hurt you," I said. "The only reason I shot Chandler was because you had Katy and I didn't have a choice." I paused, my brain whirring. "I'd like to help you out. Will you let me?"

"How?"

"Get the help you need. Make sure you're safe. Stop them from throwing you in jail and flushing the key down the toilet."

She frowned, but she was listening.

"We'll get Chandler in the car and get his knee fixed. Then we'll find a safe house for you two."

Her face changed. It was a curious expression, like she was vacillating between fear and anger.

"The sooner we get him to a hospital, the sooner he will recover," I added.

Tiffany shook her head, almost violently.

"No!"

"You don't understand," I said. "If we leave him here, he'll bleed to death in the woods."

"Let him."

I looked at her, my eyes narrowed.

"How did you move the car so quickly just now?" I said. "Last we saw, Chandler and you were shoveling the snow from the back wheels. You were stuck."

"That's what I wanted him to believe," she said in a low voice.

She tapped a foot on the brake pedal.

"One foot on the brake and the other on the gas. He never knew."

I remembered seeing Chandler beside the car. He wasn't right behind it, so he never registered the brake lights.

My mind cleared.

"You were planning to push him off the cliff," I said, a chill going down my spine. "That's why you were pretending to be stranded here."

Silence.

I frowned. "Why kill Chandler? What did he do to you to betray him like this?"

No answer.

I leaned closer. "I thought he was your lover."

To my surprise, she lowered her weapon. She placed her sidearm on her lap and hung her head.

"I just want to get out of here," she said in a soft voice, staring down at her shaking hands.

Gone was the deranged killer I saw earlier. In its place was a fearful young woman who looked like she'd had more than her share of hell on earth.

Tiffany turned a tear-stained face to me. "Will you help me?"

I scanned her face.

Was she acting again? Maybe she had a human side to her after all.

I lowered my weapon to my lap, but kept it aimed at her.

Just in case I was reading her wrong.

Chapter Fifty-eight

"They kept us locked up," Tiffany muttered, more to herself than me.

She turned away to stare out of her window. I almost gasped out loud when she moved her leg.

An ankle monitor.

She wiped her eyes.

"Was it Robert?" I said. "He put that monitor on you, Rebeca and Mia, didn't he?"

Tiffany nodded.

I glanced at the sidearm on her lap. I was itching to reach over and pluck it out of her hands. Tears were running down her cheeks, but she didn't try to wipe them anymore.

"Him and the others," she replied through her sniffling, still not looking my way.

"The whole family?" I said.

She gave an imperceptible nod, one finger absentmindedly playing with the rivets on her gun.

I glanced over her shoulder to see if I could spot Katy, but the trees created a dark curtain that wrapped along the road. I had no idea how she was doing or if Chandler had even survived his injuries.

The vehicles faded in and out as they took corners around the mountain. The open landscape amplified their sound, so it was difficult to say how far they had to get here.

I wondered how much longer I could keep Tiffany engaged without getting into a stalemate again. "Robert and Barbara adopted you when you were just kids, didn't they?"

Tiffany spun around to face me, her face flushed a deep red.

"Adopted?" she spat. "Is that what you call it?"

"Stolen?" I said, trying again. "Kidnapped?"

Her shoulders drooped.

"They lied to the hospital. Told them we were going to have a family." She shook her head like she couldn't believe what had happened herself.

"And what a family it was," I said, lowering my voice to her level.

The obsessive-compulsive clicking of her fingernails on the gun was getting on my nerves, but I said nothing.

"They're all evil," she said with a sniffle.

"Did Chandler hurt you too?" I said, observing her carefully.

She was silent for a minute.

"I didn't know anything," she said finally. "I was the oldest, so I was the first one."

"First one? What do you mean?"

"He was just a teen, but he used to come into my room at night and tell me his father told him to... I didn't know how to say no. I was scared. I was alone...."

So Chandler was just as revolting as Robert, and Victoria had thought the world of him. I wanted to push the door open and vomit.

"I hated him so much," Tiffany was saying. "But I hated his father more."

"Barbara knew about all this?"

Tiffany just stared out the window.

I took that to be a yes.

"And she did nothing?"

She turned to me.

"Chandler thought I loved him. He told me I was his first love. Can you believe it?"

"It was you who he was kissing behind the rhododendron bushes when we arrived, wasn't it?" I said.

She gave a half-hearted shrug, like that didn't matter anymore.

"He made us do things... him and his father.... I told Barbara once, but she told me she'd sell me if I ever brought it up again."

"Sell you?"

"Back to the hospital so they could do experiments on me. I was ten. I believed her."

"I'm so sorry," I said, putting a hand on her arm, inches from her gun. She flicked my hand away like she was swatting a fly.

I pulled back.

"You'll be okay," I said. "No one's going to put you on death row or prison for life, if that's what you're scared of."

"Can we just get out of here?" she said. "Please, let's go."

"Go where?"

"Away from this horrible place."

"If that's what you want."

The vehicles were getting closer.

"Why don't we start by you handing over the gun?"

"No!" Tiffany snapped at me through her tears. "No!"

"Okay," I said, gesturing with my hands to let her know I heard her. "It's okay. I just don't want you to hurt yourself."

She put her shaking hands on the wheel.

"I just wanna get outta here!" she said, blubbering now.

"Let me drive and you can relax," I said. "I'll take you wherever you want."

That was when she jumped on the gas pedal.

The Humvee leaped forward, throwing me against the dashboard. She spun the car to the left and braked hard, sending me reeling back.

"Hey!" I shouted. "What are you doing?"

Tiffany was grasping the wheel with a dark expression on her face. It was like she couldn't see or hear me at all.

"Stop the car!" I yelled.

But we were speeding forward.

In the wrong direction.

"Watch out!" I screamed as we crashed through the trees.

A loud bang made us careen over to one side. I covered my head as I smashed against the door. We hit a tree, but the mighty Humvee kept going. Another bang, and the vehicle swung in the opposite direction.

"Stop!" I hollered, reaching over to the steering wheel. She pushed me away.

"What the hell do you think you're doing?" I shouted.

Tiffany's face was taut, and her eyes were icy cold. She was leaning forward and holding on to the wheel like her life depended on it.

Katy's frightened face appeared ahead of us.

I pulled the window open and screamed.

"Katy! Watch out!"

Her eyes widened as she saw us barrel through the woods. She jumped out of the way and dove behind a tree just in time.

"Asha!" came her panicked yell from behind us.

I sprang over to the driver's side and seized the steering wheel. I turned it sharply to the right to avoid hitting Chandler, who was still lying on the ground. We missed him by inches.

I looked up.

We were heading dead straight to the ravine.

"Stop the car now!" I hollered, pushing Tiffany's hands away from the wheel. She struck me with her elbow.

I lifted my Glock and whacked her on the side of the head.

She covered her head with her hands, but that didn't stop the car. Her foot was stuck on the gas.

I clubbed her leg with my Glock and slammed her against her door. She flailed like a wildcat, clawing at me and pulling my hair.

Ignoring the pain as she punched and pinched, I scrambled on top of her and jumped on the brakes.

The vehicle screeched to a stop.

A scream died in my throat.

The Humvee tilted forward. Then it sat back with a thud. Something groaned underneath us.

Tiffany merely stared ahead.

I didn't breathe.

All I could see in front of me was the wide-open ravine.

Chapter Fifty-nine

The Humvee teetered on the precipice.

I stiffened, unsure how much of the car was on the ledge and how much was straddling open air.

Tiffany was staring out of the windshield, her face expressionless.

I was sitting in between the two front seats, my feet on the driver's side and the rest of me straddling the gear and the cup holders.

From somewhere behind us, Katy was screaming for help. I couldn't make out all her words as my blood was pounding in my ear.

Every cell in me had gone numb, but my brain was whirring a million miles a second. Thoughts of rolling over the cliff and crashing into the gully, getting swirled up in the freezing, torrential waters below us, kept flashing through my mind.

Get yourself together, girl.

A nervous twitch had started on the back of my right hand. I wanted to curl my hands into fists and bang them on the dashboard. Instead, I clenched my teeth and didn't dare move.

Think, girl, think.

Humvees were built for war zones, not the streets of Falcon Hills or even the mountains of New Hampshire. It was folks like Robert who had more money than they knew what to do with who purchased them. Their heavy-duty engines meant these machines were front loaded.

And that wasn't a good thing.

One small move and we could upset the delicate weight balance keeping us on the razor edge of this canyon.

I turned to Tiffany. She sat frozen, squished on her end, her face dull, like a robotic phantom.

She turned to me, her pale blue eyes wide open, but it was like she wasn't really there.

Did she know what she had got us into?

"Don't move," I whispered. "Stay still."

Her eyelashes fluttered.

Then she moved her leg.

I whipped up my gun and pressed it against the side of her neck.

"You move one inch, and you'll get a bullet right into you, you hear?" I whispered, gritting my teeth.

She stopped.

Moving slowly, I reached over with my other hand, and gently pulled on the handbrake.

The Humvee pitched forward.

Tiffany took a sharp breath in.

I stopped breathing.

The vehicle settled back again with a loud groan.

I let out my breath, my heart hammering.

The absurdity of our situation slowly sank into my head.

The muzzle of my weapon was pressing against Tiffany's throat. She had dropped enough hints about finishing it all off, and here I was, threatening to shoot her. If she had been honest about this to me and to herself, this was a futile mission.

Did she change her mind?

My only hope was her brain was too muddled to think straight, and the horror of a bullet ripping through her skull would be enough to stop her from doing anything stupid that would push us over the edge.

A panicked yell came from nearby, making us both flinch.

My door clicked open.

The vehicle dipped an inch.

I cringed.

Tiffany gasped.

"Watch it," I whispered, not daring to turn around to see who it was.

"Asha!"

It was Katy's horrified voice.

"Don't touch anything," I whispered. "How far are we out?"

"B... both front wheels," stammered Katy. "G... get out. Asha, please get out now."

I could hear the distress in her voice, but whatever we did next had to be calculated. One wrong move and I'd have to say goodbye to Katy forever.

Suddenly, hollering came from somewhere behind us. They were loud, unfamiliar voices. It was like a small army was invading the woods.

The convoy of cars.

I didn't take my eyes off Tiffany. She was sitting limp, but I didn't trust her.

"This way!" shouted a male voice.

"Help!" cried Katy, whipping around. "Over here!"

"Who's that?" I whispered.

"Jensen," said Katy. "Jim and Nancy called him—"

"Tell them not to get too close. The last thing we need is a stampede around the car."

"I'm here!" Chandler's voice came from close by. "By the tree. Someone help me!" he screeched. "I've been shot!"

He was still alive.

I had expected him to have bled to death by now. If I lived through this, I'd have some explaining to do to Officer Jensen and his colleagues.

"Sweet baby Jesus," came a familiar voice from nearby.

Officer Jensen.

Katy turned away from me.

"Please help," I heard her say in a high-pitched voice. "*Do* something. Get them out—"

"Stay back, ma'am," he said, stopping her in mid sentence. "Get back in your vehicle now."

I gritted my teeth.

"Get sandbags and ropes!" hollered a female voice, an authoritative one that sounded like she knew what she was doing.

A smidgen of hope swirled up my spine.

"No...." whispered Tiffany.

I turned to her and narrowed my eyes.

"D... don't want to..." she stammered, fidgeting in her seat.

"Stop moving," I said in between clenched teeth.

"Oh no," gasped Katy from beside me. "What's she doing?"

"Are you trying to kill us both?" I whispered hoarsely.

Tiffany turned to me. The glaze in her eyes had cleared, and in its place was a hard and furious glare.

A frisson of fear ran up my spine.

Chapter Sixty

"Do you really want to kill yourself?" I whispered.

Tiffany didn't reply, but her stare was unsettling.

"You'll be taking another life with you, you realize that?"

"If you didn't come to the wedding, you wouldn't be here now," she whispered back, her eyes dark and angry.

The door on my side was still ajar and I could hear Katy pleading with the first responders to hurry. It sounded like a construction crew was getting into place around us.

I pressed my gun to Tiffany's neck.

"I swear to everything holy, your death will be more painful than you can ever imagine if you make any stupid moves."

A shadow crossed the window on her side.

Jensen's jaw dropped as he took in Tiffany, the gun, then me.

"Don't touch anything," I mouthed.

Jensen rubbed his face like he couldn't believe what he was seeing. Before I could say anything, he grabbed the handle and opened the door.

The Humvee tilted forward.

Jensen let go of the door and jumped back in horror. The door closed halfway back on its hinges.

The car groaned loudly. We were still on the bluff, but it was only a matter of time before we rolled over for good.

I turned my furious eyes on him.

"Are you trying to get us killed?"

Jensen stared at me in shock.

"What in goodness's name do you think you're doing?" he said, through the half-open door. "Put your weapon down."

"This is a suicide mission," I snapped.

His eyes widened even more.

"We need to get her out of here before she takes us both down," I said.

He opened his mouth as if to say something, then closed it. He turned to Tiffany, who was staring dead straight ahead, her face expressionless again.

"Ma'am?" said Jensen, leaning in, his face paler than before. "Ma'am? Can you hear me? We need you to get out of the vehicle slowly."

No answer.

"Er... ma'am? Are you okay?"

Jensen gave me a confused look.

I gave him an *I-told-you-so* glare in response.

Someone hollered his name. He spun around.

From the side mirror, I could see uniformed officers running around behind the Humvee, carrying ropes, pulleys, and sandbags. They were crowding around the female officer who was pointing at the car.

But none of them seemed to know what the stakes were. They didn't know Tiffany was the wild card here. She could wreck this rescue operation in a heartbeat, before this lot got their stuff together.

Katy had probably told them what was going on inside the vehicle, but I could just see them dismiss her hysterical pleas for help.

"Tell them, Jensen," I said, looking at the officer.

He turned to Tiffany.

"Ma'am, I want you to stay completely still. We'll get you out. Easy does it, okay?"

Tiffany didn't even turn her head.

Jensen stepped away from the car and joined his colleagues.

This was going to take time.

Both doors were open halfway. I could jump out on my side, leaving Tiffany to her fate. But I knew I'd never be able to live with myself if I did that.

Katy's face appeared by the driver's side.

"Tiffany," she hissed. "Kill yourself if you want to, but leave Asha out of this. Get out of the car now!"

Tiffany didn't reply.

"Katy," I said, turning my eyes on my friend. "Can you open her door a bit more?"

"What if she—?"

"I got her," I said. "Go very slow."

Katy reached for the handle and pulled it open an inch. She paused for a second before pulling it another two inches, moving like she was in a video in slow motion.

So far, neither the Humvee nor Tiffany had protested.

I locked eyes with my friend. "When I say go..."

She nodded.

The door was open three quarters of the way now. Katy was holding the handle with her fingertips, sweat streaming down her face. She had one arm extended toward Tiffany.

"Hey, what are you doing?" hollered the female officer from behind us. "Didn't I tell you to get away from the vehicle?"

Katy didn't reply.

"I said step away from the vehicle!"

That seemed to awaken Tiffany. She straightened up like she'd got injected with a jolt of energy. She reached for the steering wheel.

Katy gasped.

"Now!" I screamed as I lifted my leg and kicked Tiffany on the side.

Katy grabbed her by the shoulders and pulled her out.

A blur of uniforms rushed over.

Chaos erupted around us.

The Humvee groaned and its nose slanted at a forty-five-degree angle.

I rolled out just as the car tilted. I clutched at the slippery slope but felt my feet slide on the snow.

"Asha!" screamed Katy.

Someone grabbed me by my arms.

Beside me, the Humvee rocked forward. I watched in horror as it tumbled over the cliff with a thundering crash and disappeared into the abyss.

Silence fell around us.

Two seconds later, the ominous splash came from below.

Then quietness descended in the woods again.

That was when I realized my feet were dangling over the edge, but something or someone was holding me back.

It was Katy and Officer Jensen. They were hanging on to me.

They hauled me away from the ledge. I struggled to my feet, grabbing on to the nearest tree trunk. It was only when I stood hugging that tree that I realized my entire body was shaking.

I looked around me in a daze. The Humvee was gone.

Two paramedics were running through the woods with a stretcher.

"Make way," they shouted.

They were heading toward Chandler, who was at the base of a tree curled up in pain. Tiffany crouched on the ground next to him, with the female officer's arms on her shoulders, like she was restraining her.

"Let's get out of here."

I turned to Katy.

She put her arms around me and nudged me away from the tree and away from the cliff.

"You need a warm blanket and a place to sit for a minute."

Leaning on her shoulder, I stumbled through the woods.

From behind us, I heard Tiffany's heart-wrenching sobs.

She had finally broken down.

Back in New York

Chapter Sixty-one

"Who sent those texts?"

Win had been pestering me with that question all day long.

She had been glued to her laptop, pouring over news reports of the family tragedy in New Hampshire, mad at herself for not having dug out useful information to help us out while we were stuck on the mountain.

It wasn't her fault. There had been nothing incriminating on any members of the Rupert family. Even if she had uncovered anything useful, our phones had been down till Katy and I reached Falcon Hills.

The Ruperts had hid their secrets well.

Katy and I had accompanied Victoria, Nancy, and Jim to Cedar Cottage soon after giving our statements to Officer Jensen and his colleagues.

"You ladies are nothing but trouble," Jensen had groused as he had hurriedly scribbled notes in his little pad.

"These crimes happened under your watch, Officer," Katy had quipped.

"Next time you two come to town, I want you to register with my office," he'd said gruffly.

"Register?" I'd said. "Whatever for? We haven't done anything wrong."

"That way, I'll know to get my paperwork done ahead of time."

He'd turned away with a frustrated huff, but the glint in his eyes told me he'd appreciated our work.

He'd even escorted Victoria and us to Cedar Cottage that afternoon, his light flashers on. We knew he was going against his superior's orders, who thought he had more important work to do at the crime scene.

Victoria had refused to come to New York with us, even after we promised her, Nancy, and Jim an extended holiday to forget what they had all gone through. They needed a break, time to clear their heads.

But our enticing offers to pile them with cakes, to take them to a spa, a Broadway show, or to one of the best museums or art galleries in the country had fallen on deaf ears.

All three wanted nothing more than to return to the safety and comfort of their home and get back to their normal lives. The horrors of that weekend would take time to peel away, especially for Victoria, but she had ultimately accepted the truth, however harsh it had been.

Katy and I had returned to New York late that night.

As soon as I stepped inside my bakery the next morning and smelled the heavenly goodness of sweet sugary cakes and buttered buns, all the anxiety and terror of the weekend rolled off my shoulders.

I was glad to be among family and friends again.

"Hey, so did you find out who sent you those texts?" said Win, jabbing me on the arm, just as I reached for a warm muffin on the counter.

We were all gathered in the kitchen in the back of the bakery. Between Katy and me, we had told everyone what had happened during our trip. But there were still several questions which may never get answers, like why Robert Rupert had engaged in such a repugnant and insidious crime and why Barbara had let it go on for years.

We would also never know if Chandler felt remorse for what he had done. He'd glared at us as the paramedics put him in the ambulance. He was on police watch while in hospital. They would take him to jail as soon as he recovered from his injury.

Tiffany had a lot to answer for too, but her past was so horrific, a part of me wished she'd get some leniency. Once the hearings began in court, Katy and I would have to travel back to New Hampshire and share the story from our point of view.

But that would come later.

I returned to the present.

It was good to be home. The nasty graffiti on the bakery wall had been cleaned up and there had been no further threats. Life was back to normal.

Or so it felt like.

Luc, my head chef, was now busy with an order for high tea for a fashion show, while his sous chefs, Rosalie and Sarah, were icing a wedding cake on a corner table.

The only time Luc and his crew allowed us in the kitchen was when I had finished a mission, and they wanted to hear the juicy details. This was especially true if they'd heard snippets of it on the news channels the night before.

Bibi, the bakery's delivery queen, was drinking cola near the back door, making every excuse in the world to delay her next trip. She was dying to know the rest of the story, too.

Katy sat perched on a stool next to the counter with her husband, Peace, watching a video of Chantelle's nativity play on her tablet. Chantelle sat in between her parents, a proud smile on her face as they oohed and aahed at her performance.

David was teaching a martial arts class at the dojo next door, but had promised a lunch date with me as soon as he was done. I couldn't wait for time alone with him, and to talk about anything other than what had happened in the White Mountains.

Tetyana was at an FBI training session that day. She'd come to the bakery early in the morning to confirm we had survived our unexpected mission and to scold me for not being better prepared.

She'd strutted back out in her brand-new uniform to join her partner waiting for her in the squad car, while the rest of us poured more tea and wondered how long her new bosses could handle her fiery and independent personality.

I was sad she was no longer available to join me on my private investigative missions, but I knew she yearned for this work. It was what she'd trained for, for years. In her new position, she had access to resources, teams, and equipment, unlike me, who had to rely on my gumption and wit more than anything else.

We had done one thing right in the end.

Katy and I had saved Max from being stuck in an animal shelter. He was sleeping off his long and confusing trip in David's office at the dojo, and didn't know we had all spent most of the morning arguing over which one of us would make the best adopted family for him.

I felt another jab in my arm.

I looked up to see Luc standing next to me in his tall chef hat.

"Well?" he said. "If you're not going to tell us, we've got work to do."

"It was Tiffany," I said, sitting back to peel the baking liner from my muffin. "She sent me those anonymous messages. Jensen confirmed it an hour ago. He had a long talk with Tiffany at the station last night."

"Tiffany sent those weird texts?" said Bibi. "You've got to be kidding me."

"Jensen sent the phone I found in the Humvee to their forensics lab," I said. "They confirmed all the messages."

"Why on earth would she do that?" said Rosalie, looking up from her cake. "If she was behind everything, wouldn't she have wanted to stay quiet?"

"She knew she had to pivot when she saw Katy and me arrive at the lodge—"

"And we hadn't rolled into the gorge like they had planned," said Katy, shooting me a dark look.

I nodded.

"She sent those texts to deflect attention away from her. She was trying to get us to focus on Chandler. She didn't care for the man. He abused her too, remember?"

Katy pulled a pair of headphones from her purse and plonked them on Chantelle's head.

"Adult talk," she said with a stern look at her daughter, who turned back to her tablet.

"I thought you said they didn't have phones at the lodge, other than that broken landline," said Win, frowning at me over the top of her laptop.

"Chandler kept his. He's a big city boy and there was no way he'd give up his phone, but Tiffany found it and used it against him."

"She's the one who encouraged Rebeca and Mia to talk to Victoria. Then she goaded Robert to kill them before she pushed Chandler to kill his parents," I said.

"She's a master manipulator," said Peace, shaking his head.

"Anyone who grew up in a family like that would get totally messed up," said Sarah.

"Man, talk about dysfunctional," said Bibi.

"Who cut the landline?" asked Win, frowning, always more interested in technology over the affairs of people.

"Tiffany again," I said. "She couldn't have anyone call for help as she put her game plan in action."

"She must have hated you two," said Rosalie. "You gals turned everything upside down. Good for you."

Katy and I exchanged a glance.

We were silent for a while. I wished I could enjoy the same excitement as my friends, but all I felt was a raw sadness.

"What about that hatch in the woods?" said Bibi, crushing her soda can and throwing it into the recycle bin. "Sounds like something straight out of a serial killer movie."

"The girls had taken turns to dig that tunnel," I said. "They started on it years ago when they were kids. They thought they could use it to escape one day. They were just waiting for the right time."

"They wouldn't have got far," said Luc, closing the oven door. "They'd have frozen to death."

"They could have made it in the summer by sticking to the trees and hiking down the mountain," I said. "Except they had on those ankle monitors, which meant Robert knew exactly where they were at all times."

"But you didn't find a computer at the lodge," said Win, frowning. "How was he tracking them?"

"From his office at the ski resort at the bottom of the mountain where he spent most of his time," I said. "Officer Jensen and his team discovered the software on his office computer, so there's no denying what he was doing."

"Poor girls," said Sarah, shaking her head. "That's worse than being in prison."

"That's why Tiffany decided on an even bigger escape plan," I said.

"Got a bit carried away with it, if you ask me," said Katy.

"If you two hadn't taken off to the woods to look for the missing girls, she'd have got you too," said Peace, with a shudder. "Probably have lured you into one of those burning cabins."

He turned to Katy, a concerned expression on his face. "You promised me, hun. You promised me you'd stay out of danger."

"We went to a wedding, babe," said Katy, reaching for his arm. "How would I know things were going to turn into a horror show?"

"It's all Asha's fault," said Luc, giving me a friendly nudge as he passed me on his way to the oven, his mitts in hand. "Trouble follows her around the country like a homesick puppy, I swear."

"Who are you talking about?"

I turned to see my fiancé, David, enter the kitchen, still in his sweaty dojo uniform. He grinned at me. He knew Luc was referring to me, and he, like Peace, would rather I did any other work than what I did.

I jumped down from my stool to embrace him.

"If that's true, then you're in big trouble, mister," I said, jabbing him playfully in the chest and reaching up for a kiss.

I felt his arms enveloping me and shivered in pleasure.

It was good to be home.

Continue the adventure!

Read the next Merciless Murder Mystery Thriller and find out what Asha and Katy confront next at Hidden Cove, an affluent float-home lake community on the outskirts of Seattle.

A missing heiress. A mangled body. Hidden Cove holds deadly secrets...

Flip to the end of this book to read the first chapter.

Or, get Merciless Deaths right now, right here:

www.TikiriHerath.com/Mysteries

Author's Note

D ear reader,

Did you enjoy this book?

My promise is to give you an exciting escape with every novel I write, and I sure hope I have done so.

If you have a minute, I'd much appreciate it if you would leave an honest review of this book on Amazon, Goodreads, or Bookbub. Just one sentence would do.

Honest reader reviews help my books get selected for international book promotions and I get to reach more readers.

Thank you so much.

One more thing.

If you'd like to learn the backstory of Tetyana, Asha, and Katy, flip to the end of this book to learn about the spin-off series that tells their stories.

The Red Heeled Rebels is an international crime series and is the origin story that shows how they all met. It spans four continents and features the back stories of everyone in this found family.

The Tanya Stone FBI K9 Thriller series features Tetyana as Special Agent Tanya Stone and her German Shepherd partner, Max, hunting a devious serial killer in a small seaside town on the West Coast.

Enjoy the reads!
My very best wishes,
Tikiri
Vancouver, Canada

PS: Join the VIP Red Heeled Rebels Club and receive your exclusive gift!

HER DEADLY END is a 250-page twisty thriller about an unusual murder-suicide case that Agent Tanya (Tetyana), Asha, and Katy accidentally stumble upon while vacationing in Paradise Cove. It's a pulse-pounding, nerve-shredding mystery of a devious serial criminal stalking a small seaside town in Washington State.

Click the link below to join the club and get your free gift book.

HER DEADLY END: A gripping thriller with a twisty end
https://books.tikiriherath.com/ts-b0-mmm-herdeadlyend

PPS/ If you didn't enjoy the story or spotted typos, would you drop a line and let me know? Or just write to say hello. I would love to hear from you and personally reply to every email I receive.

My address is: Tikiri@TikiriHerath.com

Continue the Adventure with Merciless Deaths!

MERCILESS DEATHS, the next book in this series, will give you more spine-tingling intrigue, mystery, and lurking killers whom Asha will ferret out in the end.

Get the next mystery thriller here:
www.TikiriHerath.com/Mysteries

⸺⸱✠⸱⸺

Read the first chapter of Merciless Deaths here:

⸺⸱✠⸱⸺

The Belly of the Beast

The young woman's anguished screams echoed, reverberating off the heavy steel walls that enclosed the chamber.

The men ignored her.

They had a job to do. And their boss was watching.

"Stop it!" she cried, tears streaming down her face.

Her thighs and shoulders were bruised, and her long, blond, and disheveled hair had fallen over her eyes.

She couldn't see much, but she couldn't push her hair off her face either, as her hands and feet had been bound by a yellow marine cable. The rope cut deep into her flesh, creating raw, red marks around her wrists and ankles.

She struggled to get to her knees, but she was exhausted from the beating they gave her only moments ago. She could hear the waves slam against the outer hull, and the constant swaying was making her nauseous.

She was the one they were after. She knew they would kill her and dump her body into the ocean.

That was, before the men turned on her boyfriend.

The two thugs were now hitting the young man on the ground, their fists pounding on his rail thin body. One punch was so fierce he jerked up like a ragged puppet on strings and landed with a dull thud on the hard floor.

Her boyfriend was an innocent artist.

He smoked weed on weekends, loved to go mushroom picking in the woods, and graffiti painted peace signs on the large corporate buildings of downtown Seattle. The worst violence he'd experienced in his life—until now—was the day his puppy got hit by a car when he was seven years old.

"Let him go!" screamed the girl through her sobs. She turned to the third man in the room. "Why are you doing this to us?"

The third man was sitting in a chair by the spiral steel stairway, carefully positioned away from where the beatings were taking place.

In faded blue jeans and a golf shirt, he looked like a suburban dad—a typical middle-aged man you'd find yourself seated next to at a weekend football tournament. He was observing the events, like he was watching a game.

He hadn't said a word since he came into the room, but the girl knew he ran this macabre show.

Something glinted under the morbid yellow light on the floor by his chair.

It was a knife.

No.

It was a cleaver.

"He did nothing to you," shrieked the girl. "Tell them to stop!"

The man in the chair merely raised an eyebrow.

"I told you, I don't remember it!" she cried.

One thug stopped his punching to wipe the sweat from his brow. "Stop screeching like a wildcat in heat." He shot an ugly smirk her way. "No one's gonna hear you down here anyway, sugar."

The young woman kept her face pointed at the leader of the crew. "How many times do I have to tell you I don't remember all of it? Let us go! Please!"

"Try harder," the man replied, speaking for the first time since his arrival.

His voice was calm and low, but firm, like he knew he was a respected man in his community, someone others always listened to.

The woman broke into sobs. She was breaking.

"Enough," said the man in the chair to his goons. "I think she got the message."

The thugs stopped kicking the man on the ground.

The man on the floor moaned in pain. Trails of blood trickled down his face and shoulders onto the floor, mixing with remnants of diesel and engine oil. His breath was harsh and raspy, and he was convulsing in pain.

He didn't look like he would survive this day.

But all three men's eyes were now on the girl.

"Do you remember it all now?" said the man in the chair, his voice as cold as the steel walls.

"No!"

"Try, if you want to live. Start from the top."

"Four, four, I think...," she stammered through her tears. "But I don't remem—"

"Will this help?" One thug raised his foot over the young man's head.

"No!" she yelled, her voice high-pitched, shrill. "Let me think!"

The men waited.

"Four... four.... six... nine...." She stumbled over her words, her voice cracking, her chest heaving. "I'm trying..."

The man in the chair looked bored, like the game he'd come to watch wasn't fun anymore.

He straightened up. "Remember, if it's wrong, it's not you, but others who will pay for it."

"Four, four, six, nine, zero, one, eight," blurted the girl.

She turned to the man in the chair, blinking away her tears.

"Please let us go now," she whispered. "Please."

He turned to his thugs.

"You know what to do," he said.

They nodded.

One goon swooped down to pick up the cleaver and raised it high in the air. He walked over to the young man on the floor, towering over him.

The girl collapsed to the ground. She couldn't save her boyfriend now.

The man swiped the cleaver down.

Outside those thick steel-hulled walls, no one heard her heart-wrenching screams.

***

New York

Chapter One

"Delivery for you, Asha!"

I looked up just in time to see the mail carrier wave from outside.

It was a cool Monday morning in April, and I'd been staring out of the open window, my troubled mind elsewhere.

Outside, gentrified Harlem was bustling with people and traffic, all hustling their way to work or school. Normal folk with normal lives.

There were days I wished I could be them.

"Thanks, Tyrone!" I yelled before the postal carrier disappeared around the corner.

I walked over to the front door and opened it. The package had fallen at the feet of our new street board. Katy, my bakery's finance manager, had put it up just outside the front door that weekend.

The sign said; Life is Short. Eat cake first. Welcome to the Red Heeled Rebels bakery.

Katy had thought it was the perfect message to attract more clients. My head chef, Luc, had thought it made his upscale cakes sound cheap.

I had stayed out of the debate, my mind swirling around the strange message left on my phone the day before.

It had been from Mary Hudson, an old friend I hadn't heard in years.

I'd thought she and her husband had retired to Portland and were living with their children and grandchildren. They were finally safe and sound, but her confusing message hinted at something terrible happening.

I'd called back five times since then, but no one had picked up the phone. That had been even more disquieting.

Her voice in the message had been muffled and the number unlisted. I was no longer sure if it had even been my friend.

I stepped around Katy's board and picked up the brown package on the ground.

"Hey!"

Win was running toward me along the sidewalk, dodging other pedestrians, a bright smile on her pretty face and her short black hair bobbing up and down.

Luc's wife, Win, was my resident computer expert who worked for a cyber security company in the city. Or the White-Hat-Hacker-Babe, as she liked to call herself.

Her petite frame and casual dress meant most people mistook her for a teenager and sometimes didn't believe her Stanford education and higher-than-average IQ.

She stomped up to me, out of breath.

"Come to see Luc?" I said, straightening up with the package in my hand.

"He said you got a weird call. Want me to trace the number?"

I nodded and opened the door for her.

Win skipped past me, her excitement to solve yet another one of my puzzles palpable. She was always bright-eyed and bushy-tailed, even when I roped her into the most challenging investigations.

I closed the front door and followed her into my office.

I stepped behind my desk and laid the package on my lap, my mind still whirring. Win plopped on the seat across from me, picked up my phone without even asking, and started clicking away.

Normally, I wouldn't let anyone touch my mobile, but this time, I let her do her thing. Win had hacked into the highest security networks in the country. My phone would be a breeze for her brilliant mind.

"Did a squirrel die in the chimney again?"

I looked up to see Katy walking into the office.

My best friend, Katy, always looked elegant in her hand-tailored, plus-sized dresses and her Irish red hair in a beautiful up do. She came to work every morning looking like she was headed to a fancy soirée instead of a bakery.

"Now you mention it, it stinks in here," mumbled Win, but her eyes remained glued to my phone.

Katy sniffed the air suspiciously. There was an odor coming from somewhere, but I had more important matters at hand.

I turned the package around with a frown. The postmark was from a local postal station, but there was no sender address.

That wasn't a good sign.

I placed the parcel on the table, plucked a pair of scissors from the drawer, and cut through the soft cardboard.

Katy peered over my desk as I opened the top flaps.

"A box in a box," she said, raising a brow.

I pulled the smaller packet from the cardboard package. The second box was wrapped in dark red paper, the kind you'd buy from a dollar store.

I ripped it open.

Katy clinched her nose with her fingers. "My goodness, what did you get?"

The smell was stronger now. It was the vomit-inducing smell of rotten flesh, and it was coming from the box.

I snipped through the smaller box and pulled the flaps down.

"Eek!" screamed Win, jumping out of her chair, dropping my phone on the desk.

"What in heaven's name!" cried Katy, stepping hurriedly toward the door, stumbling over her own feet.

I stared at my delivery.

Why would anyone mail me a dead rat?

Get the next mystery thriller here:
www.TikiriHerath.com/Mysteries

Available globally in e-book, paperback, and hardback editions on all Amazon stores. Also available for free in libraries everywhere. Just ask your friendly local librarian to order a copy via Ingram Spark.

Merciless Legacy

This is Victoria's story.

Learn what happened to her and her parents and why she was abandoned so brutally but eventually inherited Cedar Cottage. Read the first chapter of Merciless Legacy here:

The Anonymous Letter

"If you tell anyone what you saw that day, I will cut your throat while you're sleeping and leave you to bleed to death. Don't ever think I can't do it."

"Watch out!" shouted Tetyana.

I swerved the car and struggled to straighten the vehicle. I glanced at my rearview mirror, my heart pounding.

"What was that?" I asked.

"A pothole the size of Mexico," replied my friend, who was sitting in the passenger seat next to me. "Slow down, Asha. We're not in a NASCAR rally."

"We're running late. We have to get there by five thirty."

I peeked through the windshield.

There was still some afternoon light left.

New Hampshire's magnificent White Mountains gazed down at us, their peaks glistening against the setting sun on the distant horizon. This was a beautiful place. But I couldn't help but feel those mountains were warning me.

This was dangerous terrain.

We wouldn't want to get lost here.

Or get stuck.

In the dark.

"At this rate, we'll never get there," grumbled Tetyana. "Should have rented an all-wheel drive."

"We're driving in style," piped Katy from the back, pushing her head in between the front seats. "They don't even make these cars anymore."

"Give me function over form any day," said Tetyana gruffly.

I had to agree.

The back of this vehicle was so small, Katy's modelesque frame and fiery red hair obscured my view through the back window. I knew we shouldn't have asked her to choose our ride.

When we arrived at the airport rental company, and she'd squealed with delight to see this retro machine designed like a 1930s gangster getaway car, I hadn't had the heart to say no to my BFF.

But now, as I navigated this unpaved road through this unfamiliar mountain pass at dusk, I wondered if we'd made a big mistake.

"Everyone will know we're out-of-towners," Tetyana groused.

"What's your problem?" said Katy.

"The official vehicle in this state is a super-duty truck with a gun rack in the back."

"Do you know what I think—"

"We're in horse country, that's for sure," I said, trying to deflect the argument brewing between my two best friends. "Breathe that fresh air in, will you? It's good for your health."

I turned to them and grinned.

"We made it, girls. Finally. From New York to Twin Mountain. From Twin Mountain to Falcon Hills. We're almost there."

"How long before we get to Cedar Cottage?" asked Katy. "It's getting a bit dark, isn't it?"

Tetyana looked down at her phone. "We're already on the estate grounds," she said, zooming in on the GPS map.

"I saw a *Private* sign when we turned from the main road about five minutes ago," I said.

"My GPS says ETA in fifteen minutes."

"Sit back and relax," I said, looking at Katy through my rearview mirror, "and enjoy the view."

"It's stunning here. I'll give you that," she said, leaning back in her seat with a sigh.

"You needed the break, hun," I said.

Katy's life had turned upside-down recently. I knew she hadn't been sleeping well for weeks, so it was good to see her smile again.

"Plus, you only get to turn thirty once. We need to celebrate it."

"That was three days ago."

"It's your birthday *week*, girlfriend."

Katy finally cracked a smile.

"These mountains remind me of home," said Tetyana, gazing out her window. She sounded wistful, unusual for her.

"Ukraine, you mean?" I asked.

She nodded.

"My brother and I used to ride our horses to the glacier streams every Sunday. We even caught a few fish for supper." She paused and her voice dropped several octaves. "At least, we used to, until the Russians came."

The car fell silent.

Tetyana hadn't just lost a brother to the brutal Russian militia, but her mother too.

"Why don't we go on a mountain hike this weekend?" I said, hoping to distract her from her dark memories. "Maybe they have a riding stable at the estate. Our job shouldn't take that long. It's not like we're trying to catch child traffickers this time."

"Don't speak too fast," replied Tetyana, her voice somber. "I have a feeling this assignment of yours is bigger than you think."

Tetyana always looked at the harsher side of life. Given her past, I didn't blame her. Katy and I hadn't escaped our childhoods unscathed either, but we were more optimistic.

It was overkill to bring along a former rebel-soldier-turned-weapons-trainer for this simple job. But David, my fiancé, who had his own top-secret military past, almost had a panic attack when I told him I would solve this case of poison pen letters all by myself. And drive up to a mysterious mansion in the woods in another state, all by myself.

"I'm a grown woman, for goodness's sake," I told him, but he only relaxed after Tetyana promised to accompany me and Katy.

The further I drove into the heart of this remote mountain region, the more I was glad she was sitting next to me with her subcompact Glock on her belt.

I didn't realize it then, but it would come in handy soon.

To be continued...

Continue the adventure!
You can find MERCILESS LEGACY here:
www.TikiriHerath.com/Mysteries
Private eye Asha Kade travels to a remote mansion to fulfill a wealthy woman's dying wish—but when the household staff begins to drop dead, her journey becomes a hunt for a ruthless killer....

Happy reading!

Available globally in e-book, paperback, and hardback editions on all Amazon stores. Also available for free in libraries everywhere. Just ask your friendly local librarian to order a copy via Ingram Spark.

Debate this Dozen

Twelve Book Club Questions

1. Who was your favorite character?
2. Which characters did you dislike?
3. Which scene has stuck with you the most? Why?
4. What scenes surprised you?
5. What was your favorite part of the book?
6. What was your least favorite part?
7. Did any part of this book strike a particular emotion in you? Which part and what emotion did the book make you feel?
8. Did you know the author has written an underlying message in this story? What theme or life lesson do you think this story tells?
9. What did you think of the author's writing?
10. How would you adapt this book into a movie? Who would you cast in the leading roles?
11. On a scale of one to ten, how would you rate this story?
12. Would you read another book by this author?

The Reading List

T he Red Heeled Rebels universe of mystery thrillers, featuring your favorite kick-ass female characters:

Tanya Stone FBI K9 Mystery Thrillers
www.TikiriHerath.com/Thrillers
NEW FBI thriller series starring Tetyana from the Red Heeled Rebels as Special Agent Tanya Stone, and Max, as her loyal German Shepherd. These are serial killer thrillers set in Black Rock, a small upscale resort town on the coast of Washington state.
Her Deadly End
Her Cold Blood
Her Last Lie
Her Secret Crime
Her Dead Girl
Her Perfect Murder
Her Grisly Grave
Coming soon!

Asha Kade Private Detective Murder Mysteries
www.TikiriHerath.com/Mysteries
Each book is a standalone murder mystery thriller, featuring the Red Heeled Rebels, Asha Kade and Katy McCafferty. Asha and Katy receive one million dollars for their favorite children's charity from a secret benefactor's estate every time they solve a cold case.

Merciless Legacy
Merciless Games
Merciless Crimes
Merciless Lies
Merciless Past
Merciless Deaths
One more to come.

Red Heeled Rebels International Mystery & Crime - The Origin Story
www.TikiriHerath.com/RedHeeledRebels
The award-winning origin story of the Red Heeled Rebels characters. Learn how a rag-tag group of trafficked orphans from different places united to fight for their freedom and their lives, and became a found family.

The Girl Who Crossed the Line
The Girl Who Ran Away
The Girl Who Made Them Pay
The Girl Who Fought to Kill
The Girl Who Broke Free
The Girl Who Knew Their Names
The Girl Who Never Forgot

This series is now complete.

<u>The Accidental Traveler</u>

<u>www.TikiriHerath.com</u>

An anthology of personal short stories based on the author's sojourns around the world.

<u>The Rebel Diva Nonfiction Series</u>

<u>www.TikiriHerath.com/Nonfiction</u>

Your Rebel Dreams: 6 simple steps to take back control of your life in uncertain times.

Your Rebel Plans: 4 simple steps to getting unstuck and making progress today.

Your Rebel Life: Easy habit hacks to enhance happiness in the 10 key areas of your life.

Bust Your Fears: 3 simple tools to crush your anxieties and squash your stress.

Collaborations

The Boss Chick's Bodacious Destiny Nonfiction Bundle
Dark Shadows 2: Voodoo and Black Magic of New Orleans

Tikiri's novels are available around the world, on all Amazon stores everywhere. The nonfiction books are available on Apple, Kobo, Barnes & Noble, Indigo Chapters, and all good bookstores around the world.

All these books are also available in libraries everywhere. Just ask your friendly local librarian or your local bookstore to order a copy via Ingram Spark.

Happy reading.

Asha Kade Private Detective Murder Mysteries

How far would you go for a million-dollar payout?

<u>The Merciless Murder Mysteries</u>

Merciless Legacy

Merciless Games

Merciless Crimes

Merciless Lies

Merciless Past

Merciless Deaths

More to come!

Each book is a standalone murder mystery thriller featuring the Red Heeled Rebel, Asha Kade, and her best friend Katy

McCafferty, as private detectives on the hunt for serial killers in small towns USA.

There is no graphic violence, heavy cursing, or explicit sex in these books. What you will find are a series of suspicious deaths, a closed circle of suspects, twists and turns, fast-paced action, and nail-biting suspense.

www.TikiriHerath.com/mysteries

A newly minted private investigator, Asha Kade, gets a million dollars from an eccentric client's estate every time she solves a cold case. Asha Kade accepts this bizarre challenge, but what she doesn't bargain for is to be drawn into the dark underworld of her past again.

The only thing that propels her forward now is a burning desire for justice.

What readers are saying on Amazon and Goodreads:

"My new favorite series!"

"Thrilling twists, unputdownable!"

"I was hooked right from the start!"

"A twisted whodunnit! Edge of your seat thriller that kept me up late, to finish it, unputdownable!! More, please!"

"Buckle up for a roller coaster of a ride. This one will keep you on the edge of your seat."

"A must read! A macabre start to an excellent book. It had me totally gripped from the start and just got better!"

"A great whodunit with a lot of twists and turns along the way. The story was amazing!"

"I could not stop reading it. It was as if I was there witnessing the murders myself. The characters had depth and personality and backgrounds that were explained nicely. It was awesome!"

"Nothing is more terrifying than the fear of the unknown. Do you have any nails left? Another NAIL-BITING story from a very talented master storyteller!"

A brand-new murder mystery series for a pulse-pounding, bone-chilling adventure from the comfort and warmth of your favorite reading chair at home.

Can you find the killer before Asha Kade does?

To learn more about this exciting series and download the FREE novel—HER DEADLY END—as a gift, go to www.TikiriHerath.com/mysteries.

Sign up to Tikiri's VIP reader club to get the chance to win personalized paperback books, chat with the author and more.

Available globally in e-book, paperback, and hardback editions on all Amazon stores. Print books are available for free in libraries everywhere. Just ask your friendly local librarian or your local bookstore to order a copy via Ingram Spark.

Tanya Stone FBI K9 Mystery Thrillers

How far would you go to avenge your family's brutal murder?

<u>Tanya Stone FBI K9 Serial Killer Thrillers</u>

Her Deadly End

Her Cold Blood

Her Last Lie

Her Secret Crime

Her Dead Girl

Her Perfect Murder

Her Grisly Grave

To come!

A brand-new FBI K9 serial killer thriller series for a pulse-pounding, bone-chilling adventure from the comfort and warmth of your favorite reading chair at home.

Can you find the killer before Agent Tanya Stone?

www.TikiriHerath.com/thrillers

Some small-town secrets will haunt your nightmares. Escape if you can...

FBI Special Agent Tanya Stone has a new assignment. Hunt down the serial killers prowling the idyllic West Coast resort towns.

An unspeakable and bone-chilling darkness seethes underneath these picturesque seaside suburbs. A string of violent abductions and gruesome murders wreak hysteria among the perfect lives of the towns' families.

But nothing is what it seems. The monsters wear masks and mingle with the townsfolk, spreading vicious lies.

With her K9 German Shepherd, Agent Stone goes on the warpath. She will fight her own demons as a trafficked survivor to make the perverted psychopaths pay.

But now, they're after her.

Small towns have dark deceptions and sealed lips. If they know you know the truth, they'll never let you leave...

Each book is a standalone murder mystery thriller, featuring Tetyana from the Red Heeled Rebels as Agent Tanya Stone, and Max, her loyal German Shepherd. Red Heeled Rebels Asha Kade and Katy McCafferty and their found family make guest appearances when Tanya needs help.

There is no graphic violence, heavy cursing, or explicit sex in these books.

The dogs featured in this series are never harmed, but the villains are.

To learn more about this exciting new series and download the FREE novel—HER DEADLY END—as a gift, go to www.TikiriHerath.com/thrillers

The Red Heeled Rebels International Mystery & Crime

The Origin Story

Would you like to know the origin story of your favorite characters in the Tanya Stone FBI K9 mystery thrillers and the Asha Kade Merciless murder mysteries?

In the award-winning Red Heeled Rebels international mystery & crime series—the origin story—you'll find out how Asha, Katy, and Tetyana (Tanya) banded together in their troubled youths to fight for freedom against all odds.

<u>The complete Red Heeled Rebels international crime collection:</u>
Prequel Novella: The Girl Who Crossed the Line
Book One: The Girl Who Ran Away
Book Two: The Girl Who Made Them Pay

Book Three: The Girl Who Fought to Kill
Book Four: The Girl Who Broke Free
Book Five: The Girl Who Knew Their Names
Book Six: The Girl Who Never Forgot
The series is now complete!

An epic, pulse-pounding, international crime thriller series that spans four continents featuring a group of spunky, sassy young misfits who have only each other for family.

A multiple-award-winning series which would be best read in order. There is no graphic violence, heavy cursing, or explicit sex in these books.
www.TikiriHerath.com/RedHeeledRebels

In a world where justice no longer prevails, six iron-willed young women rally to seek vengeance on those who stole their humanity.

If you like gripping thrillers with flawed but strong female leads, vigilante action in exotic locales and twists that leave you at the edge of your seat, you'll love these books by multiple award-winning Canadian novelist, Tikiri Herath.

Go on a heart-pounding international adventure without having to get a passport or even buy an airline ticket!

What readers are saying on Amazon and Goodreads:
"Fast-paced and exciting!"
"An exciting and thought-provoking book."
"A wonderful story! I didn't want to leave the characters."
"I couldn't put down this exciting road trip adventure with a powerful message."

"Another award-worthy adventure novel that keeps you on the edge of your seat."

"A heart-stopping adventure. I just couldn't put the book down till I finished reading it."

"Kept me mesmerized and captivated with the rich descriptions which made me feel like I was actually inside the story."

"This is a fantastic read that will have you traveling the globe. I absolutely loved this book. You won't be able to put it down!"

"A real page-turner and international thriller. Reminds me of why I've always loved to read. Because I can visit worlds and places, I wouldn't ordinarily get to see."

Literary Awards & Praise for The Red Heeled Rebels books:

- Grand Prize Award Finalist - 2019 Eric Hoffer Award, USA

- First Horizon Award Finalist - 2019 Eric Hoffer Award, USA

- Honorable Mention General Fiction - 2019 Eric Hoffer Award, USA

- Winner First-In-Category - 2019 Chanticleer Somerset Award, USA

- Semi-Finalist - 2020 Chanticleer Somerset Award, USA

- Winner in 2019 Readers' Favorite Book Awards, USA

- Winner of 2019 Silver Medal - Excellence E-Lit Award, USA

- Winner in Suspense Category - 2018 New York Big Book Award, USA

- Finalist in Suspense Category - 2018 & 2019 Silver Falchion Awards, USA

- Honorable Mention - 2018-19 Reader Views Literary Classics Award, USA

- Publisher's Weekly Booklife Prize - 2018, USA

To learn more about this addictive series, go to **www.TikiriHerath.com/RedHeeledRebels** and receive the prequel novella - **The Girl Who Crossed The Line** - as a gift.

Sign up to Tikiri's VIP reader club and get short stories, exotic recipes, the chance to win paperbacks, chat with the author and more.

Available globally in e-book, paperback, and hardback editions on all Amazon stores. Print books are available for free in libraries everywhere. Just ask your friendly local librarian or your local bookstore to order a copy via Ingram Spark.

Acknowledgments

To my amazing, talented, superstar editor, Stephanie Parent, thank you, as always, for coming on this literary journey with me and for helping make these books the best they can be.

To my international team of beta readers who gave me their frank feedback, thank you. I truly value your thoughts.

In alphabetical order of first name:

Carolyn Pennett-Staresinic, Canada

Kristen Harnish, United States of America

Laura Edwards, United States of America

Michele Kapugi, United States of America

Congratulations to the winners of the dog-naming contest! Max is the perfect name. The indomitable German Shepherd in this story will now also appear as an important sleuthing character in my future novels.

The winners, in alphabetical order, are:

Andres Cortes
Juan Stein
Russ Frank

To all the kind and generous readers who take the time to review my novels and share their frank feedback, thank you so much. Your support is invaluable.

I'm immensely grateful to you all for your kind and generous support, and would love to invite you for a glass of British Columbian wine or a cup of Ceylon tea with chocolates when you come to Vancouver next!

About the Author

T ikiri Herath is the multiple-award-winning author of international thriller and mystery novels and the Rebel Diva books.

Tikiri worked in risk management in the intelligence and defense sectors, including in the Canadian Federal Government and at NATO. She has a bachelor's degree from the University of Victoria, British Columbia, and a master's degree from the Solvay Business School in Brussels.

Born in Sri Lanka, Tikiri grew up in East Africa and has studied, worked, and lived in Europe, Southeast Asia, and North America throughout her adult life. An international nomad and fifth-culture kid, she now calls Canada home.

She's an adrenaline junkie who has rock climbed, bungee jumped, rode on the back of a motorcycle across Quebec, flown in an acrobatic airplane upside down, and parachuted solo.

When she's not plotting another thriller scene or planning another adrenaline-filled trip, you'll find her baking in her kitchen with a glass of red Shiraz in hand and vintage jazz playing in the background.

———❦———

To say hello and get travel stories from around the world, go to
www.TikiriHerath.com

www.ingramcontent.com/pod-product-compliance
Lightning Source LLC
Chambersburg PA
CBHW051119190726
48290CB00006B/1605